DATE DUE

APR - 9 1998	
NOV 2 6 1998	
MAR - 3	
MAR 2 3 1999	
MAR 3 1 1999	
APR - 7 2000	
APR - 9 2000	

BRODART   Cat. No. 23-221

Alter egos:
multiple personalities

Books by David Cohen

Being a man (Routledge, 1990)
Development of the imagination (Routledge, 1991)
Body language in relationships (Sheldon, 1992)
How to succeed in psychometric tests (Sheldon, 1993)

ALTER EGOS:
MULTIPLE PERSONALITIES

David Cohen

Constable London

First published in Great Britain 1996 by Constable & Company Ltd
3 The Lanchesters, 162 Fulham Palace Road, London W6 9ER
Copyright © 1996 by David Cohen
The right of David Cohen to be identified as the author
of this work has been asserted by him in accordance with
the Copyright, Designs and Patents Act 1988
ISBN 0 09 474070 4
Set in Linotron Sabon 10$\frac{1}{2}$pt. by
Rowland Phototypesetting Ltd,
Bury St Edmunds, Suffolk
Printed in Great Britain by
St Edmundsbury Press Ltd,
Bury St Edmunds, Suffolk

A CIP catalogue record for this book
is available from the British Library

To my son, Reuben, with love

Acknowledgements

Obviously, this book couldn't have been written without the help of many psychiatrists and patients who confided in me. I want to thank them for their time and patience, especially Frank Putnam and Richard Kluft. In Amsterdam I also had very useful discussions with Suzette Boon and Catherine Fine, as well as with an old friend, Hanya Kaufman, who uses some of these techniques in her work. My main debts editorially are to my son Reuben who scouted many references and did much useful additional research. He also read early drafts critically. The book is dedicated to him. I am very grateful to my copy editor, Gemma Forster, and to Miles Huddleston for critique and support. Julia Ross lived with the writing of this book and raised many interesting points. Finally, Dr James Mackeith made a number of valuable comments. The mistakes, of course, are mine.

Contents

CHAPTER 1

Multiple Theories

THE MEANING OF VOICES

David was thirty-one years old. He shambled into the transport café. Short-cropped hair. A slightly uneasy look towards me. He was growing stubble. I suspected he hoped it would help hide a strange discoloration on his face. David was half black but there was a pink patch of skin on his cheek. At first, I thought he had a birthmark. You couldn't help staring at it. It was oddly beautiful, young skin.

David didn't see it like that. Much later, when I knew him better, he said he hated it. He hadn't been born like that. His skin had peeled off exposing the pink when he was sick. He was sure it was because of the many medications he had been given.

I had traced David through a lawyer who represented patients who had been in special hospitals like Broadmoor or Rampton.

We sat down in the café. David talked quietly and reasonably, as many patients and ex-patients or so-called 'survivors' of the system do. He struck me as rather gentle. I had no idea why he had ended up in a special hospital and I had learned that this was not the first question to put. If I was lucky, he would slowly get round to telling me, maybe even the second or third time we met. I was used to the fact that it is never easy for people who have been in a special hospital to confess what they have done.

So we talked about the dreadful conditions David had lived in for two years in the special hospital. He had often been terrified that the wardens (they were nurses but he saw them as wardens) would beat him up.

'I didn't actually ever get beaten up because I said, "Yes sir," and, "No sir".' He had learned to act the good patient. He thought if he played it right he had a better chance of getting out quickly. 'I needed to get out. I'm an artist,' he said.

I was sceptical about this claim but over the next few months I found out that he wasn't boasting, let alone deluded. David was a talented artist with a real gift for rather grim cartoons. His best ones caught something of the moods of mental illness. He would draw little men trapped in a cage or in a coffin. He would draw a body being pumped full of drugs by strange mechanical contraptions. He would draw idealized lovers. That's what he wanted – love.

David lived alone in a small, messy room. Here, he would spend hours turning out one drawing after another. He often drew in the middle of the night as he couldn't sleep. He was on social security, too poor to buy artists' materials, so sometimes he had to draw on toilet paper. Sometimes even that ran out. The frantic drawing – some nights he would churn out a hundred drawings – gave him some comfort.

David did not look like a madman; he seemed a little odd, a little raw. He talked about his suffering. He had bad headaches. The drugs he took affected his memory, he said, and his sex drive.

It was only the third time we met that he told me why he had been committed. He said he had a 'jealous streak', and when he thought his fiancée might be trying to leave him, he had stabbed her. He had been tried for attempted murder. He was vague about the details; he recalled his own anxiety more than the actual violence. At first, I thought he was deliberately vague.

But David insisted he wasn't being evasive, he just couldn't remember much about the stabbing. His mind went blank when he thought about it. He believed the drugs didn't help because of their effect on his memory.

As I slowly got to know David better, I saw there were times when his personality changed. Everyone's personality is different at different times but I had never seen shifts as radical as David's. He would become very depressed, and edgy. He started to talk of ways people had hurt him. Doctors told him he changed when he did not take the medication they prescribed for him. They tried to persuade him to take his medicine.

But David hated the drugs. He believed they caused massive side-effects like the headaches, memory loss and peeling skin. He didn't want to look the way he did when he took them. The side-effects were worse than the symptoms, he said.

David also heard voices. He felt ambivalent about some of them. I found out gradually that they scared him but some voices also interested him. One, in particular, suggested that he might have been alive in the past in the Caribbean; maybe as a pirate.

Anti-psychotic drugs suppress hallucinations and, often, flatten emotions. Many patients resent their side-effects. Some 'survivors' or 'users' complain, as David and a number of patients have done, that the drugs do more than suppress. They are so potent they produce personality changes. A Liverpool patient, John C, told me the drugs turned him into a zombie.

So David took holidays from medication. He knew that on these 'holidays' he was much more likely to hear voices in his head and be frightened but he also felt he was more himself. He spoke of voices *in* his head, not voices that were coming from outside his head. It's a distinction some psychiatrists are beginning to think is important. He would rather cope with himself like that: hallucinating, but himself.

Other people did not like him when he was off the medication. In time, I began to understand why. When David was, as he put it, more himself, he lost his usual vulnerable, slightly quirky charm. He would speak more urgently, he would smile less. There would be more, and stranger, moments of silence when I felt I had no idea what he might do next.

His illness didn't make him lose all touch with reality. David even had some social graces. Once he gave me a present – a Book of Jewish Thoughts, which was a very well chosen gift. Usually David didn't make a pest of himself, as if he understood the limits of our relationship perfectly well.

Then, that changed. Once he rang me very late at night to tell me what he was drawing and how bad he was feeling. It didn't occur to him that at 1 a.m. I might not be too keen on talking about it. He didn't want to get off the phone. I was sure he had stopped taking his medication.

A few days later, he turned up at my house uninvited and unexpected. I wasn't there, but my wife and children were. They had met him because he had come round to see me previously when we had arranged it. They liked him. Now, David was different. They couldn't get him to go. Usually, David was good at picking up cues and didn't push the limits of tolerance, but this time he just stayed, insisting he had to talk to me. He sat himself in our living-room and wouldn't leave.

Aileen became worried. She wanted to ring me to say what was going on but she felt that might push him into doing something violent. She knew that he had stabbed his girlfriend. It took her about two hours to tell him she thought she should ring me to say he was there. On the phone she sounded a little frightened and she didn't frighten easily. I went back immediately.

By the time I got back to our house, David had gone. Aileen and the children were shaken; they had never before seen David behave the way he had done. The man who wouldn't leave was a 'different person'. He certainly was not himself.

I don't want to get bogged down in semantics at the start of this book but the vocabulary becomes tangled. Certainly, Aileen and the children felt they had been with, if not, a different person or a different personality, at least someone who was showing them a side of himself they had never seen before. Often, of course, that is part of normal behaviour. You make me furious and I show you a side of myself you've never seen before. Only my parents and lovers have seen me when I get really upset. But there was no obvious reason why David should have been in this different state. He gave no explanation even when he was asked why he was so agitated.

Later that evening, David rang me. It was hard to follow what he was saying. He tried to describe the drawings he was doing. He didn't seem to have any sense of having frightened Aileen and the children.

'Shouldn't you go back on the drugs?' I said.

He said he was drawing. The drugs would stop him drawing. He wasn't going to let them stop him.

Three days later, I learned his behaviour had so worried his neighbours they had contacted the police. David was known to them because he was out only on parole. He was still under a section of the Mental Health Act which allowed him to be recalled into hospital. He was duly recalled.

The hospital insisted on putting him on long-term depot injections which are slowly released into the bloodstream, their effect lasting for about four weeks. David had no choice. The next time I saw him he was calm but very worried about the condition of his skin.

For the next two years, there were constant battles about the medication. David would not turn up at the GP's clinic when he was due to get his dose of depot. He would again become very disturbed. He would hardly sleep. He would behave in the darker, more potentially dangerous way he had shown when he appeared uninvited at my house. The voices in his head would get more insistent.

After the visit where he had scared Aileen, my relationship with David changed. I was much more careful than before in dealing with him. I made it clear that I didn't want him to come round to my house unless he was asked.

David didn't like that. He felt I didn't trust him. He was right, I had seen a side of him I didn't trust. I wasn't comfortable in dealing with it myself and I certainly didn't want to expose my family to such disturbing behaviour.

There is an old saying in psychiatry – fashions in therapy can change, but fashions in diagnosis should not. Perhaps, but I am quite sure that in America in 1996 David would have been diagnosed very differently from the way he was in Britain.

In Britain, David was diagnosed as a schizophrenic who might also be suffering some form of personality disorder. In America today, David would probably be diagnosed as having some form of multiple personality disorder. Without any probing or prompting, he had sometimes behaved in two quite different ways, as if there were two different persons or personalities in him. He could be the intense but gentle artist who talked lucidly about different styles of painting and drawing. He could also be a man on the edge of control: the man who had stabbed; the man who spent hours in my house, the house of a friend, and scared his family; the man who had maybe once been a pirate.

Worryingly, David seemed to rather like the second, rougher person.

'No one wants to buy my stuff,' David complained. It made him feel bitter. He ended up working in a kitchen washing dishes. No one paid any attention to him as an artist. They took more notice of him when he was menacing.

David had had almost no treatment but drugs. He had no counselling and no psychotherapy. He talked very little about his childhood though he did say he had a bad relationship with his father. No doctor had probed that to see if there might have been a history of abuse. David had not been subjected to techniques many American psychiatrists use as they have become more interested in dissociation and multiple personality states. David had not been hypnotized, for example, to see if this division – the gentle artist, the edgy, violent, even sinister, man – indicated different moods or different personalities. No one had tried to make contact with the pirate 'persona' through hypnosis, relaxation or any other therapy.

David's experience of psychiatry is fairly typical. A number of psychiatrists in the States claim many men who suffer from multiple personality syndrome are not diagnosed because they are in prison, on the streets or in indifferent, overstretched systems of care. As a result they are not asked relevant questions.

Relying on drugs to contain schizophrenia is standard practice all over the world, even though there are considerable concerns about the side-effects of anti-psychotic medications. The Royal College of Psychiatrists in Britain set up a working party to look into the issue of heavy prescribing of such drugs after evidence came to light from a number of sources including a programme on Channel 4's 'Dispatches', which suggested that at least one patient a week dies as a result of such treatment.

Such horror stories emphasize the power of the drugs. 'Ordinary' people often say they become different when they're under the influence of that other drug – alcohol. They become rowdy, talkative, violent; they say things they daren't say when they're sober. If alcohol has that effect, it's hardly surprising that drugs specifically designed to change moods and suppress feelings should have some impact on personality.

In Britain psychiatrists also constantly complain of overwork. They have too little time and too many cases. They can't go into people's experience in any depth. But even when, for a variety of reasons, they do have the time to probe more deeply, they tend to ignore experiences and evidence that would now make many American psychiatrists consider at least the possibility of a diagnosis of multiple personality disorder.

A STABLE PERSONALITY: THE TWO SIDES OF JUDITH WARD

One dramatic case that illustrates this is that of Judith Ward, who was wrongly found guilty of bombing the M62 coach in 1974. In her book *Ambushed* (1992), she describes herself as two very different persons. On the one hand she talks of herself as a timid, frightened young woman who wanted nothing more than to look after horses. She saved money to buy the riding kit she needed and went to work on a farm. As she left for her job as a stable girl, she writes, 'The train snorted and hissed along the tracks singing a little song "This is it, This is it".' She was entranced by the trees waving 'Hello' and, when she arrived in Wiltshire, she thought this was 'my big day', like a girl in an old Mills and Boon. She liked the work so much that she studied for exams to qualify as a horse-riding instructress. After her first job finished, she went to work at a stable in Ireland.

But then, remarkably, even though she was a Catholic who had grown up in a community with Republican sympathies, Ward decided to join the British Army. The change was remarkable. From horse-girl to signals operator; from Irish sympathizer to British Army operative. Ward spent a year learning how to be a signals operator and passed all her exams. Then, she says, she was disappointed not to get a posting in Cyprus or Berlin, places where there would be real excitement. She never suggests she wanted to work with horses in the army.

One weekend she went AWOL. Ward writes that she was very depressed. But depression doesn't really explain the next set of major switches. 'Switching' is a term psychiatrists interested in multiple personality use to describe changing from one personality to another. You switch personas, you switch identities. Just like you switch clothes.

Having gone AWOL, Ward drifted into a very unstructured life, quite different from the disciplines of either the stable or the barracks. After the bomb killed twelve people in an army coach on the M62, she was picked up. The confession evidence presented at her trial was dramatic. In *Ambushed*, Ward notes first that she was still very depressed at this time. Second, that, 'Most of my remand period remains a blur.' (These memory losses are seen by Americans as typical of multiple personality disorder.) Third, she tried to slash her wrists. Her view is that when it came to her trial she wasn't really there. She writes:

> Only my physical form, my head gone away, retired, retreated, redundant. They're not talking about me, this is not me. I'm not listening. They want you to go into the witness box and speak. No I can't do that, what do I say. Say anything, it doesn't matter anyway and so I did, said anything and nothing, they're not listening anyway except for the sensational, the claims of bombing, the 'marriage' to a young man who had been killed whilst on active service for the IRA. Why did I say that, I don't know, don't even know where his name came from, it has been said that it was suggested earlier but I have no memory of this. All I can say is that this is a pointer to my mental state I was in. (p. 39)

Ward acknowledges she confessed, though not how full and sincere her confessions sounded. She says she made these admissions to get the police off her back.

After Judith Ward was convicted, Dr James MacKeith and Dr Gisli Gudjuddson of the Institute of Psychiatry in London began to study why some people made false confessions to the police. Often, it was the result of undue pressure. But they also found that some individuals were highly suggestible and liable to spin elaborate fantasies. In their confusion they often came to believe these fantasies. From Ward's own account of herself, she was clearly capable of behaving as, and of thinking of herself as, two very different kinds of women. In the end, of course, Ward suffered terribly for her confusion because she served nearly twenty years before her innocence was proved. Despite the evidence of her conflicting personalities, of her switches of interests, of her changes of loyalty, no one ever raised the possibility that she might be suffering from any kind of multiple personality state.

Maybe it's Robert Louis Stevenson's fault. Perhaps *Dr Jekyll and Mr Hyde* has left British psychiatrists very diffident about multiple personalities. In America there is no such diffidence.

FIFTEEN SELVES – FIFTEEN LAWYERS?

Early in 1994 James Carlson went on trial in Arizona for a series of rapes and burglaries. When his trial opened, his lawyer, Anna Unterberger, claimed that Mr Carlson was body host to fifteen separate personalities. These included Laurie Burke, a seventeen-year-old lesbian prostitute; a seven-year-old boy who wanted a puppy; a policeman called Brian who was twenty-four years old and a character called Bud Bundy who was named after a character in a TV sitcom. Anna Unterberger argued that the personality who had committed the crimes was twenty-two-year-old Jim. She told the jury, 'The body you see sitting there was at the places the prosecutor says he was. What is crucial was what mind controlled the body you see sitting there.'

People in court noted three of the personalities had quite different patterns of speech and appearance. Carlson was the latest in a long list of accused who claimed that while one of their 'selves' may have committed a crime, the whole person did not. The alters put on a good enough show of differences for the judge to agree each of Carlson's personalities should be sworn in separately.

The Arizona police were less impressed with Carlson. They claimed Carlson was faking multiple personality in order to be found not guilty. But a number of psychologists were willing to testify on Carlson's behalf, affirming that he really did have a number of selves competing for control of one body.

By the time of Carlson's trial, multiple personality had become a hot issue in the States. British critics have tended to deride this as yet another American fad, but in doing so they ignore the fact that there are now serious studies in rather less faddish countries – Holland, Norway, Belgium, Turkey, Spain, Germany and Central America. The divide in attitudes between British sceptics and others was very obvious at a large conference in Amsterdam in 1995.

MULTIPLE PERSONALITY OR DISASSOCIATION – A QUESTION OF APPEASING THE CRITICS

This is Amsterdam without the canals, windmills or tulips.

The Free University of Amsterdam is The Netherlands' premier Catholic University. The Aula, the main auditorium, is grand. Plush seats. The latest audio-visual aids.

In May 1995, four hundred psychologists, psychiatrists and social workers gathered from all over the world to take part in the spring meeting of the International Association for the Study of Dissociation. Until 1993 this group was the International Society for the Study of Multiple Personality and Dissociation. But then it dropped the words 'multiple personality'.

These delegates were sober and serious. This was no Psychic Fayre. Forget Amsterdam's reputation as a city where soft drugs are legal and hippies sleep in Vondelpark. No one looked like a New Age Nirvana nerd. The one woman whose dress had a New Age hint told me she was very sceptical. She taught schizophrenics to listen to their voices. Dissociation seemed bizarre to her.

If there were patients here, they were pretending to be professionals.

One soon revealed herself. A plump blonde American told me she disassociated. She told me that she had blocked out many incidents of abuse in her own childhood which had caused her many problems, and her family, too. Her daughter had started to disassociate. 'She was being abused in child care, but I didn't notice. She'd started to develop alters. I came here because I wanted to find out about it.' There wasn't any shame or embarrassment.

Why was 'multiple personality' dropped out of the Association's name? Was it because there had been a dramatic change in the symptoms therapists were seeing? Over the course of the three days there, I asked a number of participants that question. Dr Catherine Fine, a psychiatrist from Philadelphia, said what most of the Americans said, 'It was political.'

One of her colleagues, Dr Suzette Boon, who is recognized as one of The Netherlands' leading experts, agreed. 'It was political.' Unlike most Americans, Boon has received much public funding to research the subject. She's co-author of *Multiple Personality Disorder in The Netherlands* (1990), a book crammed with sober statistics. It becomes clear during the conference that almost none of the delegates have stopped believing in multiple personality. But there have been so many attacks on them that they decided to drop the term and use the less emotive word 'dissociation'. So multiple personality disorder is also now known as dissociative states.

'So it was appeasement,' I said.

'Yes, appeasement,' Dr Fine agreed.

Dr Catherine Fine is a bubbly blonde Irish Catholic who works with Dr Richard Kluft, one of the pioneers of modern work on multiple personality. He sports a little moustache and peppers all his presentations with jokes. Many of them at his own expense. He told me he had a brilliant career in front of him in the early 1970s. He had been to Harvard Medical School. Then one day a patient started to switch to a distressed four-year-old personality in the middle of a therapeutic session. Kluft decided to ignore this high drama. He had been taught not to reward patients for acting-out and seeking attention, so he thought the best tactic was not to pay any heed to what looked like a perfect example of a small child screaming for attention.

A few minutes later, the adult patient complained she wanted to kill herself and that Kluft was not listening to her. The patient also complained there had been a gap in the session. Kluft was surprised. He told me he went on to make a fool of himself: he told twenty colleagues what had happened and asked for advice. Some told him that if he had seen a multiple personality, he needed treatment just as much as if he had hitched a ride on the Loch Ness Monster.

One colleague admitted he had no idea what the patient's behaviour meant, or what to do, but added that Kluft should probe, rather than ignore. That man, Kluft told me, is now recognized as the best psychotherapist in Philadelphia.

So, Kluft told me with a smile, he embarked on his first treatment of a multiple personality case. It meant he made his most basic mistakes in the 1970s when no one was looking. But it wasn't easy. He wrote papers and had them rejected. 'I was used to that,' he said, because at college he had wanted to be a poet and his walls were lined with rejection slips. Kluft burned all his poems, eventually. For five years after taking his first multiple case, Kluft could get nothing published. He laughed at the notion that it was lucrative to find multiples: he had lost patients. He couldn't even, though he was a car freak, afford to buy the Porsche he wanted. If he had only stayed busy with lucrative neurotics, he would be wallowing in Porsches.

Catherine Fine came into the field much later, in 1987, but she too was annoyed at the gossip about money. She had been an expert in depression – 'I could have pocketed fat cheques for dealing with depressed patients,' she said, adding that such patients were much less trouble.

But the symptoms, the illness, the suffering were all very much there. Brave pioneers, they had no choice but to follow what they saw.

Suzette Boon accepted that the Association had changed its name to pacify the many critics who rubbish the idea of multiple personality. In The Netherlands, however, there is much less need to appease. Boon claimed the Dutch have always been more open to the study of trauma than the Americans. In 1984 the Dutch Ministry of Health commissioned a national survey of cases of incest. As a result, the government came to accept that dissociation wasn't a cranky modern idea, but a respectable diagnosis with a long history going back to the nineteenth century. They then commissioned a survey of multiple personality cases in The Netherlands. Nel Draijer and Suzette Boon (1990) found that about 19 per cent of psychiatric patients had serious symptoms of dissociation and multiple personality.

Kluft, Fine and Boon were all clearly passionate about their work. They were pleased there were delegates from many countries where the subject is being researched. The level of official endorsement at the conference surprised me. One of the people who gave an opening address was Dr Rob Smeets, the Chief Psychiatrist to the Ministry of Health in The Netherlands. Smeets admitted that he started out as a sceptic but said he had now seen enough respectable work to believe that the diagnosis had serious validity.

Three months before this conference, the editorial in *The British Journal of Psychiatry* attacked the whole notion of multiple personality as a delusion.

Before looking at these arguments in more depth, let's switch from academic to personal.

DO YOU ALWAYS FEEL YOU'RE THE SAME PERSON?
WHAT DOES YOUR DIARY SAY?

From the time that Robert Louis Stevenson popularized the idea of the split personality such cases were seen as hardly human, but much recent evidence suggests that while multiple personalities are often very bizarre, they are not an alien species.

Many of us have some slight sense of what having more than

one personality might be like. I have no problem identifying the following character, for example.

Diary of many selves 1

6.44 a.m. I wake up. I'm grouchy, as usual. I don't like waking up alone. I can't think of anything.

8.12 a.m. A shower and three coffees later, I'm more human. Serious thought no problem. I can rattle my way through Freud and Sartre. Theories of, influences on, effects on the modern soul and culture.

1.05 p.m. Lunch with mother. I regress to five-year-old behaviour. She complains my hair is too long. I'm thirty-seven years old and have published eight books. Feel like a bad little boy. Order crème brulée to cope. Refuse to cut my hair. Thinking impossible, though I believe my mother consulted Freud to get his advice on how to give her son a mega Oedipus complex.

2.20 p.m. Back in class – no sign of paranoia or of behaving like a five-year-old. I act so mature I could be embalmed.

8.00 p.m. Hang about outside cinema to meet a date. She's late. Is she coming? I'm just divorced. This angst was there when I had pimples. Now I have a paunch. Which is less sexy? Emotional state about sixteen. Sexy fantasies of date interrupted by the fear that one of my students will see me. Or worse, my mother will.

Now, this one person that I am wonders: Am I really the same person when I behave and feel so very differently?

The question isn't academic. My brain and body are changing. My skin cells are moulting every few months. My brain cells are dying. The myelin sheath wrapped around the brain cells and dendrites to protect them sheds and regenerates like a snake's skin.

How can I really be myself when everything in me, everything that makes me, is changing?

It was fine for the Victorians to believe in the unity of the self; they didn't have our insights. They hadn't sliced the mind into compartments like ego, id and super-ego, which we have located thanks to Freud, Jung and their scrapping disciples. In one corner of the unconscious – pure lust; in another – the lust for purity. Shall we tot up the theories that break the self up into little bundles? Jung's animus and anima, archetypes and collective unconscious; Eric Berne's rather more homely Child, Adult and Parent. Many other theories also fragment the self.

Psychology: the science of chipping away at the self.

Therapy: the art of chopping away the self to rebuild it in different superior shapes.

Both Freudians and behaviourists like B. F. Skinner proclaim a sad fact. You may think that you are in control of yourself and that you determine your actions, but this is pure illusion. You're a slave to your conditioning and complexes.

Oddly, as the self isn't in charge of itself, it is also being pampered as never before. Not happy with yourself as you are? Then shop for the self you want. Don't stint. Turn to the Yellow Pages. Turn to the listings in *Time Out* or *Village Voice*. Turn yourself on to you, the 'you' you could be if only you explored your hidden depths.

Courtesy of Epic Psychobabble, I now draw your attention to the following methods of changing yourself.

Aromatherapy; EST; Rolfing; Mystic Therapy; Truth Therapy; Authentic Experiences; Role Therapy; Psychic Make-Over (you get a free lipstick every time you conquer a complex); Neurolinguistic Programming, which also helps you become a super salesman!

If you want you can discover the dolphin in yourself.

You can be more than you are now.

There's nothing you can't do.

Our sense of self has become very unstable. In the rich West most of us put on and shed many personas every day. To us, living at this time, that feels both normal – and new.

TEXT AND CONTEXT

Which is not to be taken as meaning the text is a con. At this early stage, I want to do what academic authors increasingly do in the introduction – tell the readers what the book is about. This always feels a little like an admission of failure but one of the media buzzwords of the last decade is signposting. The reader is a pilgrim of the pages and badly needs roadsigns.

Essentially the aim of this book is simple. It is to examine what seems to be a growing and heated controversy about multiple personality disorder. It's an argument which can only be understood in the context of history as there have been reports in the psychiatric literature of dual personalities since 1816. Since 1980, the controversy has become more acute. In the next sections I look at the history of the condition, at two books that made it famous and at the idea that it is child sexual abuse which somehow 'causes' the creation of multiple personalities. Much of the current controversy centres round this and, as we shall see, psychiatrists in opposing camps pull no punches.

I then go on to give in detail a number of case histories which highlight some of the complicated issues around this diagnosis. One of the most problematic is the validity of memories recovered in therapy. Are they true, false or, at least, 'sincere'? These case histories don't have clear lessons always but I hope to give readers a good idea of what the condition feels like. I also look at treatment in Chapter 13.

I also argue that given the many roles we all have to play, it is worth looking at a related field – that of subpersonalities. Normal people who never come into contact with a psychiatrist can now, courtesy of some therapy groups, go on a tour of discovery where they meet their own subpersonalities.

Let me introduce you to yourself. You will find many surprises.

To know that there are many sides to yourself is not, of course, the same thing as having a multiple personality. But I want to suggest there is a link between our increasingly chaotic and self-conscious sense of self and the increase in multiple personality cases. In the past, it was different.

Psychiatrists have been studying cases of double personality since 1816 when an Irish girl, Mary Reynolds, caused something of a stir. She seemed to have a conscious personality that was very dull and placid. But sometimes she was said to be quite different – vivacious, coquettish and quite disreputable. Until the 1880s, such cases always revealed just two personas – one of whom was usually a little outrageous. Few of these cases were studied systematically until the 1880s when William James (1842–1910) at Harvard and Pierre Janet (1859–1947) and Jean Martin Charcot (1825–1893) at the Salpêtrière Hospital in Paris started to work in the field.

William James, who set up the first psychological laboratory in the United States, was the first well-known psychologist to report on the subject. His status lent authority to the phenomenon. A man as learned as James was not likely to be fooled.

WILLIAM JAMES AND AN EARLY WELL-DOCUMENTED CASE

In 1890 William James went to see the Reverend Ansel Bourne of Greene, Rhode Island. When he was thirty, Bourne had become a fervent Christian and made a living as an itinerant preacher. Physically, Bourne was strong, but he had psychological weaknesses: he often had headaches; he suffered from recurring bouts of depression; from time to time he would become unconscious for periods of an hour or more, or even longer.

James was interested in the minister because of a bizarre set of events that started in January 1887.

On the morning of 17 January Ansel Bourne went into Providence, Rhode Island. He drew out $551 from his bank, paid some bills and got a horse-car from Pawtucket, about twenty miles away. That evening Bourne did not return home.

His family became very worried. The next day they went into Providence but could find no trace of him. They placed advertisements in local newspapers for information on why Bourne should have disappeared. He was happy, ordinary, a pillar of his community. They were afraid he had been murdered.

On the morning of 14 March, two hundred miles away at Norristown, Pennsylvania, a man calling himself A. J. Brown woke up in a panic. The townspeople there knew Brown as a timid man. Six weeks earlier, he had started to rent a small store selling stationery, confectionery, fruit.

Brown attended church every Sunday and one day the congregation was invited to make comments. He made what worshippers thought was a rather good speech for such an apparently shy man.

But on 14 March, Brown woke up desperately upset and confused. He walked out of his store saying he could not understand what he was doing in Norristown. His real name was Ansel Bourne. His real home was in Greene. Why did people keep on calling him Brown? The citizens of Norristown thought that Mr Brown had gone mad, but they telegraphed Greene. To their surprise, they discovered the storekeeper had been telling the truth. He really was the Reverend Ansel Bourne.

The Reverend Bourne had no memory at all of what he had been doing in Norristown. He also had no memory of drawing $551 out of the bank or of running his store. Bourne went back to Greene and resumed his old, or his real, life.

About eighteen months later, William James went to see Bourne. Bourne had agreed to be hypnotized. James hoped to find, buried somewhere in the mind of the Reverend Bourne, the personality that had been Brown and which Bourne claimed not to remember.

The experiment is described at some length in the *Proceedings of the Society for Psychical Research*. William James hypnotised Bourne and achieved contact with the elusive Mr Brown, who knew perfectly well what he had been doing in Norristown. Bourne, however, never recovered any memory of that. For him, the period between 17 January and 14 March remained a total blank. Brown's personality did not seem to be flamboyantly different from that of Bourne, but Brown saw himself as a quite different person. He told James that he had heard of Bourne but added that he 'had never met the man'. In one body, there were two separate selves, though Brown had been dormant for eighteen months in the mind of Bourne.

James never found out what had prompted Bourne to create and flee into this second self. No one ever found out what Bourne/Brown had done in the two weeks between leaving Greene and turning up in Norristown. Nevertheless, William James was convinced that Bourne was quite truthful in saying he knew nothing about Brown.

William James was fascinated with the make-up of the self. He had argued in his great book *The Principles of Psychology* (1890) that our personality is bound together by the stream of consciousness. Normally it feels as if there are no breaks in that stream. I wake up, know and remember perfectly well that I am the same person who went to sleep the night before. My identity remains solid even though there is a time break in consciousness. James did not know how the self achieved this feat. The case of Bourne seemed to be a real, unsensational example of Dr Jekyll and Mr Hyde. One body, one brain, could hold more than one self and the two selves didn't have to be total opposites.

THE ARCHBISHOP AS SHRINK

In the debate around multiple personality today, history has become a weapon. The enthusiasts try to show that in the past many cases were missed. Some of them have examined cases of women who were questioned by the Inquisition, cases reported in books like Emmanuel Le Roy Ladurie's *Montaillou* (1975) and Gustav Henningsen's *Basque Witchcraft and the Spanish Inquisition* (1983). The enthusiasts' claim is that many cases of demonic possession were really cases of multiple personality. The demons in the soul were, in fact, splits in the mind.

Jean Goodwin offered two nice examples of such historical revisions in Amsterdam. The image of the Inquisitor as shrink is not new. But Goodwin had found one nearly perfect case from 1584 which offered allegations of child abuse, plenty of multiple personality, a caring Inquisitor/therapist figure, juicy conflicts – and even a happy ending.

Jeanne Fery was a young woman who was brought before the Inquisition accused of being possessed by demons. The cast list of demons included Namon and Garga, a particularly vicious devil with an oral fixation. 'With my mind in the gutter,' said Dr Goodwin, 'I deduce that as a child Jeanne was abused and forced to perform oral sex.'

Namon was something of a crossword devil. Goodwin pointed out Namon was No Man written backwards. The clue was that British soldiers had been in Jeanne's native town, Mons. So the child had decided to give one of its fragments a concealed English name. Jeanne also heard the voice of Mary Magdalen who, Goodwin argued, was a folkloric multiple personality: whore and priestess.

Goodwin added that Jeanne had a 'treatment team' which turned out to be the local Inquisition led by the archbishop. There were rumours about him and Jeanne. People gossiped then about that relationship. Now they gossip about therapists and their clients.

The team eventually got to the trauma. Jeanne's father was a drunk who insisted on having sex with his wife while she had the baby at the breast. Not even Freud conceived quite so lurid a primal scene, but Goodwin had actually found a seventeenth-century print to illustrate it.

Exorcism worked. Jeanne was healed. The demons disappeared.

Goodwin has also studied the sadder case of Sister Benetta, an abbess whose alters took the form of beautiful little angels. These angels set about screwing the pretty nuns in her abbey. Her case was seen as a scandal, a question not of demons but of desire. The Church punished the lustful Sister.

Another enthusiast found a mention in Paracelsus of a barmaid with two souls. The more ancient the historical evidence produced, the more credible the phenomenon is. If multiple personalities go back to the fifteenth century, there must be something to it.

INTROSPECTION – THE CASE OF THE TWO WARRING SELVES

Six years after the Ansel Bourne case, William James got to hear of another case. Curiously, it again concerned a clergyman. The Reverend Thomas Hanna fell as he clambered out of a carriage. For hours, he lay unconscious and seemed to be at death's door. When he woke up, he was extremely aggressive – something the Reverend Hanna was not known for. It took three strong men to subdue the violent vicar.

Once subdued, Hanna went to sleep. He woke up in a very strange state. He could not talk. He could not walk. He did not know how to chew food. He was also no longer toilet-trained, which caused some embarrassment. The Reverend Hanna was engaged to a lady known as Miss Cobut. In his new state he had absolutely no memory of her or of anything that had happened to his previous self.

The extraordinary regression of the Reverend Hanna made his case interesting. Dr Boris Sidis who was at Harvard, and Dr Simon Goodhart from Brookline in Massachusetts, were summoned to try and help him. They kept daily notes of what happened, as Sidis knew that the case would be of the greatest concern to James. Hanna soon made progress. He gathered that when food was put into his mouth he was meant to chew it. He soon learned to talk. Despite these 'new' skills, Hanna was like a child with no memory of his past. He said he felt like a completely newborn person.

If Hanna had remained profoundly amnesiac, the case wouldn't be of interest to students of multiple personality. But after three months he was taken to New York to see yet more specialists. One night he became extremely quiet. While Sidis and Goodhart were in the hotel room with him he fell asleep. He woke up and suddenly started to remember some of his previous existence as the Reverend Hanna.

For four hours, Sidis and Goodhart observed, Hanna seemed to be on the brink of recovering or remembering his old self. Then exhausted, he fell asleep. When he woke up the next day, Sidis and Goodhart assumed the person who woke up was the same person who had fallen asleep – a man with some sense of once having been the Reverend Hanna. They were soon disillusioned. Hanna had reverted to his second personality. He had absolutely no memory of Hanna and no memory of his behaviour the day before when he had remembered being Hanna. Later in the day, they gave him cannabis. The only effect was to make him euphoric. It did not, as they had hoped, put him back in touch with his previous personality.

In a few days Hanna fell into what the scientists described as a deep sleep. Sidis and Goodhart went on to quote what the Reverend Hanna had told them:

> While I was sitting in the chair and fell into that deep sleep from which you made so many efforts to awaken me, the two lives, that of the primary state and of the secondary state, came up for the first time. The problem which agitated me most was the problem, which of the two lives I had been living, should be continued, which experiences I should accept as my own and make continuous. I had to choose between the two which seemed to me impossible. (p. 193)

Hanna had been told by Sidis and Goodhart that he wavered between two different personalities. Now, on 14 June, he told them he had been confronted by both these selves at the same time: 'Hence when two individualities both known as my own appeared together, I thought they must be mine. There was also an unexplainable feeling that both were mine.'

Hanna felt he had to reject one personality, but also felt unable to be so ruthless as to kill off one of them. He added he felt 'as if these were two bodies alike, like twins, perhaps beings that had lived entirely separate lives or like the twins of the same body'. But while physically the two selves were linked, 'mentally the two lives were very different'.

Hanna turned to Goodhart and said that the only way he could explain to them was to ask him to imagine what it would be like for Goodhart to feel he were Sidis. The researchers asked him which of the two selves he preferred: 'The struggle was not so much to choose one as to forget the other. I was trying to find the one I would most easily forget. It seemed impossible to forget one: both tried to persist in consciousness. It seemed as if each memory was stronger than my will.' (p. 194)

Hanna said he felt he was living through the most profound crisis of his life. He wanted either to lose one personality or to unify them so that he would have one self in one body. He knew that trying to live within, between, through, two warring personalities would be too painful. He was frustrated. Neither Sidis nor Goodhart, each a single, whole being, could understand the dreadful state he was in. He told them he felt there was a battle raging for his soul. Given the state of knowledge then, neither Sidis nor Goodhart realized how unusual Hanna was in being conscious of this conflict.

Hanna eventually managed to choose between the rival selves. He resumed an identity much like that he had had previously, as a preacher. As with Ansel Bourne, no one could really explain why all this had happened.

William James was the father of American psychology. He accepted both the cases that came his way as strange and illuminating. They didn't, however, form the heart of his work. With a French psychiatrist it was different.

PIERRE JANET

As the pioneers have looked for old cases, they have also looked to early psychiatrists to give authority to their ideas. In doing so they have insisted on the importance of the work of Pierre Janet. Janet isn't a forgotten name in the histories of psychiatry but he had been very much in the shadow of Charcot, Freud (1856–1939) and Jung (1875–1961). There are good reasons to re-examine his contribution.

Janet described hysteria and many unconscious phenomena a few years before Freud, and always felt that Freud got too much credit for these discoveries. For those interested in dissociation, Janet's work on hysteria and with hypnosis seems remarkable.

When Janet was only twenty-two, he studied a woman called Léonie who lived in Le Havre (Janet, 1887). Léonie was well known to local doctors because she sleepwalked from the age of three. Janet hypnotized her and found Léonie housed a complex system of three different personalities.

In her ordinary state, when she was conscious as Léonie, she was a rather dull, peasant woman. In the hypnotized state she became an altogether livelier person who was aware of Léonie 1, her waking self, but insisted it was someone else, and refused to identify with it. In this condition, Léonie 2, the woman, was also less suggestible. The third self, Léonie 3, knew of the existence of the other two, but they did not share her memories. Léonie 2 could be contacted by Janet's usual hypnotic methods. Léonie 2 could also be led to perform acts that Léonie 1 remained ignorant of. Janet also found that when Léonie 2 was dominant, Léonie 3 could be made to do certain things which Léonie 2 would know nothing of. Janet eventually described Léonie as having three separate streams of consciousness – a phrase that owes much to James' ideas, but Janet described her before James published the Ansel Bourne case.

Janet's work with Léonie brought him into contact with Jean Martin Charcot of the Salpêtrière Hospital in Paris. Charcot was the great authority on hysteria. Janet set about examining many of the hysterics in Charcot's care. He concluded that hysteria was the result of splitting of the personality. Unbearably traumatic material was pushed out of consciousness. If you want to use the metaphor of streams of consciousness, a new river bed. Janet spoke ambiguously. Sometimes he wrote of 'shrinking' of consciousness to exclude material: at other times he spoke of alternating selves; at other times, he spoke of 'currents' of the self.

When Janet worked at the Salpêtrière, a number of doctors suggested there might be a 'doubling' of the personality. This double was 'a new psychological existence no longer alternating with the normal existence of the subject, but absolutely simultaneous'. You had to recognize this simultaneous self to understand 'the behaviour of neuropath and aliens'. Janet had plenty of examples from his casebook. For example, Irène was twenty when her mother became dangerously ill. The two women lived in a garret and the mother was dying from consumption. Irène struggled for sixty days to cope. By day, she worked to earn a pittance; by night, she nursed her mother and hoped for a miracle. When her mother died, Irène couldn't adjust; she even tried to revive the corpse and to make it breathe again. Then, black comedy: her mother's corpse fell out of the bed and Irène found it hard to lift it back.

The funeral was not the end of Irène's troubles. Soon after, she started to sleepwalk. She then developed amnesia. Even more worrying, Irène started to have fantasies of committing suicide. She imagined walking in front of a train. But her conscious self had no memory of such self-destructive fantasies. Janet could only access them through hypnosis. Janet argued that Irène had such an intense need to blank out the terrible memories of her mother's sickness and death that she developed two separate streams of consciousness.

Janet's work also highlighted the uses and dangers of hypnosis. It raised issues that are still central. What is the status and reality of selves who are contacted only when the subject is in a trance-like state? Are they real? Does hypnosis make it easier for psychiatrists to suggest events and memories to their patients? Can these suggestions lead to the creation of alters? One leading critic of claims about multiple personality disorder, Dr Tom Fahy of the Institute of Psychiatry in London, claims that multiple personality therapists often unwittingly create the condition in their all too suggestible patients.

Janet was the first eminent researcher to claim a link between trauma and the existence of these buried selves in the unconscious.

MULTIPLE PERSONALITIES, MULTIPLE CAUSES

It's not easy to think our way back into the climate in which James and Janet were writing. It was a world before Einstein and Freud. The atom had not been split. Freud had not yet developed his theory of the ego, id and super-ego which divided the mind into three. Philosophers and neurologists were not questioning the unity of either consciousness or the self.

Imagine a world where the self was itself again. Whole; organic; nutty brown in the earth.

I've flaked into pastoral partly because Raymond Barglow, therapist and cultural analyst, says it's not post-modern angst that's crippling the self, but IBM and its work – and this was before IBM was back in profit. His *The Crisis of the Self in the Age of Information* (1994) accuses computers of crunching not just numbers but selves. Many of his patients suffer computer nightmares. Big Keyboard controls. We are losing our selves in the peripherals, circuits and terminals. They are destroying our subjectivity. Barglow wails this is happening because we exalt the self more than ever before. We're narcissistic, self-obsessed and insecure. He recommends, among much else, dreaming of dolphins.

Cultural analysis is more mood science than empirical investigation, so if you think it's weird to look to dolphins as symbols of the united self or of the soul, think of masks. Since the days of ancient Greece, people have been fascinated by masks. They occur in Eastern and Western cultures. In every case, the mask gives freedom.

Behind the mask, you can be a person you're usually not. You can be an elephant, a devil, a clown, a tearful lover, a harlequin – though to date not usually a dolphin.

The mask hides the everyday self. Behind your mask you can be someone else.

Think of the possibility that multiple personality isn't a sickness but a way of playing with, and extending, your identity.

Long before cultural theorists like Barglow, neurologists stumbled on a remarkable phenomenon.

SPLIT BRAINS, SPLIT MINDS

I am in my brain. If I lose my brain, I'm either dead or a cabbage. We assume that the brain glues together the self.

In the 1960s, at the University of California, Roger Sperry studied a number of epileptic patients who had had an operation in which the corpus callosum – the structure that links the left and right hemispheres of the cortex – was cut. Brain surgeons believed cutting the corpus callosum would stop the spread of epileptic discharges from one side of the cortex to the other. A simple procedure turned out to reveal a surprising psychological condition.

Sperry found that, with their corpus callosum cut, patients had literally two brains in their head. The two hemispheres did not communicate much. Isolated, each hemisphere had different skills and almost a different personality. Crudely, in right handers the left hemisphere controlled language and logical operations, while the right hemisphere controlled emotions and spatial functioning.

Normal people integrate information from the left and the right hemispheres. Everything seems to be a unity. Actions seem to be the actions of one person. But the neurology revealed something radically different. Inside each skull there were at least two kinds of 'people', 'entities', 'minds', 'consciousnesses'.

No one has ever suggested that multiple personality cases suffer some problem with their corpus callosum. But Sperry's work revealed two brains within the brain. That fine unity – one brain, one mind, one self – the Victorians assumed, was an illusion.

Sperry's research inspired young psychologists like Prof Howard Gardner and Dr Robert Ornstein. Both have developed theories which question the unity of the mind. Gardner's *Multiple Intelligences* (1994) argues we should not place too much stress on the general factor of intelligence. I may be verbally adroit and yet be a spatial idiot. Ornstein claims in his *Multiminds* (1985) that our actions are the result of constant competition between different programmes in the brain. Each programme has a different agenda. The programme that takes 'executive control' at any moment determines the behaviour of the person. The similar phrasing is interesting. Multiple personality theory speaks of 'taking control of the body'.

Daniel Dennett of Tufts University (1994) argues from a philosophical point of view that there is no such thing as the essential self philosophers long sought after. Consciousness 'emerges' out of the continuing and different operations of the brain.

Normal people don't have unified minds. So you can hardly expect abnormal people to have them.

Neurology, psychology and cultural studies all suggest our sense of self is none too secure now. None of these disciplines conceived the idea of multiple personality. That honour is due to psychiatry.

PROBLEM OF DEFINITION

What is the polite way to introduce your alter?

You can call an alter it, him or her; a split; a fragment of the personality; a fantasy self; an ideal self; ghosts in the machine, with apologies to the philosopher Gilbert Ryle; a splinter; a false self; a traumatized entity; a disassociated self.

It's not clear that these words have different meanings. I can't think of a sentence whose meaning would really change if, for example, you altered the word 'alter'. 'I have an alter who comes out and hits the doctor' is identical, it seems to me, with 'I have a fragment who comes out and hits the doctor.' The only shift in meaning comes when you speak of something disembodied like an inner voice. My inner voice can only tell me to hit the doctor. It can't deliver the punch.

The fascination of multiple personalities is precisely that they are embodied at times. That is true whatever the process is called; You can pick the terms: switching; taking executive control; taking control of the body; coming into the body. The different phrases have identical meanings.

And every way we speak of this phenomenon depends on our

traditional understanding that the self, the I, is normally whole, stable, and one!

THE RISE OF SCHIZOPHRENIA

We've seen that multiple personality researchers are trying to claim that cases existed long before there were psychiatrists to describe them. Many now date the first modern case as that of Mary Reynolds in 1816, a girl who exhibited both a depressed normal state and a much livelier alter. The pioneers also point to the work of people like Dr Eugene Azam, a physician in Bordeaux, who described a woman called Félida who had two, possibly three, personality states, and to cases like that of Louis Vivet who was photographed in a variety of different states or selves.* Given that cases were being described in the nineteenth century, given Janet's work, why did the diagnosis die out?

The pioneers' position is that the diagnosis became rare after the 1920s because schizophrenia became such a successful and all-encompassing label. Psychiatrists, influenced by the work of Dr Eugen Bleuler (1857–1939) in Switzerland and Ernst Kretschmer (1888–1964) in Germany, started to diagnose different patients with different conditions as schizophrenics. Schizophrenia no longer meant a divided personality but a disturbed one. There was much work on the first-rank symptoms of schizophrenia like hallucinations and voices in the head. No one paid attention to the fact that even if multiples had these symptoms, they didn't behave like schizophrenics in other ways. Usually, they were quite well adjusted to reality. Many managed to hold jobs and bring up families. They were not withdrawn. In the enthusiasm for schizophrenia, these not too subtle differences were forgotten.

The early enthusiasts also lacked stamina. Janet may have lived on until 1947, but he became far less influential after 1920. In America Dr Morton Prince who worked around Boston, Mass.,

---

* Azam: 1877

was still an influential supporter, but the climate was changing. A narrow behaviourism was conquering psychology, while among clinicians, psychoanalysis was chic. For Freud, hysteria had nothing to do with multiple personality. Prince died in 1929 and had no real successor.

Sceptics, like Ian Hacking of the University of Toronto, say psychiatrists were wise to dump the diagnosis. Hacking adds that multiple personality only thrives when it latches on to a current fad. Unflatteringly, he says it is a parasite which needs a host. From 1880 to 1910, there was the perfect host – paranormal research. Was it an accident that two of the most famous American cases were clergymen? Hacking suggests that as interest in the paranormal declined, multiple personality declined too. It has revived now because there is a new host – our obsession with child abuse.

Despite the decline, there were a few cases reported after 1920, but none really grabbed the popular imagination. Schizophrenia, on the other hand, succeeded even if its popular image was sometimes confused. Schizophrenia was pure madness. It was hysteria but it was also, as with Jekyll and Hyde, split personality. Today, there is much media coverage of psychiatry but many people still think schizophrenics have split personalities.

THE THREE FACES OF EVE – THE FIRST SCIENTIFIC STUDY OF THE MODERN ERA

The revival of interest in multiple personality started with a very dramatic case – that of 'Eve'. One doctor who treated her was sure he had stumbled on a remarkable one-off phenomenon.

The setting of the case was Georgia, in the southern United States, a very considerable state in the 1950s. Eve White, whose real name was Chris Sizemore, complained constantly to her local doctor of migraines, blackouts and memory loss. She also confessed her marriage was unhappy, claiming that the problem was religious. She and her husband Ralph couldn't agree on how to raise their four-year-old daughter, Bonnie. Eve wanted her raised as a Catholic; Ralph wanted her raised as a Baptist.

In 1954, Colin Thigpen and his senior colleague Dr Harold Cleckley published a paper in *The Journal of Abnormal and Social Psychology* which was the core of their later book, *The Three Faces of Eve* (1957). These publications mark the start of the study and saga of multiple personality today. The book is not clear in separating their roles but it seems the patient was referred to Thigpen, a psychiatrist at the Medical School of the University of Georgia, who then called in his once teacher, Cleckley. Cleckley was already well known for a book *The Mask of Sanity. The Three Faces of Eve* established many of the criteria for diagnosing multiple personality. The book attracted enormous public and professional interest, partly because no one had reported a case like it for nearly fifty years. It was turned into a Hollywood film starring Joanne Woodward. The case was scientific gold dust and a human interest high.

The local doctor who saw Eve felt she needed psychotherapy. He sent her to see Colin Thigpen.

At first Thigpen saw nothing strange in her case. For example, Eve soon reported a recurrent dream which troubled her. She was in a huge room. At its centre there was a stagnant green pond. Her husband and uncle stood at the edge of the pond, menacing figures. In the pool, Eve and her daughter Bonnie fought for their lives. Eve added, 'I am trying to get her out for we both seem to be drowning. Despite all I can do to the contrary, I put her directly into my husband's hands. Then my uncle whom I love dearly tries to push my head under the slimy water.'

Then in the dream, Ralph, her husband, controlled Bonnie and took her away from Eve.

Dr Thigpen hypnotized Eve and they arrived at a simple interpretation of the dream. Eve was trying to save herself and her daughter from being taken into Ralph's Baptist faith. Eve White understood and went back to her discontented life. Nothing indicated she would make psychiatric history.

About a year later, Eve wrote to a relative explaining she was going to get a divorce. She had had one battle too many with

Ralph. The letter somehow fell into the hands of Eve's local doctor. It seems likely the worried relative sent it.

However, it proved to be a trigger.

Eve seems to have been visiting a cousin when she wrote this letter. Despite vowing to get a divorce, Eve went back home and acted normally with her husband. She was placid. The next day, however, Eve started to get ready to visit the cousin she had just left, the cousin at whose house she had decided to divorce Ralph. But Eve could remember nothing about the just completed visit or her decision to divorce.

From then on, Eve's behaviour became more and more peculiar. One moment she would be affectionate to Ralph, the next, bitter and hostile. Often, she had no memory of these dramatic switches of mood. Often, too, when she started to explain to the doctor she spoke in a flat, emotionless way, making her bizarre stories seem only more bizarre.

A few days later, her doctor received a letter from Eve. She said her visit to the doctor brought her relief but she also complained that 'my head hurts right on top' and that she was developing a rash.

Then, there was an abrupt break in the letter. The style and the handwriting changed completely. In a childish scrawl, quite unlike Eve's normal writing, was written, 'Baby please be quiet dear Lord don't let me lose patience with her she's too sweet and innocent . . .'

When she was asked about this letter, Eve claimed she had never finished it in this way and also never sent it. It also emerged that Eve had done something very untypical. The rather prim, conservative housewife had spent hundreds of dollars on flashy, sexy clothes. Eve had never worn clothes like these before. Thigpen knew, of course, of many cases of designer revenge, angry wives going on a spending spree to get at their husbands. But that was conscious. This was not. Ralph was livid.

Eve went back to see Thigpen. She confessed that for months she had been hearing a female voice in her head. It was happening more and more. The voice sounded familiar but she couldn't quite place it. It scared her. Mad people heard voices. She was afraid she would be sent into a state asylum for ever. It might suit Ralph. Again, these symptoms didn't manifest themselves in a vacuum. In the 1950s, there was growing concern about huge state psychiatric hospitals in the States, the so-called snake-pits that were dramatized in films like 'Suddenly Last Summer'. Albert Deutsch wrote *The Shame of the States* (1948) which publicized the appalling cruelties in these hospitals.

Thigpen then saw Eve behave in a completely surprising way. She was not under hypnosis but she suddenly slipped into a mini-trance. As we shall see, therapists now watch for particular facial movements that signal a switch into a new personality.

'The brooding look in her eyes became almost a stare. Suddenly her posture began to change. Her body slowly stiffened until she sat rigidly erect. An alien, inexplicable expression came over her face.'

Then the doctor saw 'utter blankness', followed by a slow transformation of her face. She closed her eyes, pressed her hands against her temples as if breathing off pain. Then, suddenly she relaxed.

A few moments later, Eve White's eyes popped open and with an entirely uncharacteristic sparkle and in a voice he had never heard before, she said, 'Hi there, Doc.'

These words were to become famous as the case became famous – and the film was a success. The phrase is telling. It has an almost cartoon-like feel. Bugs Bunny was always popping up with the words, 'What's up, Doc?'

It wasn't Eve White who was speaking. The person who snapped into life introduced herself as Eve Black. She explained that it was she who had bought the expensive, sexy clothes.

Initially, Thigpen was completely surprised and I suspect didn't really know what he was seeing. That's hardly strange. The condition had scarcely been reported for fifty years. The text of *The Three Faces of Eve* doesn't quite reflect this raw surprise. By the time Thigpen came to write the case up with Cleckley they had studied the history of multiple personality and were far more familiar with 'switching' and other aspects of the condition.

The newly appeared Eve Black was anything but shy. At once,

she added: 'I'm me and she's her . . . I like to live and she doesn't.'

So Black established herself as, at least, a radically different person from the timid, nervous, repressed Eve White. Black was pert, flirtatious and not at all meek. Her gestures were not self-effacing. Black sat, spoke, moved about, in a completely different way. Thigpen was astonished.

Thigpen wanted to know if Eve Black knew about the existence of Eve White. She said she hadn't been paying much attention to her recently but added slyly that she knew a few things about Eve White. Especially that she was far more sick of her husband than she let on. Black was irritated by White's fine ladylike airs and her goody-goody attitude. Black didn't always want to do the right thing.

Thigpen asked if any of this was to do with four-year-old Bonnie who had provoked the dream about the stagnant pond. Eve Black blazed, 'Why the hell should a girl find nothing to do but fret all the time about a four-year-old child?'

Black conceded she and White shared the same body. However, there were some questions she couldn't answer – especially how, when and why she, Eve Black, had been born. It was up to 'Doc' to find that out.

While Black knew of the existence of Eve White, White did not seem to know of the existence of Black. Black asked the doctor to keep it that way. The situation was very unequal. Black had unfettered access to White's thoughts and memories; White knew nothing.

Soon Thigpen managed to piece together a sequence of events. White had had a difficult marriage. Ralph had been extremely unsympathetic. It was at this time Black had started to emerge, suggesting a clear link with marital problems. As Eve White resented her husband more, Black started to get control of the body more easily. White got more migraines as she fought to keep Black silent and suppressed.

The difference between the two personalities seemed childishly simple. They were almost crude stereotypes. White was conventional, conservative and self-effacing. Black was a party girl. She went out with men; she hung around bars; she danced. Tellingly, however, Black doesn't seem to have been completely out of control. For example, she wasn't promiscuous. Thigpen pointed out to Black that, given her personality and tastes, if White ever became aware of this alternate self, she would fight even harder to control the body. Black's reply was, 'I'll fight,' and she added, 'I'm getting stronger than she is, each time I come out she gets weaker.'

And if this shift in power were to continue?

'The body will be mine,' Black said proudly.

The other person whose life was affected was Ralph. The doctors felt he had to be introduced to Black. She was adamant she was not Ralph's wife. She had nothing but contempt for the man. Though Black flaunted the party-girl image, she was even more negative about sex than White.

White had bad dreams in which her limbs turned into snakes. Sometimes, she was saved. Strong masculine hands grasped the snakes before they could reach her. She couldn't say if they were her father's, Ralph's or Dr Thigpen's hands. There were other crises too.

On one occasion, after White had an argument with Ralph, she ran from the house and was found unconscious at the foot of a tree in heavy rain. Soon after, White was sent to a psychiatric hospital for about two weeks. She did not resist hospitalization and seems to have found it helpful. White started to remember some childhood memories. One was of a terrifying monster who lay in the ditch by her house.

The hospital also had a restraining effect on Black, who emerged from time to time, but in less aggressive form than usual. In this subdued mood, Black finally agreed White should be told of her existence.

The only way that White could find out was by Thigpen telling her there was another personality who shared her body, a personality who did some of the puzzling things that had been happening to her.

White was totally surprised. 'It just can't be,' she said.

In the hospital there was one other significant development – and in terms of understanding subsequent controversies about multiple personalities, it was a crucial one. Black started to claim that she had been a presence since childhood, alive alongside White; she claimed a separate consciousness. She gave a number of reasons for not having appeared previously. She liked the masquerade. It gave her power. Thigpen did not push for more details about childhood traumas.

After White came out of hospital, her relationship with Ralph deteriorated. Black became more dominant. But the couple stayed out of medical contact for some months. Then, Thigpen got a letter in which Black said White had tried to kill herself. Black claimed she had emerged just in time to prevent White slicing her wrists with a razor.

After the suicide attempt, White decided to leave Ralph. After doing so, she developed a strange way of life. White would move into a boarding-house and get a job. She managed to hold each job longer than one might expect. Then, Black would not be able to resist emerging and causing trouble. Black would get drunk, be found in disreputable bars or be rude to superiors. Embarrassed, White would flee to the next job or the next town. White was always afraid of Black 'breaking out' but White showed surprising persistence. She didn't give up working.

In dealing with this extraordinary case, Thigpen used conventional methods – some psychotherapy, a little hypnosis and much listening. He eventually helped the personalities work out a truce. Black would hold herself back from creating mayhem at work. In return she would be given more time in control of the body, time for herself.

Ralph had given up on his marriage when White left, but after some months he started to try to convince Eve to return to their marriage and to his bed. White was not keen, but suddenly, surprisingly, Black was. Black agreed to spend a weekend with Ralph in Florida after White had refused to go.

Black claimed she went along with this escapade because she wanted Ralph to buy her some very expensive clothes. And he did, she crowed. Black even slept with Ralph though she referred to that as distasteful. When a few days later, back from Florida, White regained control of the body, she couldn't remember anything. Ralph told her what had happened and White froze him out completely. She became icily hostile. The Florida jaunt was the death-knell of their marriage.

Soon after, White started to get migraines and blackouts again. Until now, Eve, like most nineteenth-century cases, showed two personalities – she was a double rather than a multiple. Now that changed. A new person emerged. She too had a different voice, different gestures, different mannerisms, but she had a much more metaphysical opening line than 'Hi there, Doc.' Her first words were 'Who am I?'

This new person soon called herself Jane. She was remarkably self-confident. The doctors immediately welcomed this new personality. White was repressed and often emotionally upset – a perfect neurotic. Black was irresponsible, flighty and not much more than a pert baby. Jane appeared to be warm, mature and a real woman. She also had what the doctors called 'a capacity for accomplishment and fulfilment far beyond that of sweet and retiring Eve White'.

The doctors were by now rather concerned to get some scientific as well as therapeutic evidence of the remarkable phenomenon they had uncovered. They subjected all three personalities to an EEG test. (To do that they used hypnosis to evoke each one.)

They found that Eve White and Jane had strongly similar brainwaves. In 1953, ways of recording the electrical activity of the brain, first used in 1934, had become a routine neurological tool. Psychologists and neurologists believed the rhythm of brainwaves was an important clue to the working of the brain. There were many odd theories, including one which claimed that a slightly faster rhythm of alpha waves was a sign of anti-social tendencies. The EEG evidence supported the reality of at least two different personalities – the good White/Jane duo and the bad Black. This was to be the first of a number of modern attempts to prove there were physiologically, neurologically and psychologically separate selves in the body.

Thigpen and Cleckley also contacted two distinguished experimental psychologists – Charles Osgood and Zella Luria – who had developed what they called the 'semantic differential test'. The test was, in fact, a profile of how different individuals used language. It studied whether words like 'good', 'warm' and 'kind' had the same meaning for individuals by comparing their use of them with so-called 'normal' use. Osgood and Luria gave their test to all three of Eve's personalities and also analysed how each personality spoke. Their findings delighted Thigpen and Cleckley for they confirmed the presence of different personalities.

Osgood and Luria also offered character sketches of the three personalities. White perceived the world in a normal fashion and was well socialized, but she had 'an unhealthy attitude to herself'. Black had achieved 'a violent form of adjustment in which she perceives herself as literally perfect'. But she had a quite distorted view of the world. Jane displayed 'the most healthy meaning pattern'. She managed to have both a positive attitude towards herself and a realistic attitude towards the world.

It wasn't only psychologists who were convinced. At the time, Eve White had to sign some legal documents. Given the circumstances, her lawyer insisted that all three personalities had to sign. Otherwise they might end up with lawsuits.

(It's interesting that so far in the States we haven't seen multiple personalities suing each other, but in time that will come.)

The doctors then did something which established what has turned out to be the goal of most modern treatment – they decided to heal Eve's broken self by trying to integrate her different three 'selves' into one working personality. Unfortunately, they could only agree on this goal with two-thirds of their patient. White was content to give up the ghost, as it were, and merge with Jane. She had the insight to see she would become part of a warmer, more capable woman and so was willing to give her self up.

Black was hostile, however. She could see she was going to be the loser and understandably resented therapy whose aim was to annihilate her.

Jane and White became very close. Jane wrote a number of gushing diary entries about White, such as, 'The simple girl possesses direct honesty, genuine religious faith and unfailing gentleness.' Jane began to emerge more often. She also started to share White's headaches and snake dreams. The two personalities began to see the project of Jane taking over as being a job that she and White shared. White would be improved and absorbed – not destroyed.

There was now a crucial development. White would visit her daughter at times. During one of these visits, when Jane was in charge of the body, she crawled under the house to find a ball they had lost. Under the house, Jane was overwhelmed by a brief but vivid sensation. It was intense, a little like joy, a little like terror. Under hypnosis, White recalled something that had happened when she was about four years old. She was playing with a blue china cup in the house with her cousin. White wasn't sure if there was another person present. She then began to speak chaotically of chairs, flowers, a crowd. The words tumbled out intensely but incoherently.

Then, suddenly, she became silent 'as if the zigzag path of association down which she had been racing had suddenly ended' (p. 214). Then Eve Black emerged. She was in tears, which was extremely unusual. She said, 'I feel funny, I don't like this business, I guess, I'm scared.' Then she rambled almost manically. She asked Thigpen to keep the red dress as a souvenir of their meetings. There were then a few moments of chaos till she cried, 'Mother . . . oh . . . Mother . . . Don't make me . . . Don't, I can't do it . . . I can't.' Then a piercing scream.

This was the cathartic moment, Thigpen and Cleckley believed. After this, a new Eve emerged. She was a lot like Jane but she also incorporated aspects, usually positive aspects, of the other two personalities.

With Jane the childhood memories began to be unravelled. She eventually recalled being forced to touch the face of her dead grandmother at her funeral. It was her mother who made her do it. The touching caused immense trauma. It made Eve feel very morbid and scared of death.

In 1953, Thigpen and Cleckley decided that it was time to exhibit their remarkable patient. They organized a meeting in Georgia, where all three personalities agreed to attend. The doctors admired their cool as for two hours the three answered questions. At one point, a doctor asked Jane what she thought about her situation, to which Jane joked, 'But, doctor, you forget I am only seven months old.'

The doctors wanted to repeat the performance at the 1953 Los Angeles meeting of the American Psychiatric Association. But the organizers refused permission; they felt it would breach confidentiality. So Thigpen could only deliver a paper. But even this less personal presentation made headlines as the case was so sensational.

Eve's case highlights many questions that will surface throughout this book.

Had she really split into different personalities or were the three alters just different sides of herself?

Were they an attempt to compensate for everything that was wrong or missing in her life?

What was the role of the frightening childhood experience in creating the selves?

Why did Jane appear? Was she the product of a normal evolution or was she a personality that the therapists consciously or unconsciously suggested?

What precisely had gone on in the many sessions of hypnosis?

In 1957 *The Three Faces of Eve* proclaimed Eve, i.e. Chris Sizemore, was cured. Sizemore herself wrote two books later which contradicted this optimism. In them, she revealed that she went on to develop between nineteen and twenty-two other personalities. She broke the law, couldn't hold jobs and had endless problems with men. Some of these new personalities flowered just before Eve published her first autobiography in 1977. Some sceptics sniped this revelation was a marketing ploy to boost sales.

Sizemore also began to claim Eve's initial trauma started when she was only two when she witnessed a grotesque accident at a sawmill. A man's arm was severed. There was blood all over the place. Her first alter appeared that night when her mother cut her wrist. She had to escape the frightening blood.

The status of Eve in the development of multiple personality studies is a matter of some controversy. To some, the case marks the start of the modern multiple personality study, but critics like the London therapist and lecturer Ray Allridge Morris and Ian Hacking claim that many enthusiasts now dismiss the book. Eve does not fit the later model of multiple personality. She didn't have enough alters and, even worse, she showed no signs of having been abused as a child. Both experts are being a little too snide.

Eve herself claimed in her final book to have, at last, achieved integration. She added, 'I was well and famous but facing every-day problems with few normal experiences on which to base my decisions . . .' She went on to add, 'Years later Dr Kluft would succinctly describe this by saying "the cure of multiple personality disorder is the state in which most patients seek psychotherapy".' Sizemore seems to mean that once all the personalities have become one, they're not whole. The fused self needs help. But none of this came out until well after the publication of *Sybil* (1973), a book written not by the therapists, but by Flora Schreiber, a journalist who was given unique access to what seemed a unique case.

A TALE OF ABUSE – SYBIL

Thigpen and Cleckley did not really manage to explain why Eve should have developed her personalities. The case that led to the outline of a theory of why multiple personality should develop was that of Sybil.

It was nearly twenty years after the publication of *The Three Faces of Eve* that the next high-octane account of a multiple personality was published, but Sybil Dorset had actually been in treatment since 1945 when she was twenty-two years old. The case was important as it highlighted, for the first time since Freud, possible links between multiple personality dissociation and child abuse.

Sybil told her therapist, Dr Cornelia Wilbur, that she had been aware of having blackouts from the age of eight. Then, when she was in the fifth grade (aged about ten) she suddenly found that her last memory was of being in the third grade, aged about eight. She had no memory of the time in between. In college, studying art, Sybil turned to therapy. Sybil's therapy was stopped by her mother, Hattie. She told Sybil that the psychiatrist didn't want to see her any more. In 1947, Hattie Dorset admitted that this was untrue. She had never actually spoken to the psychiatrist. She just had not wanted her daughter to have any more therapy.

Hattie Dorset died in 1948. Her death freed Sybil. She graduated from college in 1949 and got a job teaching in a junior high school. She kept house for her father, Willard, and also worked as an occupational therapist. Her problems continued but she did nothing about them.

In 1954 Sybil moved to New York. She found her therapist, Cornelia Wilbur, who in the meantime had become a psychoanalyst. The first time Wilbur saw Sybil again was 18 October 1954. At first, Wilbur assumed that she was dealing with someone who had a very troubled childhood. Dr Wilbur never seems to have imagined that she was dealing with a case of multiple personality.

All that changed on 21 December 1954. On that day, Sybil told Dr Wilbur she wanted to show her a letter from a useless, sexless man who had once been her fiancé. The letter told her he was breaking off their relationship. When Sybil started to root in her handbag, she found the letter was torn in half. She couldn't explain how. This discovery triggered a sudden change. Dr Wilbur was no longer confronted by Sybil but by a much more aggressive and assertive woman who called herself Peggy Lou. Sybil's mother apparently sometimes called her Peggy.

Peggy Lou would turn out to be one of Sybil's sixteen selves. Some, Wilbur would learn, had been part of Sybil since the age of three.

Peggy Lou expressed her fury. She told Dr Wilbur she didn't know who wouldn't be insulted by the Dear John letter in the handbag. But Sybil wouldn't be: 'She can't stand up for herself. I have to stand up for her. She can't get angry because her mother won't let her.'

Peggy Lou insisted that Hattie Dorset was not her mother.

Peggy Lou added she knew it was a sin to get angry but that people did get angry: 'It's all right to be mad if I want to be.'

Sybil did not know of Peggy Lou's existence. Just as in the Eve case, the therapist would have to decide when to reveal the truth to the 'host' personality.

Peggy Lou and Sybil continued in therapy until 6 March 1955 when in the middle of a 'joint' session, a voice that was quite unlike Sybil's said:

'She was so sick she couldn't come, so I came instead.'

This 'I' was Vicky Antoinette Schleau, who was a highly sophisticated personality. She was the only one of the sixteen to know of the existence of all the rest. Vicky described herself as coming from abroad but said she had been Americanized. She warned the doctor that many other personalities would in due course make their appearance.

Soon after this, Dr Wilbur decided that she had to tell Sybil the true nature of her condition. Sybil thought her blank spells were just that. Though she often heard descriptions of her behaviour which she didn't remember, she had 'let it go' without probing. What the doctor told her terrified Sybil. She ran out of Wilbur's office, fled back to her dorm at Columbia and locked herself in.

The revelation triggered an alarming series of transformations as Sybil switched from one 'self' into another. Then she fell into a stupor. Dr Wilbur was summoned. Seeing how distressed Sybil was, she dosed her with Seconal. Dr Wilbur also decided she would have to break some of the classic analytic rules. She would become an active presence in Sybil's life. Wilbur took her for a drive out of New York. This human act won Sybil's trust – and also the trust of the other personalities. They held what Dr Wilburn called some sort of inner conclave and decided, 'We'll go see her.' The personalities were going to co-operate.

It was at this time that Sybil started to speak of her childhood more openly. She was born in Willow Corners, Wisconsin, a small town near the Minnesota border where the local papers had headlines like MOTHERS' PICNIC AT HIGH SCHOOL WEDNESDAY. It was a solidly Republican place, small-town America. Hattie and her husband Willard belonged to an extreme Protestant sect which regarded all literature other than religious tracts as lies. Members of the sect were forbidden to read even the innocuous local papers.

Sybil's mother, Hattie, had her own traumas. She was born in the middle of a family of thirteen children. She had musical talent. When Hattie was twelve, however, her father pulled her out of school to work in his music store. Hattie was not to be allowed to flower as a musician. So Hattie took to petty acts of sabotage, such as cutting the sleeves of her father's treasured smoking jacket. Wilbur concluded frustration made Hattie ferociously angry – anger she would take out on her daughter.

After Sybil was born, her mother went into a deep post-natal depression. Dr Wilbur claimed Hattie was schizophrenic, perhaps to excuse some of her sadistic acts. For Hattie, Sybil's birth was a turning-point. She stopped being a devoted homemaker and became less attentive to her husband, Willard. To Sybil, she was cold. Sybil only got warmth from her grandmother, who died of cervical cancer when Sybil was nine. She was not allowed to attend the funeral service but she was allowed to attend the burial; there, she went berserk and had to be stopped from walking into the grave. For years, the last thing Sybil could remember, was being restrained at the graveside.

Sybil seems to have had no memory for the next two years. When she 'emerged' next, she was living in a redecorated house. She was in the fifth grade but she couldn't cope with the work, partly because she thought she was two years younger. Her classmates ignored her or, worse, made fun of her.

Willard, Sybil's father, was too weak to protect his daughter. The only person Sybil could communicate with was Danny Martin, a young school-friend who did his best to fill in the gaps of her two missing years.

Sybil's life changed again when her father bought a gas station in, of all places, Waco, Texas, where fifty years later the Branch Davidian Cult fought the FBI. When the family moved to Waco, Sybil lost Danny, her only support against total isolation.

Minutes after Sybil said goodbye to Danny, Vicky – the sophisticated alter – first managed to get control of Sybil's body.

At first, Dr Wilbur believed Sybil's condition was rooted in her grief at her grandmother's death. Slowly, however, she began to uncover a catalogue of trauma and abuse. Until she was nine years old, Sybil shared a bedroom with her parents. Several nights a week she saw them make love; Hattie and Willard might have been fundamentalist Protestants, but they didn't think it odd to have their growing daughter in their bedroom. When she was four and a half, Sybil was placed in a crib by her mother who said, 'I love you, Peggy,' and then removed the stairs that were her only means of escape. Sybil was left to smother. She was rescued by her father. Hattie blamed a boy called Floyd, the local bully. It wasn't clear whether she meant to kill her daughter or 'just' make her suffer.

Hattie also abused her daughter sexually. When Sybil was a small child her mother would often insert objects into her vagina – buttonhooks, knives, small bottles. Hattie said, 'You might as well get used to it. That's what men will do to you when you grow up. They put things in you, they hurt you and they push you around.' It was probably because of the internal injuries she suffered that Sybil could never have a child.

Hattie also beat Sybil with her bare fists. Sometimes, Hattie beat her so hard she broke bones. The local doctor didn't question why Sybil so often had broken bones.

Sometimes, in a grotesque scene that recalled her own frustrations, Hattie would tie Sybil to the kitchen table while she played the piano. Sometimes, she injected cold water into the child's rectum. Sometimes, Hattie would say, 'I'll show you what it's like to be dead or blind.' Hattie would lock Sybil in a trunk for hours, blindfold her and taunt her. Sometimes, Hattie suffocated her until she became unconscious.

Hattie's cruelty lasted for years. No one ever suggested that Sybil exaggerated. The question was more why her father did nothing to protect her. As Dr Wilbur unravelled the story of the abuse, she came to meet Sybil's sixteen different personalities. Each had not just her own distinct history and attitudes but a different voice, different mannerisms and, even, hair colour. It's worth listing the sixteen:

Sybil, tortured as a child, terrified of intimacy, a talented graphic artist. The 'real' Sybil was born in 1923. The first alters started to emerge when she was three years old. Others came later, and Dr Wilbur managed to get dates for some of their 'births'.
Vicky Schleau, born 1926, a sophisticated personality and the only one to know of the existence of all the others.
Peggy Lou, also born 1926. Peggy Lou, like Eve Black, seems to have been a personification of anger. She was assertive, confrontational and, at times, an ignorant hick.
Peggy Ann Baldwin, a counterpart to Peggy Lou, who was more given to fear than anger. Towards the end of therapy, they merged.
Mary, a contemplative, rather dull character, plump, with long brown hair.
Marcia, born 1927, openly emotional, a writer and artist.
Sybil Anne, born 1928, pale, insubstantial.
Vanessa, born 1935, dramatic and intense; a redhead.
Nancy Lou, an anti-Catholic bigot.
Ruthie, an infant.
Clara, pious and critical of Sybil.
Helen, terrified but determined. She had light brown hair and thin lips.
Marjorie, serene, vivacious and good humoured.
The Blonde, born in 1946, who did not have a name but was a perpetual teenager and blonde goddess. She was to prove a key figure.
Two male alters also were part of Sybil's constellation: *Mike*, a builder and carpenter, and *Sid* a handyman.

As with Eve, the therapy aimed at integrating these different selves into one whole personality.

Sybil was a talented artist. Every Christmas, Dr Wilbur knew she would get sixteen different Christmas cards – one from each of the personalities. Dr Wilbur felt it was important for Sybil to meet the others but any move towards that was usually traumatic. Once, after being told of one of the others, Sybil nearly threw herself into the Hudson; happily, Vicky emerged in time to ring Dr Wilbur.

In Eve's case, Jane emerged spontaneously. She may have been everything the therapists thought was healthy, but at least she wasn't their creation. Dr Wilbur was more proactive with Sybil. One problem seemed to be that all Sybil's personalities had a different age. Dr Wilbur put Sybil in a deep trance and, eventually, managed to age them till they were all thirty-eight years old.

Later in therapy another alter, the Blonde, appeared. She was young, gorgeous and seemed to represent what Sybil could be. At one point, the Blonde said, 'You and I belong together, Vicky. Unlike the others, we are not cradled in trauma but in Sybil's wish.' The Blonde claimed she had come to set Sybil free – an ambition she never fulfilled.

As Sybil began to articulate her deep-seated hatred of her mother, she alone appeared for therapy. The others could only be reached through hypnosis. The appearance of the Blonde and the ageing of all the selves led to a slow, gradual fading of the other personalities. They were assimilated in Sybil's persona. She stopped suffering bouts of amnesia and the appearance of other selves.

The importance of the case was that Sybil made explicit what had only been hinted at before – a link between being physically and sexually abused as a child and developing multiple personalities.

But Sybil, like Eve, seemed to be an extraordinary one-off.

No one had any reason to think of multiple personality as anything but very rare. One psychiatrist went through the literature and argued that the number of cases was actually falling. There had been thirty-three cases reported between 1901 and 1944. But in the next twenty-five years, to 1969, there had been thirteen cases.

Rare in the first place, multiple personality seemed to be getting even rarer.

CHAPTER 2

Stuff One-Dimensional Life

In which the Postmodern Reader is introduced to the Zen and the Yen of Multiple Personality and has to face the fact that not everything in this book is going to be serious stuff.

Are you feeling a little one-dimensional?

If so, this is the chapter for you.

I don't apologize for the fact that this chapter is quite out of keeping with the style of the first.

If an author can't peacock his own multiple personality tendencies, giving voice to all his subpersonalities' insights, surfing across Academic, Psycho-pop, Deep Soul and Mega Mind in a multiple personality book, where can he play such textual games?

Tell the different bits of me that.

So I'll start with the trick of a direct appeal from what is the author's voice – i.e. the objective me writing as sincerely, subjectively and honestly as I can – to the reader, reading as sincerely as she can.

Did you get everything you wanted out of Chapter One?

I hope (author's humble voice here, scribe – a mere servant of readers – trying to please in the best traditions of Grub Street and modern academic man in search of a grant from a government body which wants to hear research into this subject is of vital national importance and will boost exports) – I hope, as I said, you got some information, history, case-histories, theories, background out of Chapter One.

But is that enough?

What about those parts of those readers who were hoping for something more intense, more personal?

Those who want help to find their own multiple personalities?

Those who rather fancy a touch of the Jekyll and Hydes, who feel it'd be cool to have at least seven personalities to try on of a Sunday night?

Don't despair. Read on. Later you'll find one of the key instruments of current culture – the questionnaire. The author will turn into an agony aunt with a slight taste for empiricism. Based on the Dissociative Experience Scale and twelve other questionnaires which analyse the tendency to split, fantasize, fragment, disassociate, associate with weird paranormal grungy ghosts who call to you from within your soul.

First, though, we have to get back to the serious and the harrowing.

CHAPTER 3

The Discovery of Sexual Abuse

A drab road in Birmingham's suburbs. I've come to the Gracewell Clinic to meet a friend of mine who used to be an actor. Patrick used to tour prisons with a theatre group but has decided to give up the stage. The Gracewell Clinic offers treatment to people who have committed sexual offences. Some have been through the courts, some haven't. Patrick went to work there.

Through Patrick I met a man I'll call Martin.

Martin has a thin face. He wears a dark jacket. At this meeting he wants to listen. He won't say anything. He'll decide later if he will co-operate. I explain both what I've done and what I'm doing. I'm not out to make fun of him or exploit his experiences.

'I'll think about it,' Martin says.

Three days later, Martin rings me up. He wants to meet in a pub. Neutral territory.

The pub was a bad place to talk. Martin drank cider. He didn't seem to want to 'put it away'. He talked about what treatment was like. He was sceptical. Again, it took time to discover what he'd done.

We go to an Italian.

'It started when I was four,' Martin says. 'I used to bathe with my father.' They'd play with ducks and toys. Then, and he has no problem 'confessing', his father would get him to masturbate him. 'I loved my father,' Martin adds.

Martin didn't do anything to stop what was happening. He thinks he must have liked being that close to his father. But he knew that what they were doing wasn't right. His father was always careful to close the bathroom door. He didn't make any sounds. Usually, they had these baths together when Martin's mother wasn't at home. Once, she found them in the bath together.

'There was a terrible fight,' Martin said. His mother left but she eventually came back. She made her husband promise never to do it again.

'He did stop it,' Martin said, and paused.

'Did you miss it?'

'I don't know.' But what happened next was extraordinary. 'My father introduced me to someone who worked with him at the bus depot. I used to go after school to see him sometimes.' As Martin put it, it seemed likely that his father knew this man would abuse his son. 'I was eight, I think, when that started,' Martin told me.

Martin doesn't see himself just as a victim. It seems important to his sense of identity that he also had power. He added, 'I was starting to be interested in boys myself. I knew a lot about it, you see.'

Martin told me that between the age of eight and twelve, he lived a strange double life. He was both abused and abuser. He would often stay with the man from the bus depot. But Martin also became good at spotting younger children who were 'keen', as he put it.

'There was this boy, can't have been more than seven, who used to hang around me all the time. I got fed up with it. So I took him in the shed. I said I knew what he wanted and he could have it. I let him toss me off.' Martin thinks he was eleven at the time.

Martin claimed to have committed hundreds of acts of abuse without ever getting caught. He had once spent a few weeks in a relative's house in Brighton where he had to share a bed with a thirteen-year-old cousin.

'They never found out,' Martin laughed.

Martin reckoned he was more interested in boys than in girls. As a cover, he had married, but he still continued to abuse boys. His wife eventually found out but she stayed with him. In his early twenties, Martin had finally been caught. He claimed now that he had changed. His behaviour did worry him, he said. He wondered who it was who had committed so many acts of abuse. Was it really himself? It no longer felt like himself.

I couldn't make out if Martin was truly concerned or whether he thought it was best to claim to be.

We know now that there are many people like Martin – abusers who were once victims. And we feel our knowledge is progress.

Every day in Britain and America, police and social services investigate allegations of child physical and sexual abuse. The two agencies have joined forces to pool expertise. Estimates of how many children have been abused are unreliable but some studies suggest that over 20 per cent of women have had experience of some form of abuse. In America, the statistics are at least as high. Gerillyn Smith (1995) has claimed 50 per cent of women have been abused. Often, the situation is similar to that Martin described: it's a father, an uncle, a cousin.

We tend to act as if we have discovered physical and sexual abuse in the last twenty years. The Victorians, however, were well aware of both kinds of abuse. The National Society for the Prevention of Cruelty to Children was formed in 1889 after a long series of scandals about 'baby farming' – poor girls paid women to take children off their hands. These infants were often killed. Lionel Rose in *The Massacre of the Innocents* (1986) quotes the social reformer, Mary Barnes, who said that the 'Metropolitan Police think no more of finding the dead body of a child in the street than picking up a dead cat or dog.' Victorian child-killers were often not prosecuted. Thousands of babies and infants were killed each year between 1850 and 1890. Many were also sexually exploited. There were thousands of child prostitutes in London in the 1880s and 1890s.

Eventually, the government passed a series of reforms, including the 1908 Children's Act, which created Infant Inspection Officers whose job it was to protect children.

Despite these reforms and the development of social work as a profession, child abuse was ignored – considered too sordid to think about. Few believed in the 1930s that parents could be so cruel or evil and that seems to have been true even of clever, dedicated researchers. Carl Rogers, the founder of client-centred therapy, was head of research for the Rochester Society for the Prevention of Cruelty to Children in the 1930s. In his first book (1939), he looked in detail at the problems client families were bringing to the Society's office in Rochester, New York. Child abuse, physical or sexual, was hardly mentioned. The emphasis was entirely on how to make the family work well together and prevent the child being delinquent. The early editions of Dr Spock don't mention child abuse.

No one has been able to explain satisfactorily why child abuse became a forgotten issue. Jeffrey Masson (1980) blames Freud, who initially suggested that many of his patients had been molested by their parents. Masson accuses Freud of not having the courage of his data. He appeared to change his mind about the reality of the abuse and dismissed what his patients said about their parents as fantasy. Freud went further. He claimed that being seduced by parents was an unconscious fantasy for many children. Masson argues Freud did not genuinely change his mind. Rather, Freud was panicked into hypocrisy. Psychoanalysis would never have established its doctrines if the so-called 'Jewish Science' went so far as to claim parents regularly abused their children. Freud, aware of the anti-Semitism in Viennese society, dared not shock too much. So the great pioneer trimmed the truth.

Many Freudians, and many non-Freudians, disagree with Masson. Whatever the truth of this argument, the fact remains that in 1895 Freud was an obscure Viennese doctor. His visions and revisions weren't of much import. The reasons why child abuse dropped off the agenda seem more mundane – complacency, a distaste for anything so 'vile', society looking the other way.

The Three Faces of Eve was published in 1957, before the revival of interest in physical abuse. In 1961, the American press drew attention to some appalling cases in Denver. In Britain, the rediscovery of child abuse owed much to the tragic death of four-year-old Maria Colwell in 1974. After she was battered to death, social workers suddenly became more aware of the dangers of physical abuse.

Sybil was published in the United States in 1973. Professionals were ready to believe in the trauma that physical abuse might cause. Though Sybil was also sexually abused, as it was by her mother, the case didn't make sexual abuse a central issue at once. It was only later in the 1970s in the States, and in the late 1970s and early 1980s in Britain, that social workers and doctors started to look regularly for evidence of sexual abuse.

In 1991, I made a film called 'The Last Taboo' for 'Dispatches' on Channel 4. By then, sexual abuse was well recognized. Few social workers accepted another uncomfortable truth, that in about a third of cases, it is children who sexually abuse other children. Sometimes, the abusers are as young as eight – and know quite well what they are doing.

While making 'The Last Taboo', I interviewed two distinguished social workers involved in the Cleveland inquiry, which investigated why over two hundred children had been taken into care in the Middlesbrough area as a result of allegations of sexual abuse. Both these social workers independently told me they had sat on an inquiry into the death of a child in north-west England in the late 1970s. They both realized now that they had missed obvious evidence of sexual abuse. Julia Ross, now the director of social services in the London Borough of Hillingdon, told me that she drew the attention of the local police in Hammersmith to a case where a girl complained that her father was feeling her up. Ross was shocked herself. She had never heard any similar allegations. The police were sceptical. They had only just begun to absorb the lessons of the Maria Colwell case. Beating children up was bad enough.

The history is important because if professionals didn't think such things could happen, imagine the pressure on the children living through an experience that no one believed was possible.

One victim of abuse has given me the following account of her experience as a seven-year-old. Her mother would go off shopping with her friends. Mother's new boyfriend, who she was going to marry, would look after her '. . . every Saturday afternoon. He would tickle me in private parts of my body, he'd hold me in all the wrong places, he'd try to insert his fingers in us as well.' The boyfriend gave her money, but the victim said, 'He had never threatened me but somehow I felt threatened just by him being there. I always accepted his money but wasted it straight away just to be rid of him.'

The seven-year-old didn't say anything to her mother. The boyfriend was good at finding ways of being alone with her. This pattern continued until the girl was eleven. Then, she said, 'He lay on top of me touching me all the time. I tried to block it from my mind and I succeeded. I was frightened because when I cried "no" he didn't stop. I couldn't remember, I didn't want to.'

The girl kept her secret for four years. She was frightened no one would believe her, felt guilty about taking the boyfriend's money and confused about the fact that he also offered her some appropriate affection. The girl did eventually tell a teacher at school and bitterly regretted the chaos and investigations that followed.

Every case of abuse is an individual tragedy but there are patterns. Children as young as six know that what is happening is wrong and has to be kept secret. Often, they are bullied into the act by an adult they love and respect as well as fear. Sometimes, they also get closeness, warmth and, even, some pleasure from it. Often, they feel guilty, too. Nearly always the abuser will put them under intense pressure to tell no one. It's their great secret. Hidden from the family. Hidden from the world.

The child cannot bear facing up to what's going on. The father – occasionally the mother – is doing things that shouldn't be done. To cope with this impossible situation, the child cuts off. There is no physical escape from the out-of-control father thrashing you, no physical escape from the father getting into bed with you while mother is at evening classes, or shopping, or at chapel. The only escape is to pretend it is not happening – to cut off, to deny, to withdraw where you can't be reached or hurt. Fine, they shout inside, fine, hurt me but you're not really hurting me. I've shut my eyes. I've shut my mind. I've shut my door. It's not me you're doing it to.

But what happens inside the slammed-shut, closed self?

Father gets dressed. He leaves my room. Mother comes back

from evening class. I pull my pants back on. We have dinner. As a family, we watch television. I go to bed. Mother comes to give me a kiss. Father comes to give me a kiss. I let him. I do not think about what he has just done. I do not think about what I dread – next Thursday, when mother's off again to her evening class, he'll be back in my room. Coming to 'play' with me when I have a bath. Coming to 'play' in bed.

When abused children get warmth, even some love, it makes it only more confusing. Such situations give rise to two psychological processes – denial and repression. These are concepts which have extensive literature but their core is not hard to summarize (Sue Walrond-Skinner, 1988).

Denial is simply: this is not happening to me. I have no awareness of it, no memory of it. My mind is blank about it.

Repression is more complex and controversial: this is happening but I cannot bear to know the fact, so somehow my mind protects me. It pushes my awareness, my memories, my painful, unspeakable feelings down and down. Into oblivion. I forget, or I pretend to forget. The feelings don't bother me. I don't know how this happens and I forget that it has happened.

In discovering repression, Freud was building on ideas that Pierre Janet had already written about. Ellenberger (1970) in *The Discovery of The Unconscious*, gives a good account of the discovery of the unconscious in the nineteenth century. Repression isn't destruction. The memories, feelings and pain try to get back to the conscious mind but they are censored, sometimes mangled. Freud called this process 'the return of the repressed'. Often, repressed ideas return in the form of conventional psychiatric symptoms – tics, obsessive behaviours like repetitive hand-washing, peculiar fetishes like being unable to leave a room without touching the mantelpiece three times, or terrible recurrent nightmares.

As more cases of multiple personality came to light in the 1970s, some American psychiatrists started to put forward a theory. The abuse some children suffered was so traumatic it led, first, to memory disturbances and blackouts, like those Eve and Sybil suffered from. Then, the repressed material led to splitting and the kind of dissociative tendencies Pierre Janet had first described.

'Splitting' is used in at least three different senses in psychiatry. The first refers to the split between the conscious, unconscious and preconscious levels of mind which Freud first mapped out in *The Ego and the Id* (1923). The second use of splitting refers, not to the geography of the mind, but to the process by which the ego can give two different responses to events: for example, I admit spending thousands on new clothes, and then, I forget that I have done so.

The analyst Melanie Klein (1948) used splitting in a different way yet. For her, splitting meant dividing objects into the absolutely good or the absolutely bad, exactly as in the story of Jekyll and Hyde. Multiple personality workers tend to mix these three uses. Nevertheless, they have put together a fairly clear account of how abuse leads to splitting. The blindly angry nebulous 'Not Me' of denial starts to take on a positive identity. It becomes more than a mere 'Not'. It splits but it also grows into an entity with a 'life' of its own. Often, this 'life' means it takes on all the outrageous wishes and angers the conscious 'host' self can't bear to admit to. This theory involves a number of stages.

1. Incidents of abuse, nearly always abuse the child can't escape from.

2. Repression, so that the child has no conscious memory of the abuse. As a result, memories are only accessible through techniques like hypnosis.

3. A crucial transformation of these buried and repressed memories, in fact a quantum leap. In many cases of trauma and post-traumatic stress disorder, patients suffer flashbacks, intrusive memories, nightmares. Sometimes they have a sense that if they survived a kidnapping or a bomb, they can survive anything. With dissociation and multiple personality, however, this theory supposes the repressed memories transform

themselves into the representation of some psychological being – alters, splits, fragments of other selves. These may express what is also expressed in a dream or a nightmare but an alter is not like a dream. However vivid your dreams may be, however much you may feel you are in them, they are not personalities. An angry alter screaming, 'I'm going to kill you,' is a different entity. The nightmares and flashbacks happen to you but you construct the alter out of them.

4. Frank Putnam of the National Institute of Mental Health in Washington, D.C., suggests that if the abuse takes place before the child is six or seven, splits into multiple personalities will take place as described. If the abuse happens later, children react to the trauma in different ways.

5. The changes I have described in point 3 above take place roughly when the child is abused. The dissociation isn't a product of memory. It happens, more or less, when the child is abused to help her or him block the trauma – and escape it.

Somehow, though, once they have been created, these alters remain buried for years, usually only to reveal themselves in the teens. It is this theory that the pioneers defend and the critics attack fiercely.

Eventually both Sybil and Eve suggested their multiple personalities had first developed in childhood. But at the time no one knew, or noticed, what was going on. Both children were thought of as rather odd but they were never caught out with one of their other selves on display. Their most obvious problem was loss of memory.

Was neither Sybil nor Eve found out because both managed to hide the fact they had alternative selves, or was it because the alters only developed when they were much older – either as the memories were worked through or in response to other stresses? The books unfortunately don't make it possible to answer these questions. They also don't allow one to answer to one other crucial point. When Eve and Sybil 'integrated' or 'fused' was this a natural evolution or was it the result of suggestion on the part of their therapists?

RISE IN NUMBERS

While the number of cases was small, these were largely academic questions. It was only at the end of the 1970s that Richard Kluft began to attend conferences on hypnosis where his ideas on multiple personality didn't get scorned. He stopped feeling like an outcast. By 1980, one study noted that perhaps five hundred new cases had been reported in the previous decade. Greaves (1980) published this result and began what some see as an important new movement in psychiatry. The sceptics, on the other hand, see the growth of multiple personality as a perfect example of modern medical hype.

However, it's probably worth telling the story first from the side of the pioneers. By the mid 1970s, a small number of psychiatrists were beginning to have a certain enthusiasm for the diagnosis of multiple personality. One of these was Eugene Bliss of Utah who developed the theory that those who suffered from multiple personality disorder had learned how to hypnotize themselves, and had probably started to do that very young. Bliss argued in 1985 that patients literally entrance themselves and, in that state, produce alters.

Today, one of the most energetic members of the multiple personality 'movement', as some critics call it, is Dr Colin Ross. Ross, a trim Canadian, saw his first multiple personality case in 1979 when he was a third-year medical student. One of his early cases was a woman he calls Jenny Z who was admitted to his hospital in Winnipeg. Jenny Z turned out to be a complex case.

Everyone had assumed that she suffered from borderline personality, a diagnosis American psychiatrists started to use in the late 1970s. Jenny Z had been in trouble with the law. Ross was intrigued by her lapses of memory. He didn't think that these were necessarily cynical, though they did help to cover up a

number of small frauds and the theft of $1,600 from her boy-
friend. There were legal cases against her pending both in Winnipeg and Vancouver. Over a period of weeks, Ross became
convinced Jenny wasn't manipulating him or putting on a performance. She really had a number of different personalities. At
the last count, Ross had made contact with seven of them.

Ross told me that he spent much of his first five years working
as a general psychiatrist dealing with the run of cases that arrive
in any large hospital. Jenny Z did not turn out to be an excep-
tional freak as people had believed Eve to be. Of all the pioneers,
Ross is perhaps the most ambitious. He argues one reason the
diagnosis has been attacked so fiercely is that it may trigger a
major shift in the way we think of psychiatric illnesses and their
causes. Ross comes in for a good deal of flak from the critics.
Some, he argues, is based on prejudice and poor scholarship.
Making enthusiasts like him sound silly is good 'scientific' tactics.

A pioneer who gets a better press from the sceptics is Dr Frank
Putnam. Putnam is more cautious than Ross but that may not
be the only reason. Ross has worked at relatively out-of-the-way
clinics. Putnam works for the National Institute of Mental Health
in Washington. He has status and prestige, so whereas Ross is
derided, sometimes very viciously, Putnam is sniped at in a rather
more academic manner. (After all, Putnam might have coffee
with a man who might be on the panel dealing with your next
grant applications.)

Putnam told me he became interested in multiple personality
after he successfully treated a woman who had been considered
untreatable. That patient showed him the reality of multiple
personality.

Following this, in 1986 Putnam wrote to ninety-two clinicians
asking for details of their multiple personality cases. Putnam
added that he felt it would be wrong for him to study his own
patients, given the controversial history of the subject. He might
be too biased. Putnam claimed that his survey was the first scientific review of recent cases.

He made two startling findings. First, he discovered that nearly
everyone who was eventually diagnosed as having multiple per-

sonality disorder had previously been diagnosed as having some other psychiatric condition. Patients had been said to be depressed, schizophrenic or borderline. It was more than possible that conventional psychiatry was misdiagnosing these patients. This is not something psychiatrists like to hear. They particularly didn't like to hear it in the late 1970s and early 1980s. After the huge publicity that anti-psychiatrists like R. D. Laing and Thomas Szasz attracted, an international project was started by the World Health Organization. Its aim was to make sure that schizophrenia was diagnosed according to the same criteria all over the world. The last thing establishment psychiatry wanted to confront was the possibility that people who were not schizophrenics were being diagnosed as such.

Putnam found that on average patients had spent over six years in the mental health system before they were recognized as having multiple personality disorder. On average they had had 3.6 previous diagnoses. Many did hear voices and that started a controversy that has continued. The borderline debate matters because of arguments as to whether schizophrenics hear voices coming from outside – messages from God or little green men who are residing in the TV set – while those suffering from multiple personality disorder hear voices coming from inside. These are the alters talking to, and through, them.

Putnam also latched on to another strange development. Eve was really parsimonious – at least, the three-faced Eve of Thigpen and Cleckley was. Putnam's sample showed the average multiple sprouted 13.3 alters. The cast had expanded dramatically.

Putnam also confirmed a finding going back to William James and Morton Prince. The conscious self or host personality hardly ever knew of the existence of the other personalities.

Putnam then set about doing something quite routine. He wanted to devise a test. He hoped to identify the kind of person who had a tendency to develop alters. He became convinced there was a continuum between, at one end, individuals who were so self-solid that questions of self and identity never flashed through their splendidly rock-like personalities, to flakey multiples who fragmented like sparks out of Catherine wheels.

TESTING FOR MULTIPLE PERSONALITY

In the best traditions of American psychology, Putnam first – and Ross after him – set about devising Tests of Dissociation. A few sample questions to whet the appetite.

Have you ever noticed yourself in the mirror and not recognized yourself?
Do you ever speak about yourself as 'we' or 'us'?
Do you ever find yourself in an unfamiliar place and are not sure how you got there?
Have you experienced a sudden inability to recall important personal information or events that are too extensive to be explained by ordinary forgetfulness?
Do you sometimes hear voices from inside you speaking to you?
Do you suffer from hallucinations?
Do you have long periods when you feel unreal, as if in a dream, not counting times that may be due to alcohol or drug use?
Do you feel there are other people inside you?

Putnam argued that his test results suggested there was a continuum of states from amnesia to frank multiple personality syndrome. It is worth setting out these states in some detail.

Amnesia. There is no controversy about amnesia. Patients lose their memory; they don't know who they are. They wake up after a road accident or a stroke and they have forgotten their name, their profession, their wife. Most will recover most of their memories in a short period of time. They will become 'themselves' again.

Fugue. The second state is fugue. Some sceptics claim that Ansel Bourne wasn't a real multiple personality at all but a fuguist. The typical fuguist 'flees' and assumes a new identity. They forget who they were and have no idea, it seems, that their second identity is brand-new. Charcot was struck in the 1880s by how resourceful these fuguists could be. They were, he wrote, 'mad people in full delirium, yet they buy railway tickets, dine, sleep in hotels'. No one they met ever seems to have noticed that they were off their heads because, Charcot noted, while they were fleeing their normal lives, they had apparently sane conversations with ordinary people. They sometimes seemed odd, but not crazed.

Depersonalization Syndrome. The third state Putnam identified was depersonalization syndrome. This is a state in which an individual feels unreal. I do not feel like I am anybody at all. I wake up in the morning. I look in the mirror. I have no idea who is staring back at me. We assume, for the diagnosis to hold, that I am not drunk and I have not recently been on drugs.

Freud threw some interesting light on this state. In 1936, in an open letter to the writer Roman Rolland, 'a disturbance of memory on the Acropolis', Freud admitted to having had a strange experience which had bothered him since 1904. Freud went on a holiday to Greece with his brother. Freud told Rolland that as he stood on the Acropolis 'and cast my eyes around . . . a surprising thought suddenly entered my mind. So, all this really does exist just as we learnt at school.' What surprised Freud was that the person who saw this 'was divided, far more sharply than was usually noticeable, from another person who took cognizance of the remark.' The divide between the person who saw and the person who thought about the remark jolted him because it was as if this second person had been unaware before of the real existence of Athens and the view from the Acropolis. But the boy Freud knew it was there hence the disturbance of memory – and sense of strangeness.

Freud concluded that his odd experience was an experience of 'derealisation', a feeling that 'what I see is not real'. It unsettled him, though making him wonder just what he had learned at school about the Acropolis. He explained to Rolland that in many mental illnesses patients felt that some perceptions, some moments of life were unreal but that this could also afflict normal people. Freud analysed this feeling further and concluded that his bizarre experience was a defence mechanism. When he had been at school, the young Freud did not really believe he would ever get to see the Acropolis. He was a not very well off Jewish boy whose father had a chequered business career. But Sigmund prospered mightily and, as he looked down upon Athens from the Acropolis, he knew he had committed one of the great Oedipal sins. He had bested his father who had never stood on this great site. That awareness made Freud feel guilty and it triggered defence mechanisms which was why he started to wonder about his memories.

Freud was careful to say he had not experienced a double personality but it is interesting that he should have tried so hard, so long afterwards, to explain the odd feeling and, also, that he anticipated the idea that dissociative thinking is often a misguided way of defending the self. (Freud, 1936).

Multiple Personality. The final state is full-blown multiple personality in which alters appear or can be teased out.

As more psychiatrists saw more patients who seemed to have multiple personality, they put pressure for it to be recognized as an official psychiatric condition. When I first realized how much controversy there was about the diagnosis, I was surprised to find that it had actually been recognized by the American Psychiatric Association as early as 1980. It was then included in the American *Diagnostic and Statistical Manual of Mental Disorders.* DSM III was then the bible of psychiatry. It offered two definitions of multiple personality and required three conditions to be fulfilled for a patient to be so diagnosed:

A. The existence within the individual of two or more distinct personalities, each of which is dominant at a particular time.
B. The personality that is dominant at any particular time determines the individual's behaviour.
C. Each individual personality is complex and integrated with its own unique behaviour patterns and social relationships.

This last condition turned out to be rather stringent. Eve Black, for example, would not have qualified. She certainly had unique behaviour patterns but she didn't really have social relationships of her own, apart from a few casual encounters when she went partying. Many other alters are as limited. In many patients, each multiple personality has no full blown life of its own. Rather, each personality has a few strong, almost cartoon-like traits which do not add up to a separate being leading to a separate life.

In 1987, multiple personality syndrome got a second, rather less demanding, definition from the American Psychiatric Association in its revision of DSM III. This now only insisted on:

A. The existence within the individual of two or more distinct personalities or personality states, each with its own relatively enduring pattern of perceiving, relating to and thinking about the environment and itself.
B. Each of these personality states at some time seems to have taken full control of the individual's behaviour.

Conditions A and B are obviously less strict than the 1980 ones. In 1993, DSM IV revised the definition further, excluding the words 'multiple personality'. It now spoke of a 'dissociative disorder', though it still insisted patients had to have different personality states or alters having control of the body.

But in one way the 1993 definition is tougher. The patient must not be able to report that they have alters and, also, must not be able to report that most of the alters are unaware of the other alters. You couldn't be dissociating, therefore, if you turned up complaining of having alters. (What did you suffer from then?)

DSM IV also spoke for the first time of children dissociating. It emphasized that this symptom should not be confused with having imaginary playmates.

Usually, when an illness is written into any of the *Diagnostic and Statistical Manuals*, there are few arguments about its existence. The pioneers must have believed that after inclusion in 1980 they would be free to ask conventional questions like: how many people suffer from multiple personality? What distinguishes them from other patients? What is the best treatment?

Instead, they keep on having to prove the syndrome exists. Ross has tried to establish how common multiple personality disorder is in North America. His conclusions are remarkable and so it's not surprising that he should arouse a good deal of criticism. Ross has done two studies, in one, repeating Putnam's methods, sending questionnaires to clinicians to get a profile of their patients with multiple personality disorder. The second was a survey of 454 American students using a variety of questionnaires.

The second study yielded Ross's most challenging result. He claimed that 14 of the 454 students reported symptoms of multiple personality disorder. Students tend to be more disturbed than the normal population, but even so, if replicated his results would mean that 3 per cent of the American population suffers from multiple personality syndrome. Therefore, more than six million Americans are splitting!

Ross claims to have tapped what he believes is enormous unrecognized suffering. The critics pan his study as a total hype, however. One critic, Ian Hacking, both mocks Ross and also has a delightfully zany explanation for the growth in cases. Blame television! Remotes swapping from channel to channel encourage splits. Give up channel surfing, surf among your selves. You're never alone with your personalities. They're more fun than Larry King Live!

Ross admitted to me that the figures look amazing but he maintains that in his own experience in Winnipeg such statistics are not ridiculous. He saw over fifty multiple personality cases but he did not think, even though he was known locally as an expert who ran a dissociation clinic, he had seen as many as 10 per cent of all Winnipeg's cases.

Ross believes there are a number of reasons why many multiple personality cases bypass the system. Some individuals, even those far along the dissociation continuum, can manage their condition. They collapse into depression, use that to recover, and then feel galvanized back into action. He noted that a number of multiple personality cases he had seen could be better described as manic-depressives.

Ross also believes many people on the streets suffer from multiple personality disorder. No one questions the need to research the mental health of the homeless population both in Britain and America. But in my own *Forgotten Millions* (1988) I noted how many people on the streets flee any kind of help, let alone investigators. Ross has certainly not proved his point but it is not a ridiculous hypothesis.

Third, Ross argues there are multiples in the American prison system. They suffer in silence and get no help. It is easier to study the existence of multiple personality disorder in prison than on the streets, but in Britain there is so much embarrassment about mentally ill people finishing up behind bars that research projects studying the mental health of prisoners are rare.

Ross initially argued that psychiatrists often missed the condition either because they were sceptical or because they didn't know what to look for. His study of 236 cases treated by other doctors found that the average age of patients when first diagnosed was thirty. The vast majority of patients were women. Only one in nine patients was male. Like Putnam, Ross found most of them had been in treatment for over six years before the condition was diagnosed. Again, the host personality had no idea of the existence of the other selves.

Ross, like Putnam, believed he was doing a routine study. DSM III and DSM IV had accepted the disease. It wasn't an illness on probation. In 1984, four learned journals devoted special issues to multiple personality. That same year, the International Society for the Study of Multiple Personality and Dissociation was set up after a lunch at Mama Leone's in New York. In 1986, it was estimated there were perhaps 6,000 cases in treatment in America. Today, the figure is far, far higher. There are special clinics from California to the Carolinas.

Ross has now moved from Winnipeg to the Charter Health Behavioral Institute in Dallas, Texas, where he runs a Dissociative Disorders Unit. They get referrals from all over the States. Those who come include many people who have mutilated themselves badly, who arrive with cuts all over their bodies. Cut arms. Cut wrists. Cut vaginas, even.

Health insurance companies now recognize the condition. In 1992, one of the speakers at the Association conference was a vice-president of Aetna, a big US company. In 1995, Wyeth Laboratories sponsored the Amsterdam conference.

The multiple movement, as some critics call it, mushroomed in the 1980s. But how real were the cases on which it was all based?

There have been sceptics both inside and outside America. They range from the cool and polite to the downright vitriolic. One of the earliest and most hostile was the therapist and lecturer, Ray Allridge Morris. He made fun of the proliferation of cases and criticized the quality of the research. Allridge Morris attributed a range of bad motives to the pioneers. They were gullible, deluded, slipshod, or, worse, out to make money. Allridge Morris sniped there was nothing more lucrative than to find a nice juicy plum of a multiple personality. Plenty of selves, plenty of sex, plenty of trauma. It might be a best-seller, a mini-series, a re-make of 'The Three Faces of Eve' as 'Fifty-Seven Aspects of Anna'. If Andy Warhol were still alive, he couldn't resist turning himself into a multiple.

Rather curiously, Allridge Morris argued that one impressive piece of counter-evidence was that Colin Thigpen now said he was sceptical about the explosion of cases. He would, wouldn't he? Not only had his previous prize patient, Eve, announced that she had dozens of alters he had never uncovered, but she claimed to have been sick for another twenty years. A case, perhaps, of hell hath no fury like a therapist scorned!

Tom Fahy of the Institute of Psychiatry in London is another critic and argues (1988) that the diagnosis is contrived. He claims suggestible therapists mould suggestible patients into multiple cases. Fahy criticizes the quality of the data which he dismisses as '. . . dire. The science is very soft', as he told me for an article for the *New Scientist* (June, 1955).

The debate has become much more acid as it has become enmeshed with issues of child abuse, including Satanic child abuse. Hypnotizing patients has been one flashpoint. As therapists interested in multiple personality used hypnosis and made contacts with alters and splits, they discovered many thirty- and forty-year-old patients who 'recovered' traumatic memories of being abused as children. Therapists did not usually question whether these memories were true, so many patients got furious with their parents and a significant number employed lawyers and started to sue their parents.

Few parents admitted the abuse. Most dismissed the memories as fantasies and claimed that their children had been seduced by therapists into making false allegations. A parallel debate about whether therapists sexually abuse their patients when so 'seduced' hit some anxieties. In 1992, a number of parents set up the False Memory Syndrome Foundation in America. In 1994, a similar society was set up in Britain. In America, the attacked parents also went to their lawyers and counter-sued the therapists. If their children hadn't been bamboozled in therapy they would never have falsely accused them.

So, the question of whether or not the multiple personality was a real diagnosis became entangled with the saga of child abuse. Was middle America so evil that inside many lovely suburban homes there were phallus-mad fathers? As it turns out, many of the key believers in Satanic abuse were right-wing Protestant sects. It could be argued that since the Cold War was over and there was no longer the great Satan in Moscow to battle, they had to find another devil.

If the patients were telling the truth, their parents owed them fortunes for having abused them, causing long-term trauma.

If the memories were false, the parents were victims of their children and of the children's therapists. They could sue the therapists for millions.

In Amsterdam it wasn't hard to pick up sensitivity on these issues. In one session, Colin Ross explained that they hardly ever encouraged patients to confront their parents with accusations. Catherine Fine told me she was tired of having to be constantly aware of potential legal problems while conducting therapy. When patients tell you what is going through their minds, the best way to ruin therapeutic progress is to ask, 'Is it true?' Questions like that undermine the whole therapy. You have to go with what the patient is saying. It may not be the truth but it is *their* truth.

Respected psychiatrists have often been less than totally honest in the interest of their patients. Janet, for example, reported curing two patients of traumas by hypnotizing them into believing the frightening events that made them hysterical had never happened. Was this lie unethical or very humane?

Catherine Fine said to me that what is important is to listen to the patient, to get to the heart of the trauma. You can't do that with the mind-set of 'L.A. Law'.

The sceptical view is very different. In March 1995, Harold Merskey of the University of Toronto published an editorial in *The British Journal of Psychiatry*. This was no slim volume in an academic imprint – Merskey attacked in one of the world's prime psychiatric journals. He rubbished the whole notion of multiple personality as a diagnosis. He pointed out that some of Ross's claims, in particular, were implausible, even ludicrous.

Merskey focused on the dangers of panic about child abuse. A study in Britain of eighty-four cases of Satanic ritual abuse found no reliable evidence of it ever having occurred. Dawn raids by social workers in the Orkneys and in Cleveland on homes where children were alleged to have been abused led to children being suddenly taken from their homes. Long legal and political battles showed social workers and doctors had behaved irresponsibly. Worse, in interviewing children, the 'professionals' used leading questions. Studies of the interviews made it clear that some children were frightened and likely to say what they believed social workers wanted to hear. A recent Scottish case in Ayr confirmed these dangers. Social workers there believed that five-year-olds had been abused while flying in a hot-air balloon! If you ask an eight-year-old what kind of mask his abuser wore, it will take a tough, self-confident child to ask what you're talking about if there hasn't been any abuse. I sat in on one interview where a well-meaning police constable told a little girl of three she could go home as soon as she had confirmed that she was abused and that when she said, 'Uncle touched the piano,' it really meant that he'd asked her to touch his penis. Investigation became interrogation. Protecting children became abusing children. In Sweden, social workers' zeal has created worse problems. Of about 400 men in jail for child abuse, 200 are maintaining their innocence and claiming are now victims themselves.

Catherine Fine told me that Americans hate thinking their society is riddled with abuse. If children could be so misled, vulnerable adults who were hypnotized could also be.

In his *J'Accuse*, Merskey claimed that hypnotizing patients and seeing if they, or their alters, recalled incidents of abuse was a perfect way to plant memories. Any recovered memories were more likely to be false than true. Psychiatrists like Ross were not curing trauma but creating trauma. If patients didn't reveal the expected recollections of trauma or splits 'more pressure is exerted', Merskey said.

Merskey quoted a line from Ross which implies the poor shrink was so deluded he even argued the CIA had encouraged the development of multiple personality in children. Nothing was spared in fighting the Cold War! Ross himself told me that Merskey 'is no great intellect' and that he never checked the context in which Ross spoke about the CIA. Ross had taken part in a Canadian TV programme about multiple personality. He alleged to me that he had been misled by the producers. In the programme, Ross had been asked some hypothetical questions, including some about the CIA. He had answered, only to find that his 'as if' questions were used in the programme 'as if' they were the replies to real, not hypothetical, questions. Ross was furious and vowed never again to have anything to do with television unless he could control the final cut.

Ross accuses the sceptics of being as guilty as the pioneers of hyping the evidence and distorting the truth. For Ross, making the case for multiple personality is important, not just to win the argument and be Proud Top Shrink – all the American therapists in Amsterdam poked fun at their own pretensions, almost too much – but because the argument may change the future shape of psychiatry. It will force psychiatry to pay more attention to trauma as a cause of psychiatric illness.

The controversy has also led to bitter dispute about the tests for dissociation and multiple personality. Ian Hacking attacks their quality. He has some sharp points but many of his criticisms could be made against other psychological tests. Douglas Shelley and I in *Testing Psychological Tests* (1986), tested eighty different psychological tests. The most famous and reputable – the Wechsler and Stanford Binet IQ tests, Cattell's and Eysenck's personality tests and Stanford Binet IQ tests – had some flaws. Most other tests suffered serious methodological problems. One of my favourite tests is the Columbia Driver Judgement Test which I pass with flying colours. In fact, I failed my driving test twice on every count except parroting the Highway Code. The last time someone tried to teach me to drive – we were very much in love – I nearly drove her Renault into a tree on an entirely deserted common!

The various tests of dissociative experiences are far from perfect scientific instruments. Later on, I show they have as many holes as a colander. However, Hacking ignores the fact that many tests with as many, and indeed some with far more flaws, are used every day in American psychology and psychiatry. Without such tests, these disciplines would look much less scientific.

So sceptics range in attitude from the decently cool to the outraged empiricist who has never seen such rubbish masquerading as science. The hostile view is that all diagnoses of dissociation and multiple personality are false positives. No one has ever had the disease. What nineteenth-century doctors saw as hysteria was a form of schizophrenia. In 1995, any doctor who diagnoses multiple personality is incompetent. The softer position is that the disorder does exist but is very rare. David Halperin, an American psychiatrist the American Psychiatric Association encourages journalists to contact as one of their experts, agrees there may be a few cases. He personally has seen one. The 'softer' sceptics refuse to believe there are now so many cases, and cases with so many bizarre twists. In pillorying the American 'zealots', the sceptics ignore the rather dull, conventional European psychiatrists who also present solid evidence that multiple personality disorder affects a significant number of people.

The Amsterdam conference heard papers on how many people who go to Amsterdam's central walk-in clinic have dissociative disorders, on the use of art therapy and on a number of cases diagnosed in Dutch prisons. In one interesting case, a prisoner pleaded not to be released even after completing twelve years of his sentence. The Dutch investigators found he was suffering from a severe multiple personality disorder. He was rightly terrified that once out of prison, one of his vicious alters would take control and 'make' him commit murder against his will. There were many papers on eating disorder and dissociation, too.

A number of studies from Norway looked at the prevalence of the disorder there. A team from Istanbul Medical University presented reports on multiple personality in an Islamic culture. Suzette Boon and Nel Draijer reported a follow-up to their large survey of multiple personality in The Netherlands. A different study of 101 Dutch patients who had dissociative experiences found that 41 could be considered multiple personality cases.

The Amsterdam conference was not getting reports from far-out, freaky therapists but reports of routine work into what they saw as a routine illness. 'Neutral' psychiatrists, who neither believe nor despise the diagnosis, are now studying the existence of multiple personality disorder. Latz *et al* (1995) looked at 176 women admitted to a state asylum and found 12% did have multiple personality disorder. Critics complain these 'neutral' studies use the tests the pioneers devised, and so they're flawed. How can there be such a radically different view of an illness?

THE PASSIONS OF PSYCHIATRY

Both psychology and psychiatry are highly political and ideological. In the 1970s, I interviewed David McClelland of Harvard University who commented that many of those who go into psychology and psychiatry want power and influence. Such motives lead to intense quarrels about the nature of these disciplines. Biologists quarrel about theories but they don't usually quarrel about the nature of their subject. Geologists don't debate whether they're studying rocks or rocks with souls. The titles of books published in the last twenty years confirm psychology's passion for controversy. Stephen Williams,' *Psychology on the Couch* (1988), Paul Kline's *Psychology Exposed* (1990), Anthony Clare's *Psychiatry in Dissent* (1976) all suggest a love of conflict about the nature of the subjects.

With multiple personality, the controversy is specially acute as the existence of multiple personality suggests a society in which millions of children were abused while their parents were either guilty or uncaring.

Multiple personality disorder is a new battleground. It reminds me of some issues raised twenty years ago in the battles between psychiatry and anti-psychiatry. R. D. Laing, Thomas Szasz and David Cooper were bitterly attacked by conventional psychiatrists as frauds, sick themselves and gullible for claiming that schizophrenia wasn't a disease.

Twenty years on, however, there has been an intriguing change. Though Laing is now attacked as out of date, some of his insights are now routine. Ordinary psychiatrists look for triggers that set off psychotic episodes. They talk to families to see what stresses in the family might provoke an episode. As Laing wanted, there is more concern for human rights, reflected in Britain to some extent in the 1983 Mental Health Act. No one now questions that schizophrenia is an illness but anti-psychiatry has had an impact on treatment and attitudes.

Laing was, and Szasz is, a scholar and doctor with much historical and clinical insight. No book yet written by a multiple personality enthusiast is a patch on Laing's *The Divided Self* (1961) or any of Szasz's work. But the Dutch work can't be dismissed as wacky; Putnam told me British and Canadian critics seem to ignore the fact that there are hundreds of reputable studies into the condition.

There are good reasons to worry over the 'boom' and good reasons to question the standard of some studies, but that does not justify rubbishing the whole theory. Some of the ideas the multiple pioneers have developed may seem bizarre but they are not without foundation. They deserve serious study.

As will become obvious, I think patients and doctors I have talked to report phenomena that deserve investigation and don't deserve to be dismissed out of hand.

It's now time to get out of 'Academic' and enter the spirit of child's play.

CHAPTER 4

Playing and Fear of Playing

GAMES ARE FUN

A little boy, twenty-two months old, says, 'I fly.' He flaps his arms and yells, 'Batman.' The boy seems to forget who he is.

When young children play, Pitcher and Schultz (1983), two psychologists, claim, 'Characters are usually stereotyped and flat.' Boys take on the roles of cowboys, Superman, Batman and other superheroes. Girls prefer traditional roles and still play mother, daughter. 'Even at the youngest age, girls are quite knowledgeable about the details and subtleties of these roles.'

'I'm the flying cucumber,' says my two-year-old son. Of all would-be alters surely one of the strangest? My oldest runs round his young brother's play-pen. Nicholas is six, but an expert game player. He pretends to be a bird, an elephant, a buffalo. Each different animal is represented by a different walk, a different sound. Both kids love this.

Not all play is so innocent. Not all children who are abused develop either multiple personality or disassociated states. So why do only some children express their distress in this way?

As I said, play is not always sweetly innocent. Games fathers and uncles and stepfathers play with little girls.

We're going to have fun, Lily. Oh yes, this is fun. You want me to hold your hand. That's what grown-ups do, Lily. Hold hands. My hand's big. Yours is very small. You feel safe, don't you.

Let's pretend we're on the moon. You're Lunar Lily. You've

86

got to breathe in a big spacesuit, Lily. We're heading for Moon Station Zero.

I've got to lift you up and we've got to run to get away from the Moon Baddies. They're trying to shoot us. I know. You'd like a hug. Makes you feel good. You'd like a kiss. No time for a kiss now. Daddy's too busy saving our life, shooting the Moon Baddies. We're safe. This is Moon Base.

I know it's your room, Lily. But in our game it's Moon Base.

It's cosy here. We can take off our big spacesuits. Daddy's going to help you off with your spacesuit. We're going to pretend to be Moon Beasts now. Moon Beasts need to lie down and rest.

You're scared. Scared of the Moon Beasts?

Don't be scared, Lily. Daddy's here, Daddy's hugging you. Daddy's stroking you. Daddy's loving you. You like being loved. Daddy likes being loved, too. You can love Daddy. Stroke Daddy's stick-man. It makes Daddy feel happy. Kiss it. Daddy knows you want to kiss it.

Does Mummy kiss it? That's Mummy and Daddy's secret. This is our secret.

Mummy's shopping at Tesco Lunar. You mustn't tell Mummy. If you tell Mummy, Daddy will be very angry. You don't like Daddy to be angry. No, Daddy doesn't like being angry with his lovely girl. That's fun. And you like it when Daddy strokes you. Oh, look, there are Moon Beasts outside. But we're safe in here.

Perhaps it's not surprising that Lily gets nervous about playing games.

If the scene I've just described happens all too often, the following one seems weirdly rare. It's another fiction but it illustrates one of the paradoxes of the whole field.

THE THERAPIST'S DOUBTS

In the consulting-room of Allen Woody. Once a rather orthodox Freudian, he got bored with listening to his patients and therefore 'invented' insult therapy, a form of treatment in which he nags, criticizes and verbally mugs his patients. He claims, of course,

*that his treatment works. What is true is that he is less bored. It
is Kate's fifteenth visit.*

*She is twenty-nine years old. She is small, and has short-
cropped hair. She wears overalls but has had a manicure and has
red fingernails. She claims to have a number of alters. The one
that is currently out is a truck driver, a Marlon Brando type out
of 'The Wild Ones'.*

*Allen Woody, always looking for his patient's weak spots,
attacks.*

ALLEN WOODY: You want me to believe you're a truck driver.

KATE: I just did Alabama to New York.

ALLEN WOODY: In your dreams, truck driver, shmuck driver.

KATE: I've got diplomas in truck driving.

ALLEN WOODY: No one would hire you to drive a truck. It's
one of your fucking stupid alters speaking. One that has completely flipped. Truck drivers don't paint their nails red. Truck
drivers are not little girls who work as secretaries. Truck
drivers get their hands dirty. I can no longer suspend my dis-
belief.

KATE: You wanna slob driver. OK. Dickhead, fuckbrain.

There are no exchanges in the literature like this. Most therapists
wax lyrical about the performance of their patients. As they
switch from alter to alter they bring off performances that Meryl
Streep would be happy with. The multiple personality isn't just
sick but a virtuoso. Whether or not these performances convince
those who are non-believers is an interesting point. Margaret
Boden, highly respected for her work on artificial intelligence,
notes in a paper on computer programming and multiple personality (1995) that she really could see the switches in films taken
of Eve White/Chris Sizemore. Ian Hacking, on the other hand,
is less sure he saw switching though he does worry it may be
unfair to expect disturbed patients to put on Oscar-winning performances.

Boden is far from being alone. Lawyers, judges, juries, social
workers have all been impressed by the performance of some

multiples. They seem genuine: so they must reflect real trauma.

The pioneers maintained the alters split at the time of the childhood trauma. Frank Putnam told me that critics don't realize there have been advances in developmental psychology which make it possible to be more precise. Putnam argues very young children switch between moods very easily. Something makes them laugh, then something else happens and they cry. Older children and adults don't change moods so fast. Basing himself on work by Peter Wolff at the Boston Children's Hospital, Putnam (1986) claims part of forming a stable self involves learning to bridge the gap between these different moods. It also involves learning to focus on one thing. Abuse, he thinks, interferes with this process of integration. This feels like an interesting idea, though Putnam has no model of how it might be done. He argues that it may help explain why, if the abuse begins after a child is six or seven, the trauma will not lead to splitting but to other disturbances.

But do children younger than seven have the skills to make up convincing characters, such as alters often are? And how would children bury these characters deep in their selves only for them to emerge later on? The evidence suggests they certainly have the imaginative skills needed to make up alters.

IMAGINARY FRIENDS

In the mid 1980s, some pioneers became interested in a few aspects of child psychology. In particular, they latched on to the topic of imaginary playmates. There are two sorts of these. A child may actually create a character outside him or herself. Bernie will say he has a friend called Teddy who has red hair, laughs a lot and lives on top of the Empire State Building. But imaginary playmates may also be inside the child. A little boy puts on a skirt and pretends to be a girl. But instead of pretending, the boy says he is now a girl. The boy calls himself Judy. Imaginary playmates are very real to children; they have names, personalities, histories. Three-year-olds can make up loud, brave, show-offy playmates who often make up for something missing in their lives.

Research on imaginary playmates is almost antique. There are reports going back to 1895. Jean Piaget (1952) was aware of imaginary playmates and interested in what they represented. In the 1930s, however, American psychologists became a little neurotic about them. How-to-bring-up-baby books preached the need to bring up a well-adjusted child. Well-adjusted children didn't speak to spooks who weren't really there. That kind of thing led to schizophrenia. Parents were warned to discourage their children from playing games with imaginary playmates.

By the 1960s, psychologists had changed their tune. They argued that these imaginary playmates were positive – a sign of mental health. The child could use them to deal with emotional problems. They were natural play-therapy. Studies discovered that a third of the children in Texas aged under seven had imaginary playmates. Some interesting experiments were done. Jerome L. Singer and Bella Streiner (1966), for instance, compared the fantasies and imaginary playmates of blind and sighted children. Blind children nearly always had a playmate who could see. The playmate filled a very obvious gap for them.

There were a few psychoanalytic studies which suggested that children were wily enough to make playmates to get away with being naughty. One interesting case (Fraiberg, 1959) was of a boy called Stevie. Stevie dreamed up an imaginary playmate, Gerald. Gerald was always the scapegoat for any bad behaviour. Stevie seemed to get up to all kinds of mischief, such as breaking his father's pipe. But the child responsible for this Freudian outrage was, of course, Gerald.

IMAGINARY WORLDS

To make up an imaginary friend or playmate isn't perhaps that complex an act of imagination. To make a whole world is. It's why we admire writers like Tolkien or Ursula Le Guin. Yet children can do this, too.

Together with the psychiatrist, the late Dr Stephen MacKeith, I have looked at fifty-seven imaginary worlds called 'paracosms' (1991). Each one was made up by a child. We found one child as young as four and many who were seven or eight when they first started to weave such fantasy worlds. Some of these paracosms are very complex, countries with legends, histories, constitutions. The Brontë children made up a number of such imaginary worlds, but plenty of children who do not grow up to be artists have also created them.

Two of the cases MacKeith and I reported, Deborah and Rosemary, are perhaps specially interesting in the light of the debate.

Deborah was born in 1939, the seventh child of a poor family. Her mother died in childbirth. Deborah was sent to a children's home and then she was adopted. Her new life felt quite alien to her and she had many disturbing memories of rejection and violence. She was then sent to live with an uncle and aunt. They had an eight-year-old son but they had lost a daughter and Deborah was always being unfavourably compared to her. Finally she was sent back to the children's home. At the age of twelve she was fostered by a couple who were in the Salvation Army. Again, she found that she was very unhappy. As she was good at music she was allowed to join the Salvation Army band but was thrown out for being naughty.

Deborah created an imaginary family who compensated for all these problems. 'They were my security, my friends, my guardians. It was my real world. It was the only place I felt safe.' She gave her new family different personalities. In the family, Deborah was often punished for talking to herself. Her imaginary friends allowed her to play the piano, which she was not allowed to do by her foster-parents. Deborah said:

'Music broke the coldness of the reality world. My imaginary friends often sat and listened to my singing and my piano-playing. I received trophies and rewards for my perfect musical renderings.'

After Deborah lost her place as a singer in the Sunbeam Group of the Salvation Army, she shut herself up in the garden shed. There, she entered her private world and played the tambourine in front of an appreciative audience of her imaginary friends.

Even her fantasies, however, had a dark edge sometimes. Deborah's world contained a Room of Judgement where she had to justify her behaviour to her imaginary friends. Deborah believes her imaginary world helped her cope with many traumas. Another girl who made up a paracosm, Rosemary, had the same impression. When she was six, her mother died. Her father remarried. Rosemary and her sister hated their step-mother. They created a world called Santafagasta into which they escaped. They needed the refuge. The second marriage was tense: their father became very withdrawn. Again, the imaginary world and the identity she could assume there offered conso-lation, often unconscious consolation, for Rosemary's real problems.

PRETENDING IS HEALTHY?

The ability of children to make up tales to order has been tested, too.

Finland, 1976: the University of Oulu was the site of one of the strangest experiments an education authority has ever allowed. Rena Kampman studied 1,200 local teenagers aged between fourteen and eighteen. She wanted to see how many of them would prove good hypnotic subjects. After a complex pro-cess of elimination, Kampman found that seventy-eight of them could enter a deep hypnotic trance.

Kampman put all these seventy-eight teenagers in a deep trance and then told them, 'You are going back to an age preceding your birth, you are someone else. You are somewhere else.' It was their ability to imagine being someone else Kampman wanted to explore.

She then tried to get them to explain who this other personality was. This was an experiment in pure suggestion. Could the teen-agers devise another personality? Kampman found forty-three of the subjects could not create a second personality but thirty-two of them could. (She never said what happened to the other three.) She was very surprised by how many wove quite coherent fantasies – and even more surprised when she started giving the subjects questionnaires about their mental health. It seems logical that unhappy neurotic people would find it easier to escape into imaginary situations. But Kampman found that, on the whole, the subjects who could create the second personality were less disturbed, felt less guilt and reported less shyness and less stress than the children who failed to create other personalities. Kampman's study is not much quoted. It was published in 1976 in the *International Journal of Clinical and Experimental Hypnosis*. This is not an obscure journal; some researchers like Richard Kluft have published in it. It's always interesting when a paper is ignored. Can it be that one reason why Kampman's has been ignored, even though her sample is impressive, is that it offends all sides in the argument?

The sceptics claim that either alters are fakes or, at best, they are distortions of memory produced years after any trauma. The alters are created by the demands of therapy: they have not existed in the person since childhood. The pioneers, on the other hand, have invested heavily in a link between multiple personality and trauma. Kampman's results support the pioneers' view in showing that some children or teenagers have the imagination multiple personality theory demands, but damage it in showing that the children who are better at making up imaginary beings are psychologically healthier than those who can't. (Their alters were made up as a result of being told to play.)

But Kampman's study was just the first to have made that point.

Later studies have sugggested that Kampman's improbable results were right. Lynn and Rhue (1988 and 1994) found adults who scored high on dissociation tests had fewer imaginary playmates than adults who scored low.

Peter Wolff's work, quoted by Frank Putnam (1986), on how children create a sense of self is part of an explosion of developmental research which may help resolve these contradictions. Camcorders have made it possible to catch long episodes of play and analyse them in detail. It is clear now how sophisticated three- and four-year-olds can be in their play. Young children know you can be in different states at the same time. A three-year-old knows you can cry when you don't feel sad. You can either weep as a deliberate pretence because you want Mummy or Daddy to feel sorry for you, or you can do it as part of a game. You're playing a sick girl. Some monster has bitten your foot off and is chewing it for his dinner. So you cry. By the age of three, children know how to signal they are starting to play, that there is a switch from reality self to fantasy self. Developmental psychologists speak of a play-face which signals 'This is not real, this is a game.' Another mark of games is that children put on exaggerated gestures or voices when they begin. They break into giggles. In young children's games, the wolves growl and howl evilly. The baddies always smirk.

A number of researchers have shown that most children first learn how to pretend in their families, playing games with parents and with siblings. In my thesis (1985) I gave many instances of parents teaching their children to play and, especially, to play long sequences of pretend-games. In most families, this is fun. It's often physical fun. Children bounce on the bed and turn it into a circus arena. They hide under the kitchen table because the monsters from Saturn are coming to get them. Children love these games. They're imaginative, fun and warm. Adults love them, too, because they bring out the child in them. The only excuse I had when I was thirty to crawl on the carpet and make Heffalump noises was when I was being an elephant playing Jungle with my children. In normal life, if I'd done that, I'd have been booked for the stress reduction programme.

But as suggested already, in families where there is abuse, play may be less fun. Because the adult playing will have a very different end in mind and the child has some sense of that.

Given all this, I want to suggest some questions.

Is it possible that some abused children have the normal skills it takes to pretend, but don't like pretending? Work on autistic children claims they can't pretend.* I'm suggesting something different.

---

* Studies by Dr Uta Firth (1993) have developed that idea.

Is the reason these children do not like to pretend that often their abusers have used pretend-games to get close to them as a prelude to abuse?

Is that why, though these children can make up alters, they don't have conscious access to the alters – and don't externalize them?

If any of these propositions are true, should it affect the way people are treated when they are adult patients?

Does this theory help explain the cartoon-like character of many of the alters? They are like the stereotypes Pitcher and Schultz (1983) claim normal children produce in normal pretend-play.

These are questions, not answers. But I would argue the current debate is often a little too simple. It tends to pit the enthusiasts whose equation is abuse-trauma-repressed-alters against sceptics who dismiss the entire hypothesis and claim the pioneers are so naïve they don't understand how much of what we remember is always reconstruction rather than pure, as-it-was, truth.

I can only find one study that goes against the notion that healthy children are better at creating imaginary playmates. Hornstein and Putnam (1992) looked at forty-four children who had some of the symptoms that later develop into multiple per-sonality disorder and twenty children with symptoms that develop into dissociative disorder. They had memory problems, blackouts and heard voices. The authors mention, in a rather throwaway sentence, that 84 per cent of these children said they had imaginary playmates. They don't say how the question was asked; they give no details of any playmates. Psychologists know that questions put to children have to be very carefully con-structed but here there is little indication of such care being taken. Hornstein and Putnam also don't explain why their results should be so different from Kampman's (1976) or Lynne and Rhue's (1988). It's also not clear, of course, if their sample will go on to develop multiple personality disorder. Putting their study aside, an explanation is needed for the improbable finding that healthy children produce more multiple personalities when asked to imagine them than do disturbed children.

The following seems to me a plausible hypothesis. Young children can make up imaginary companions and playmates. Most children who do that enjoy doing it and know that they are doing it. It's fun. Children won't know it's a way of letting off steam or dealing with stress. But they don't need to be fully aware of their motives to realize they are fantasizing. Most who have imaginary playmates know they are not 'real' like Mum and Dad are real.

Imagine, however, a child who is abused and whose abuser often starts the process that leads up to the abuse by playing games with the child. For them, games are different. They always have an edge, a purpose. He tells you to pretend you're riding a horse. He's the horse. It finishes up with him on top of you.

So games and pretending stop being fun. They're not safe spaces where you can explore. They are danger areas where you are explored, exploited, touched.

Children who are abused in this way may come to hate games. Pretending may come to trigger memories of trauma. So these children don't have the chance to use their creativity as part of a coping mechanism. They don't associate pretending with fun. I suggest there is a group of children whose experience of abuse hasn't just traumatized them but made them fearful of play and of pretend-play because such play often was the first step to abuse.

What would happen to a child who felt like that?

Memories of abuse would be repressed. And memories of playing – and games – would have negative emotions attached to them.

Time passes. Memory works, distorts, creates, but all of these mechanisms are unconscious and kept submerged by repression.

Time passes. The child grows up. There's no need to play or to pretend any more. But neither the trauma nor the fear of play are healed.

Yet children always want to play. It's natural.

Coming from my background in play research, I keep on being struck by how much dissociative behaviour seems like a distorted form of play, play that is scared to be fun. The manic energy needed to switch between one self and another recalls the energy small children put into games like King of the Castle or what I called 'charging' games in my thesis. In a charging game, one child pretends to be an animal and runs at another child only to veer away at the last moment and avoid a collision. Almost inevitably, it leads to manic laughter. The apparently crazy aggression of a three-year-old pretending to be a vicious rhino turns into laughter. Abused children find 'fun' more perilous. Multiple personality patients do sometimes show a frantic energy in 'switching', a distorted reflection perhaps of the energy children put into play and games. But with none of the usual pleasure that goes with games.

These ideas can be developed into a testable hypothesis. Adults who develop multiple personalities will have been abused in a way that has made them frightened to play. For them, play is not free and not fun. It is a deception. They became involved in a pattern where adults pretended to play with them, 'pretended' because there was always a hidden agenda. The games were a prelude to abuse.

The case-history that follows offers some illustration of these ideas.

CHAPTER 5

Jonah: In Search of Science

The case that follows is one of a number in which I try to explore what it is like to be a multiple personality. The story of Jonah is especially interesting because it offers one of the best descriptions of how the alters first developed as children. I hope by looking at his story to shed some light on the issues raised in the last chapter. Jonah has also been the subject of probably the most comprehensive attempt to answer the question of whether a person was a number of different personalities – each a separate, consistent being – or essentially one person whose alters were expressing different sides of his or her character.

I have had to change the names of all the people involved. In a number of the other cases, 'patients' I was put in touch with were very reluctant to talk in detail.

One proviso: there is a danger in writing up any case-history. The therapist is writing after the event. Inevitably, we structure case-histories as stories with something of a narrative. This adds its own distortions.

JONAH'S THREE CHILDHOOD SELVES

Jonah is black. He was born in Kentucky in 1948.

When he was six years old, Jonah's mother and stepfather had a violent fight. During it, Jonah's mother stabbed her husband. He was taken to hospital. Jonah's mother was put in jail. She was released after a few days as was his stepfather. The couple decided to go back and give their marriage another try. Neither can have been prepared for what happened when they met their children again. Their six-year-old started to lecture them.

It wasn't Jonah, however, who told this story. The tale only came out twenty years later when one of Jonah's alters, a superficially rational alter called Sammy, informed psychiatrists of what he had managed to pull off as a little boy. According to Sammy, he split off when his mother stabbed her husband. As he met them again, Sammy had to warn them not to behave so irresponsibly ever again. It was not wise to fight in front of their children.

But did the child really speak the words? Or did he just want to? Or did he dream he had?

Sammy claimed from the moment he first spoke up, he always had to help when Jonah got in trouble.

Fights were not the only problems Jonah faced as a little boy. His mother wasn't only violent but engaged in a habit that is more frequent than people imagine. She dressed her little boy in girl's clothes because she would have liked to have a girl. It's not hard to see that this was a form of abuse.

Jonah became confused. Little children don't say they're confused about their sexuality but in school his teachers saw he was muddled about gender. When he had to read books where Alice, being a girl, did girlish things while Jerry, being a boy, was up to boyish tricks, Jonah's teacher saw he had a hard time making out which characters were male and which characters were female. It seems likely this confusion made him feel helpless.

At school, Jonah split off another alter to help with this gender dilemma. The split was called King Young. He was streetwise and sex-smart. Girls were easy; gender had no mysteries. Girls were for love and fun.

Jonah's school took both black and white pupils and there were tensions. It is not surprising that a child who was dressed as a girl at home should be weak and bullied. One afternoon after school a gang of white boys chased the ten-year-old Jonah. They caught up with him, shoved him to the ground and started to beat him. Jonah was terrified he was going to die. He blanked out in panic. As soon as he blanked out, a third personality split off. Just as King Young coped with Jonah's sexual insecurities, this third personality, Usoffa, coped with the fact that he was a weakling.

But the conscious Jonah didn't know that an African warrior-king had come to rescue him.

Under hypnosis, Usoffa eventually revealed that he was Usoffa Abdulla, son of Omega, who was a god but not the God. Fierce, fearless and a bit the superhero, he turned on the white bullies and nearly killed two of them.

These three descriptions of how Jonah's alters first split off came, of course, years after the event. The psychiatrists studying Jonah had no idea whether:

1. These were true stories of what had happened at the time.
2. These were stories that were made up later by Jonah to explain the peculiar things that happened to him.
3. These were fulfilment fantasies. All three of these alters were powerful and each seemed to be an attempt to create solutions to Jonah's problems.
4. They were real alters but were developed long after Jonah had been a child and, then, by some quirk of memory, they acquired a history based on what had really happened to Jonah earlier in his life.

Remarkably, given his problems, Jonah went into the army. When he was twenty-one years old, he heard a close friend of his had been killed. Jonah went berserk. He poured gasoline over the camp's garbage trench and set fire to it, starting a huge fire. Jonah was sent to Vietnam without anyone being told about the arson incident. When his unit came under fire for the first time, Jonah again went berserk. He started firing in all directions and nearly killed some of his comrades. They had to struggle to bring him under control. As so many soldiers were under stress in Vietnam, it's not surprising the army didn't investigate in depth. Jonah was sent back to America with an honourable discharge on medical grounds.

He moved to New England and went to work at a beach resort. He now started to notice lapses of memory.

Then Jonah went home to Kentucky for the Christmas holidays. He had, miraculously, never been in trouble with the police. One morning he woke up in jail to find he had been accused of beating up a man and a woman in a bar. Jonah managed to avoid standing trial probably because the offence was not too serious and he did seem very confused. But the memory lapses – and the violence – started to get worse.

Two years later, the police arrived to find Jonah fighting a man by a river. Jonah was trying to drown him. He got a short jail sentence.

By the time he entered hospital, Jonah was twenty-seven years old. He came of his own free will. He was scared by what he had been told he had been doing. Again, he had no memory of the events just prior to his admission.

Three weeks before coming to hospital Jonah had attacked his wife with a kitchen knife and beaten her up, then chased her and their three-year-old daughter out of their house. His wife came back when he seemed a little bit calmer. But the calm didn't last. A few days later, he tried to kill his wife again. His wife told the doctors that when he attacked her, Jonah called himself 'Usoffa Abdulla, the son of Omega'. She had never heard the name before. After his second attack, his wife left. He became very distressed. Two days later, he tried to stab a complete stranger. The police were called and gave chase but Jonah managed to get away.

When the psychiatrist first saw him, Jonah presented a puzzling picture. He was upset and suffering blinding headaches. He said his head felt as if it had band-like pressure clamping round it. He admitted he had no idea of what had recently happened in his life. He couldn't remember attacking his wife, though he believed her when she said he had done it. The blinding headaches seemed to accompany the loss of memory.

The doctors thought at first Jonah was suffering from psychomotor epilepsy, and must be committing his acts of violence either before, or after, some form of epileptic attack that robbed him of his memory. But Jonah didn't respond to any standard tests of epilepsy.

Then, while he was under observation on the ward, the nurses saw something much more peculiar than any lapses of memory. There seemed to be a number of rather different Jonahs. His behaviour, his voice and his gestures would change drastically from time to time, though the nurses did not realize at first what was happening and that they were seeing the spontaneous revelation of a number of different personalities.

They watched him carefully from then on and came to an astonishing conclusion. Jonah's body hosted at least three other personalities. These were the splits who would claim they had existed since Jonah was a boy – Sammy, King Young and Usoffa Abdulla were still inside him.

On the ward, these alters came and went. The doctors decided to hypnotize Jonah so that they could make proper contact with these three personalities. This required some tact as, typically, Jonah had no idea he was a host personality.

Sammy claimed to be the only alter to be aware of the existence of all the others. He told the doctors of a number of other incidents when 'Jonah' had been violent.

The most dramatic incident was when Jonah suspected a new girlfriend was cheating on him. He arrived at her apartment after a man had just left. Jonah found his girlfriend stark naked. He became very upset and they started fighting. At this time, Sammy said, another one of Jonah's splits appeared. It must have been Usoffa Abdulla. Usoffa got in a rage and started to beat the girl up severely.

Sammy claimed that before this outburst, Jonah knew he had other personalities within him. After the violence, however, Jonah blanked out all knowledge of his alters. This is a very interesting claim, suggesting Jonah may have become terrified of the alter who protected him because that alter could become so violent.

To the doctors, Jonah described himself as shy, retiring, sensitive, polite and passive. He was a typical repressed host personality. He also often got frightened and confused. To the doctors, however, Jonah seemed rather shallow.

As he presented himself, Sammy was rational and cool. He said that while he knew of King Young and Usoffa, Jonah was the one he knew best. Sammy claimed that what had happened when he was six had determined his entire life. From the moment he had split to lecture his violent parents, Sammy saw himself as an entity whose mission it was to help Jonah when Jonah was in trouble with authority figures or the law. Sammy also described himself as a lawyer. And Jonah often needed a lawyer.

Under hypnosis, the psychiatrists discovered King Young had also grown up. The seven-year-old alter who, at least, knew who was a boy and who was a girl had become a dedicated ladies' man. He saw himself as a lover, fascinated by pleasure. He was much better than Jonah at dealing with women since he had a nice line in pick-up patter. King Young smiled a lot, exuded warmth and tried hard to be charming. King Young saw his mission as looking after Jonah's sexual interests. He claimed he appeared and replaced Jonah whenever Jonah couldn't find the right words to say to turn a woman on. King Young 'scored'.

The third personality, Usoffa the warrior, had also settled down into something of a stereotype. He said he knew Jonah very well but that he didn't know much about the others. Usoffa added he had appeared about seven times since the first split. He said that his appearances lasted between an hour and two days. He had to manifest himself because Jonah was not able to defend himself. Usoffa trumpeted he would deal with the threatening situation like the warrior he was and, once it had been dealt with, he would disappear. The doctors found Usoffa sarcastic, sullen, often silent, but he was totally dedicated to the task of protecting Jonah.

The first time Jonah was in hospital he stayed two months. The make-up of his alters seemed simple enough. The psychiatrists hypnotized him, and while he was under hypnosis they suggested to him that he should merge these personalities into one whole who would be more assertive and more confident with women. Despite their assurances, there were signs the therapy wasn't working. During one hypnotic session, Sammy said another personality was 'brewing' inside Jonah. This personality was still developing. Sammy described it as 'scattered but gathering'. The doctor called this personality De Nova – the new. Sammy said it would reflect the thoughts, actions and motives of Jonah as well as the extent of the harm that had been done to him. Jonah clearly saw himself as a victim. It would be, Sammy warned, 'five times worse than Usoffa'. There would be no controlling it because it would be 'probably somewhere in between dynamite, electricity and nitroglycerine'.

The doctors were not too sorry this explosive alter never actually materialized. They didn't want havoc on the ward.

So Jonah left hospital. In theory, a new self had been welded out of the fragments of the old. The optimism of the doctors turned out to have been misplaced.

Nine months later, Jonah was brought back to hospital. He had had two short jail sentences in the meantime. He was brought unconscious to the hospital's emergency room after being found lying by the roadside. He was suffering from amnesia. The last event he could remember was getting into a fight with a friend.

The psychiatrists hypnotized Jonah again. There had been no change in his systems of alters. They now felt they had a remarkable chance to investigate the key question that had dogged multiple personality research for so long.

Was Jonah one person with a number of fragmentary beings in him? Or did his body really contain three other whole personalities who had a life of their own?

THE SEARCH FOR SCIENCE

The doctors decided to give Jonah over twenty psychological, neurological and psychiatric tests. They hoped, by concentrating resources, to be able to give a definite answer. They trawled literature for ideas and they also looked in detail at the ever growing number of psychological tests. There are currently over eight thousand psychological tests on the market which claim to measure everything from IQ and extraversion to the ability to fit into a sports team. Some of the tests they decided to use dated back to 1910.

Before looking at what they did, their results, and the impact on Jonah, I want to emphasize one paradox. Jonah did not seem to be particularly intelligent. On the four IQ tests, he scored in the low normal range – around 98. Each of the personalities achieved the same unimpressive score. Generally speaking, intelligence correlates with creativity. Despite this low score, Jonah had constructed a personality system which was worthy of a good dramatist. Unconsciously, the team recognized this because they gave each of his characters roles out of a drama – Sammy was called the lawyer, King Young the lover, Usoffa the warrior. How did dull Jonah manage to achieve this creation? It's a paradox I will return to.

As the study of Jonah is the most comprehensive scientific analysis that has ever been done in this field, I want to go into it in some detail.

The MacDougall Scale of Emotions

When Morton Prince had studied Miss Beauchamp, he had used a scale which had been devised by William MacDougall, a psychologist who had developed a theory of instincts. MacDougall had listed thirty-five instincts and feelings people often feel. They ranged from 'joy', 'pity' and 'blame' to 'acquisitiveness'; another was the feeling of 'suggestibility'. Subjects have to say whether they feel each of these feelings, 'Never, infrequently, sometimes, or frequently'.

The psychiatrists gave the scale to each of Jonah's alters and got a very consistent pattern. Usoffa reported the highest number of 'frequent' feelings. He felt angry, resentful, scornful, disgusted and vengeful very often. The only emotion Sammy felt often was acquisitiveness. He never felt angry or tender or joyful, though he sometimes felt pity. King Young, on the other hand, often felt love, joy, desire and empathy, but he never felt anxiety. The only feeling Jonah reported having often was suggestibility. This was interesting and odd. Interesting, since it suggests Jonah felt he could be easily influenced. Odd, since he described himself as sensitive and one might expect him to feel a few more emotions.

The MMP I

As psychology developed, it produced more sophisticated tests of personality than MacDougall's. The MMPI (the Minnesota Multiphasic Personality Inventory) is a complex personality inventory with over two hundred questions that elicit sixteen different personality factors. They are ranged in opposition like Tough $v.$ Tender. The clearest differences between Jonah and the other three personalities were not really what the researchers hoped for because Jonah showed so many 'paranoid' tendencies. As he showed no signs of paranoia however, the doctors ignored this.

One refinement of the MMPI is that it includes questions which aim to tease out subjects who give fake positive answers, answers they believe will make them look good. Jonah turned out to give fewer of these than any of the alters. He seemed the most truthful and the most willing to accept his inadequacies. The other three presented a too positive front; beneath it, they were brittle.

The Adjective Check List

This is a test where subjects are given a series of adjectives and have to say whether they apply to them or not. The Adjective Check List again revealed predictable differences between the various alters. Usoffa, for example, endorsed the least number of favourable and the highest number of unfavourable items. He said he was impulsive, lacked control and had hostile feelings. He admitted to being arrogant, dominant, self-confident, narcissistic and poorly socialized, and had no regard for the feelings of others. The other three presented very different verbal self-portraits. Sammy highlighted the rational; King Young the affectionate and pleasure-seeking; Jonah was less defined.

Self Draw Test

Each alter was asked to draw how they saw themselves, and each produced what amounted to an effective cartoon of their dominant trait. Usoffa drew himself as a warrior with a shield and a strange hat, a little like a chef's. Sammy drew himself sitting at a desk marked ATTORNEY with a heap of files and a map of the law-courts at his side. King Young drew himself in profile, facing a woman, as if they were about to kiss. Jonah drew himself as a pinched stick-man sitting in a boat with a girl. These self-portraits were telling. Jonah's was the least substantial. There was no power in his image of himself. Quite different was Usoffa. He had a strong mask-like face with a big nose. Sammy wore a very ordinary hat and had a tiny moustache but no arms. King Young in profile seemed less Negroid than the others.

All such tests, even the MMPI, rely on subjects to be honest. If you are dishonest but smart enough to be consistent, you can present any picture you want of yourself.

I may hate having to mix with people because I am very shy but I can still answer 'yes' to questions like, 'Do you like going to parties?' As Jonah scored low on all IQ tests, he probably did not have the intelligence to choose to present different personalities. It requires some wit to be so manipulative.

The psychiatrists also gave Jonah and his alters tests used in experimental psychology which are harder to fake. Subjects aren't asked to describe themselves or their attitudes but to perform simple learning and memory tasks.

The Paired Word Task

The paired word task is a much used design in studying learning and memory. It tests whether particular words that don't have a natural association can be linked together in the memory.

The key question is simple. Usually if I am taught to associate certain words – say 'book' with 'sugar' – I will remember that association weeks later. If I am presented with the word 'book', I will respond with 'sugar' more quickly than normal on subsequent presentations.

In studies of multiple personality, the issue is whether what one personality learns to associate will transfer to all others personalities. What would happen if Sammy was asked to remember associations that Usoffa had been taught? The researchers found that the associations Jonah had been taught tended to be remembered more quickly by the other selves. But otherwise, each personality was cut off from the others. What Sammy learned, Usoffa did not learn.

The researchers went on to do a similar study of conditioning. If King Young was conditioned to respond to a particular sound, would Jonah also respond more quickly to that particular sound? Would the learning transfer from one personality or one personality state to the others?

Each alter was given a different conditioned stimulus – a tone, a gesture, a flashing light and so on. One second after each alter saw or heard their particular stimulus they got an electric shock to the outside of the calf. Normal people would learn to try to avoid the shock. Their electrical skin resistance would also show a dramatic change as the skin tensed itself to receive the shock. The results were more confusing than before. Jonah and King Young responded to the conditioned stimuli of all the alters other than Usoffa. Sammy responded to every personality's conditioned stimuli, Usoffa to all stimuli other than Jonah's. Usoffa also proved very hard to condition. It needed more than twenty-five pairings to establish proper conditioning. Some theories argue that antisocial and aggressive personalities are very hard to condition, which would fit Usoffa's performance.

Physiological Tests

The psychiatrists also gave Jonah and his alters neurological and physiological tests – including tests for galvanic skin response, an EEG to look for different patterns of brainwaves, as had been done to Eve, and a test for sensitivity to pain.

Galvanic Skin Response

The psychiatrists interviewed each of the four personalities under hypnosis and asked each to give words that had a strong emotional charge – good or bad – for them. When the other alters heard these words repeated in the midst of a list of neutral words, would their galvanic skin response show a deflection? Would something that was emotional for Jonah be emotional for Sammy?

The results were similar to the paired word task. The words Jonah chose as being emotionally charged got a high response from all the other personalities – sometimes even higher than Jonah's own response. But the words each of the other alters said were emotionally charged did not have much of an effect on the others. Jonah shared his emotions with the other three but the alters did not share their emotions with each other or with Jonah.

EEG

People can't fake their brainwaves to make a good impression. A yogi can suppress some kinds of alpha rhythm during meditation, but that is the limit of such manipulation. The team here found interesting differences between the alters.

Three things were especially significant. When their eyes were open, Jonah and Sammy – but not King Young or Usoffa – showed what is called alpha blocking. There were also significant differences in the frequency of the brainwaves of each personality. King Young showed the slowest alpha frequency, while Usoffa showed the fastest.

Sammy had less muscle activity, fewer eye movements and spent a far greater percentage of time in a different rhythm of brainwaves – theta rhythm – than the others did. The differences in brainwave activity were startling. While Sammy would spend 20 per cent in alpha rhythm, King Young spent 52 per cent.* There were huge differences in eye movements, too, between the different personalities. The significance of those differences was much harder to assess.

Pain and Emotion

Most of the very detailed neurological examination showed no differences between the different alters. King Young, Sammy, Jonah, and Jonah when he was in a hypnotic state all had normal touch and could tell when they were being touched in two different places on the skin. They reacted to painful stimuli in a perfectly normal manner.

Usoffa, on the other hand, did not seem to have a 'good' sense of pain. He was poor at noticing when he was touched. He had a more bizarre failing, too. He seemed to be unable to discriminate between sugar and salt.

The psychiatrists distinguished between neutral and emotional material. They concluded that there didn't seem to be much difference between the alters in their response to non-emotional material. Each alter scored much the same on various forms of the IQ tests, for example. But the results on the MMPI, the Adjective Check List, the Scale of Emotions and the ward observations all suggested clear differences between the alters. Usoffa's very different reactions to pain and to touch were also interesting.

* Alpha rhythm is generally associated with a normal but relaxed state: alpha blocking suggests anxiety.

We know too little about Jonah's youth to be able to answer detailed questions about any abuse beyond his mother's dressing him as a girl but the alters' dourness is striking. It offers some support, I suggest, to the ideas developed in Chapter 4, where I argued that abused children become frightened of play.

In dealing with anything emotional, the four personalities were quite distinct. They reacted and behaved as if they were separate selves. King Young, who described himself as loving, for example, gave appropriate 'warm' responses on all of the tests of attitudes and emotions. This was not true of the other tests. In other words, Jonah did have three other emotional selves but, in other respects, the evidence for separate selves was poor.

The psychiatrists wanted to repeat a number of the studies, but some of them felt it was unfair to Jonah. They guessed that he had a reasonable chance of integrating the three alters. They embarked on another course of hypnosis and claimed that they were successful the second time round. Jonah does not seem to have been followed up in detail later, so it is not possible to say.

Some of the cases that follow are more dramatic than Jonah but none has been studied with such rigour. Different experts have seen different things in Jonah. Ian Hacking claims he was expressing black power stereotypes: for example, Usoffa was a radical who wouldn't be cowed. Hacking suggests that it's not very likely such an alter would have come into being when Jonah was a child.

I'm not sure Hacking is right. The great child psychologist Jean Piaget claimed (1952) that children take out on their dolls and toys the strains they lived through each day. It's hardly inconceivable that a black child facing a world full of discrimination should make up a superhero to help him cope.

One psychologist who has been very impressed by the study of Jonah is John Morton, director of the Medical Research Council's Cognitive Development Unit in London. Morton is a very empirically minded psychologist. He is now trying to recruit a number of subjects in order to repeat the study using the very latest techniques.

Given the ideas I developed in the previous chapter, what I find striking about Jonah's alters is that there is very little sense of fun and play about them. Sammy and Usoffa are both dour. Even King Young in his self draw has no sense of joy or pleasure

CHAPTER 6

Lizzie's Ghosts

Descartes' *Cogito* can be rephrased: *Dubito, ergo sum.*

The case histories that follow are an attempt to reveal the complexity of the disorder. None of them, apart from the case of Pam (Chapter 9), have clear lessons. But each case does have something to say both about the suffering of the patients, the problems the condition causes for families and friends, the difficulties of treatment and the fact that this is not a disorder that is easily cured. Pam's case reveals dramatically too the risks therapists run – physical risks and risks to their self esteem.

In dealing with all this evidence, every time I go to meet someone who is said to suffer from multiple personality disorder I am acutely aware of two different feelings. On the one hand, I want what I am told to be true. Like all investigators, I hope that I am unearthing a real and interesting story.

I started to research this book in a sceptical frame of mind. Maybe I've been over-influenced. Maybe I should be poking more fun at these contortions of the self. But I can feel myself being persuaded.

But there is still the other side of me. Sceptical, very unwilling to be conned. I hold these two contradictory attitudes. They are not different selves, of course, but they certainly are different aspects of me.

I have been here before. In the 1970s, in journals like the American *Human Behaviour*, I wrote a good deal on the work of a French statistician called Michel Gauquelin who seemed to prove that the position of the planets at birth had a major effect on success in different professions. There has been a twenty-year battle between those who believe in Gauquelin's findings and those who argue they are nonsense. Often, when I talked to him, I found myself agreeing with both points of view.

Did that make me indecisive, or open, as a good researcher should be?

In Britain there has not yet been the development of a multiple personality movement. Many professionals are dismissive. Others, even if they encounter people who suffer symptoms, are extremely worried about publishing the fact in case they are made ridiculous – a situation that recalls Richard Kluft's experience in America in the 1970s.

Lizzie is in her early thirties. She lives in a small council flat in the Home Counties. She wears her red hair cropped. The day I first went to see her was sunny and warm. Despite that, she wore a long-sleeved shirt. At times as we talked, she wrapped and unwrapped a tartan scarf round her wrists.

Her small flat was strikingly neat and bare.

'I'm surprised Trevor sent you,' Lizzie said, a little aggressively.

'Why?'

'You know,' she smiled. 'I've read too many books.'

I could see no books in her small front room.

'I hid them,' she smiled.

The therapist who put me in touch with her insisted that I don't use either his real name or her real name. He had found dealing with her disconcerting. When I first talked to him about the subject, he said he found the whole multiple personality explosion in the States very odd. Unlike many British doctors and therapists, however, he wasn't totally dismissive. He got in contact again and hinted at the fact that he was treating someone it might be worth my while seeing. But he was not sure if she was an honest patient or not. He had made many attempts to verify parts of her history and had met with only partial success. He was fascinated by the case but he wasn't sure if her symptoms were real or if, consciously or unconsciously, she was faking. He was very nervous of being taken for a gullible fool.

He had had Lizzie in treatment for nearly two years, he said. Lizzie had been in and out of the psychiatric system since she was in her teens. She had spent some time in a psychiatric hospital on the south coast near Brighton. They had diagnosed her as having serious depression. She had made a number of suicide attempts by cutting her wrists. She was also extremely interested in fire. The hospital believed, but could not prove, that she had started a number of small fires on the premises.

Lizzie had been treated with both ECT and anti-depressants. There was, Trevor said, a fairly extensive medical history. Lizzie had been released from the hospital a number of times. The hospital was sure, according to Trevor, that Lizzie had also spent time in the North of England and in Ireland.

Trevor is a psychotherapist – not a doctor. He had been called in by Lizzie's GP. He was getting nowhere with her depression. She was complaining of dizziness and blank spells. She was picked up a number of times by the police and claimed to have no idea why she was in the places where she was picked up. Her GP wondered if some form of relaxation might help.

Knowing many young women who are abused do make suicide attempts, Trevor started to explore – or, really, fish for – memories of episodes of abuse. Lizzie completely denied that anything of the kind had ever taken place. She came from a very religious family. Her father had been an important figure in his local Baptist community. She had been good at Bible studies and had won a number of scripture prizes. Her father and mother were very happy. She had two brothers who were normal. Trevor just had no idea of her childhood if he suggested anything of the sort. She had been warned about sick therapists like him.

Trevor was struck by the fact that she seemed, however, to have no family support despite all her problems.

Trevor decided to back off for the moment. He told me he wasn't prepared for what happened next. Lizzie, who was usually polite and kept on saying that she was desperate to get better, just walked out of his office.

I waited and wondered whether she would explain to me what

happened next. She seemed to know this part of the story and to have no difficulty with it.

'Oh, I know what happened next. I ran away.'

'Did you know it or did Trevor tell you later?' I asked.

'I'm not sure but I know now.'

She didn't add to that. There was no point in acting like a cross-examiner.

Trevor was both worried and curious. He looked in more detail at her medical records with the GP and there seemed to be blank periods – as if Lizzie had gone missing. He also went to talk to the local police with the permission of the GP, who was very worried about her. She made no contact and had not been picked up again. Lizzie was eventually put on the register of missing persons but there was no intense attempt to find her. Trevor did have one strange conversation with a police constable who had talked to Lizzie when she was being held in the cells. She had insisted to him that he had her name wrong. She wasn't Lizzie at all. She knew quite well who Lizzie was. But she was Esther.

At first, the policeman thought Lizzie was joking. Eventually he asked if Esther was her first name then what was her second name? He thought, he told Trevor, she had said something like Faversham.

Trevor could find out nothing else about her. Lizzie's GP promised to tell him if she turned up again in the surgery. He sent two or three letters to her address asking her to get in touch but there was no response.

After Lizzie left his office, Trevor didn't see her again for over six months. He told me that she had made contact again by letter. This was peculiar in itself. The letter said that she was going to keep next week's appointment. Lizzie didn't have an appointment for next week. She turned up, nevertheless. Curious, as many therapists dealing with such cases become, Trevor was waiting.

'I asked her where she'd been for six months.' Trevor is sure he asked the question gently. It wasn't meant as a rebuke.

'Six months?' Lizzie seemed surprised.

She thought it had been less than a month since she had seen him. She was very sorry she had left so abruptly but she explained that she had had an appointment to keep. It took Trevor a good deal of effort to persuade her that it had actually been six months since he had last seen her.

Trevor stopped arguing about the time gap and asked her where she had been. Lizzie was evasive. She either wouldn't say or didn't know. He asked to see her wrists and saw there were recent scars which suggested that she had slashed her wrists since he had last seen her. In the meantime, Lizzie had also acquired a tattoo on her upper arm.

I asked her if it was then that she had been tattooed.

'It was then other people could see the tattoo,' Lizzie said.

Being only too aware of the gaps in the community care system, Trevor guessed she had ended up in some casualty department after a suicide attempt. Any reasonable casualty department would have summoned the duty psychiatrist and tried to get her admitted.

Lizzie told him that she wasn't sure what she had been doing. Trevor told her there was nothing to be ashamed about if she had been in hospital. He contacted her old hospital in Brighton but found that they had no record of her being re-admitted.

By the time I was talking to her, Lizzie had made some progress towards being able to explain what she had done. It's important, though, to remember the layers through which this narrative comes. Essentially I am telling the story which was extracted from Lizzie (when she was in a state of deep relaxation). Lizzie and her alters told the story to Trevor who told it back to Lizzie who told it to me.

Science, in Ian Hacking's sense, this is not. Yet the experiences felt real to those who had them.

'I just didn't want ever to see Trevor again. I know now that it's because it's so fucking painful. But I didn't think that. I just wanted to get away,' she told me.

Faced with Lizzie's evasiveness, Trevor asked who Esther was.

'Esther?' Lizzie asked. 'You must know who Esther is if you know the Bible.'

'Esther Faversham,' Trevor insisted.

Lizzie said the name did seem a little familiar but she couldn't really place it. Trevor asked her if there were any feelings, good or bad, associated with the name. He remembers Lizzie pausing and then saying very definitely, 'Bad, very bad feelings. Nightmares.'

Trevor explained to Lizzie that he wanted her to tell any nightmares she had about Esther. Meanwhile, he tried to give her some training in relaxation. He emphasized that if she ever felt she was going to cut herself or slash her wrists, she should try to use these exercises – and ring him. He gave her his home number, too.

Trevor wasn't prepared for what happened next. At seven the next morning Lizzie rang to say she had had a terrible dream about Esther. She must see him.

Trevor cancelled a lunch and agreed to see Lizzie the same day.

In her nightmare Esther appeared. She was a witch who had been dead for three hundred years. She had lived in Faversham and was called Esther of Faversham. She had been burned at the stake there.

Trevor was completely at a loss. He had some experience of regression work but he was surprised by Lizzie/Esther's intensity. Witches seemed like New Age nonsense. He wasn't sure what to do next. He does not believe in hypnotism and anyway does not know how to do it. He hesitated to consult colleagues as he didn't want to look a fool. He is experienced at relaxation and with therapies related to psychodrama, so he asked Lizzie if she would agree to be deeply relaxed. He hoped that if she was relaxed he might get more information about Esther.

Once Lizzie was deeply relaxed, Trevor urged her to be honest and not ashamed. He said to her that we all have secrets, families inevitably have secrets. Talking about secrets was always frightening, but in the end it was healing. He then asked Lizzie to describe her family. Instead of getting a new picture, he got exactly the same picture he had had from the 'usual' Lizzie. She talked about her religious parents. She talked about a few rivalries she had with her brothers but, apart from that, they were great. Lizzie seemed at ease as she described Sundays when they went to chapel. She did not act defensive. He couldn't detect any signs of repression.

Still fishing, Trevor asked Lizzie if she had ever been to Faversham.

'I once went to Margate.' Margate is about thirty miles from Faversham in Kent. 'Nan may have taken me to Faversham. We used to go on lots of picnics.'

Lizzie had never spoken about her grandparents before.

Her grandmother turned out to be a woman very different from Lizzie's prim and religious parents. She was her father's mother and used to poke a good deal of fun at her straitlaced son. He didn't know how to enjoy himself. He took after his grim father, Lizzie's grandfather, who only ever had fun when he got drunk. Lizzie's grandmother told her she had become fed up with drinking because when he was drunk, he also became violent. She had left him after one beating too many. She had met Victor, who was five years younger than herself. Victor was good fun, she kept on saying. After some summers working in the hop fields in Kent and a bit of luck on the horses, they had managed to scrape enough money together to buy a small boarding-house in Margate where they offered bed and breakfast.

Lizzie's parents often sent her down to Margate. This struck Trevor as strange. If Lizzie had been a good girl and the excellent Bible student that she said she was, why did her parents often let her go down to Margate to stay with her slightly disreputable grandmother and her 'fancy man'? Why had Lizzie not said anything about this in any of the medical records Trevor had unearthed?

From the age of eight or ten – Lizzie always had a vague sense of time – she told Trevor that she often went to Margate during the summer. Trevor kept on asking if Lizzie had done anything to annoy her parents which made them send her away.

'Mum and Dad only liked me when I was being a Bible girl,' she said.

Trevor asked if she was sometimes fed up with being the Bible girl. She said that she was sometimes and wouldn't learn bits of the Bible. Then her father would hit her for not obeying Jesus, saying it was for her own good. Her mother sometimes got frightened and would arrange for her to go down to Kent.

Trevor couldn't get any further. He asked Lizzie to describe her Nan and Victor. There were some hesitations when Lizzie started speaking about him. With so little to go on, Trevor began to suspect that if there was any abuse, it had taken place in the bed and breakfast.

'Are they still alive?'

Lizzie didn't know. She had lost touch with them years ago. She thought they hated the fact she was 'in the loony-bin'. Victor and Nan had visited her for a while but then they had stopped. Trevor asked her when she had last seen them. She couldn't remember. He asked if she would like to try to find them again. Her very definite answer struck him:

'Victor won't want to see me.'

'Why not?'

'I'm not a pretty young girl. He liked pretty young girls.'

'Did he like you when you were a pretty young girl?'

'Sometimes.'

Trevor asked Lizzie's permission to contact her parents. He tried the last address she had for them. The house they had lived in had changed hands a number of times. No one knew where they were. Trevor decided he would investigate further. He wasn't sure why he was doing this and he didn't tell Lizzie what he was doing. But it was typical of what Tom Fahy calls the 'over-involvement' of therapists.

He went to Margate and found her grandmother's house. The street Lizzie had named was full of bed-and-breakfast houses. Many had gone over to housing patients who had been discharged from psychiatric hospitals. Lizzie had remembered the number of the house. It was run by a young couple. They knew the house had been a bed and breakfast for over forty years but they had no idea about who had owned it twenty-five years earlier.

Trevor decided to tell Lizzie what he had done. He thought it was very important to be able to piece her past together.

'Did you find Victor?'

'No.'

Lizzie seemed relieved when he told her that he hadn't done so. He decided to relax her again and see if he could get her to talk about Esther. After about fifteen minutes of deep relaxation, Lizzie spoke to him. Trevor thinks her voice was much deeper, but admits that perhaps he was imagining it.

'If you want to find out about Esther why not ask her? Oh yes, Esther of Faversham. That's me.'

'Esther of Faversham,' Trevor repeated.

'I must have put myself to sleep for a long time.'

Esther's tale was so bizarre Trevor thought Lizzie might have been making it all up, but there was no indication Lizzie had the imagination or the knowledge to do that. In this deep relaxation state, Esther said that she had been a witch in the seventeenth century. She had been burned, but it's not so easy to burn witches and her soul had survived. She had spent a long time waiting to return – she couldn't explain why it had been so long – then she had decided to house herself in Lizzie's body. Esther was very concerned not to be burned again so to play safe she had chosen a religious girl.

'I wish I'd made a different choice. They were awful.' Esther said she couldn't bear Lizzie's mother and father. 'Good people,' she spat. 'Good people who did nothing but eat, piss and pray.' Esther claimed she had sabotaged Lizzie's Bible learning and so annoyed the parents. The only pleasure in Lizzie's life was going down to see Nan and Victor.

Trevor asked what had happened with Victor. Esther laughed. With very little embarrassment or apparent pain, she said that little Lizzie loved the fairground. Her Nan was busy sorting things out in the bed and breakfast. So, one day, Victor took Lizzie to the fairground. They had a marvellous time. One ride they went on was a Bouncy Castle. It was meant to be only for children but Victor took his shoes off and bounced up and down with her. He hugged Lizzie as they jumped. He got a look in his eyes that Lizzie didn't recognize but that Esther remembered from the past.

Lizzie was a little girl but she, Esther, was a woman – and a witch.

In the evening, when Nan must have been out shopping, Victor told Lizzie that he would help her dry herself. He came into the bathroom when she was washing and watched her. Then, he dried her.

'It had been three hundred years since a man touched me,' Esther said.

Trevor was flabbergasted by these memories and far from certain that someone wasn't making fun of him.

'You can tell me, Esther,' he said.

'Esther liked it.' The voice that said this didn't seem to be that of either Lizzie or Esther.

The new 'voice' didn't claim a new identity. An experienced multiple personality therapist would have asked routine questions like, 'Who are you?' or 'What's your name?' but Trevor had never been in this situation before.

The voice said, 'We didn't like it, Lizzie or me.' Then it changed back to the slightly deeper tones that seemed to be Esther's. Esther described what had been a long – and sadly familiar – catalogue of abuse. Victor had started by helping her wash and dry herself. Then he started reading stories at night to her as she lay in bed. He would have his hands on her while he read. The abuse became more intimate involving masturbation as he got her to touch his penis. Until Lizzie reached puberty, Victor did nothing else. Then he came into her bedroom one night, put a hand over her mouth and had intercourse with her. Esther did not object, she claimed now. Lizzie's reaction was very different.

As a result of dealing with this case, Trevor had started to read round the subject. He had come across the work of Adam Crabtree. Crabtree is a psychotherapist who is convinced that some examples of multiple personality are instances of possession (1985). Crabtree doesn't work by hypnosis but by trying to tease out such selves in conscious conversation. As he was worried about using hypnosis, Trevor had adopted this technique. He asked if this 'third' voice belonged to someone else. Nothing happened immediately.

The day after this session, Lizzie went to her GP. She said she was still very depressed and needed more medication. She was given a prescription. She told the GP she was not sure about continuing to see Trevor.

The next session with Trevor was very quiet. Trevor tried again to relax her deeply. Nothing happened. He was almost sure Lizzie had dozed off.

At the following session, Trevor relaxed her again and said he wanted to know more about Esther and about any other voices. He couldn't bring himself to use the terminology of multiples – the alters or other selves. Then a voice said: 'It was so painful.'

Trevor thought this was the 'third' voice he had heard before. This voice said that at first she had liked Victor holding and stroking her. Her parents never stroked her. But then Victor started saying all this had to be kept secret. He would sneak into her bedroom. He made her touch his penis and rub it. She remembered when he had first come into her. She was terrified. She hated it. She hated Esther who seemed to like it. Esther was mad with all her talk of witches. She hated and feared Lizzie because Lizzie could have told her parents she didn't want to go back to Nan. All Lizzie had to do was to parrot the Bible. That would have kept Dad happy.

Esther didn't have to put up with the consequences.

The next part of the story came through this voice. Again, Trevor was not sure how much to believe.

When she was fifteen, Lizzie became pregnant. Her parents were furious. They were convinced that their daughter had been misbehaving with some local boy. They couldn't bear the shame. It would destroy their standing in their religious community. To make matters worse, Lizzie denied she was pregnant. That was hardly surprising. She had blocked out what Victor was doing. To Lizzie's complete confusion, her bags were packed and she was sent back down to Kent.

'I heard them talking,' the voice told Trevor, 'the baby would be adopted.'

The parents told their friends that Lizzie was being sent to a special school to cram for her exams. Lizzie's father and mother hoped that Lizzie would have the baby discreetly, have it adopted and come back home. Nobody would know what had happened.

In Margate, however, Nan was suspicious. She had a better sense of what Lizzie was like. It seemed to her very unlikely that she had got herself knocked up by a boy. For the first time, Nan began to wonder about her now-husband, Victor. Victor had always been very devoted to Lizzie.

Trevor had told me Lizzie remembered some of this. And in conversation with me she seemed to. At least she told me, 'There were lots of rows, I think. I didn't know what the rows were about but I know they were about me. My Nan was very angry with me. She also kept on saying it wasn't like me.'

Trevor had asked what had happened to the baby. Did Lizzie remember? Lizzie was adamant she'd never had a child. Trevor asked her if she remembered anything about seeing doctors or a hospital. Or the colour white.

He made sense of the next part of the story largely through the third voice.

Victor persuaded Nan that the girl should have an abortion. That would have been easy to arrange at the time but Trevor wondered why it didn't show up on Lizzie's medical records. He decided eventually they had probably paid for it at a small private clinic.

But Lizzie insisted she didn't know she was pregnant, though she did have some conscious memory of being in a hospital. But, then, she had often been in hospital later. With her poor memory, it got muddled.

'I didn't know I woke up in a hospital. I had no idea I was sick. I'd had my appendix taken out.'

If the clinic explained to Lizzie what had happened to her, she had blocked it out. As far as she was concerned, she was still a girl who'd never even kissed a boy.

Despite this 'innocence', Lizzie seems to have made a huge effort now to regain control. As soon as she had recovered enough to leave hospital, she took a train to go back north to her parents. But she never got there. Piecing the story together, Trevor now guessed that somewhere between Kent and the north, Esther had sabotaged the plan and taken 'control of the body'.

It wasn't easy to find out what had happened next. Trevor relaxed Lizzie again in subsequent sessions and asked for more information about Esther. Lizzie said she didn't know anything else.

Two sessions later, Trevor had made no progress. He had developed the tactic of not pushing. When Lizzie wouldn't speak about something, he would ask her either about the present or go back over ground they had already established. But suddenly, Lizzie said, 'Ask Esther.'

Again, Esther said that he could talk to her directly.

Esther said that she was entitled to what happened next – she had a good time in London. She joined a commune which included a number of people who were very interested in astrology. Esther had been able to teach them a few things. She had also enjoyed the men, though she had the sense to have a coil fitted. Then, to spoil the good time she was having – the first for three hundred years, she kept insisting – Lizzie started to come back. Esther found that Lizzie was resuming control of the body.

Both consciously and in the relaxed state, Trevor asked Lizzie if she had any memories of living in London in a commune, any memories of being disturbed.

All Lizzie said she could remember was how horrible it was when she went north. She couldn't understand why her clothes had become muddled up in the hospital. They weren't the ordinary clothes she normally wore. Lizzie remembered going back to her parents' house wearing flowered skirts and funny jewellery like hippies.

'All I wanted was to go back home,' Lizzie told Trevor.

Her parents couldn't cope with her return though. Lizzie had only vague memories of how they treated her. There was a lot of shouting. She was a disgrace. She had sinned. Her brothers had been told not to talk to her. The family had been so worried.

Trevor asked if she understood they were worried because she had disappeared. But Lizzie seemed to think that she had left her

Nan, gone to London and, after a day or so, gone north. That wasn't Esther's time frame. The only explanation the family had for what had happened was that Lizzie had gone mad. She was only sixteen. They took her to their GP who had known her as a child.

The next thing Lizzie remembered was a big building like a hospital – and corridors. It was a description of a typical psychiatric hospital. Lizzie remembered that they were unkind to her there.

At a later session, the third voice explained that Lizzie had asked for it. She hadn't managed to keep Esther in check. Esther had started a series of fires. 'She was always going on about fire being sweet to witches.' But Esther, who had been subdued now for a matter of months, took the attitude that she wasn't going to put up with it. Security at the hospital was fairly poor and Esther/Lizzie walked out and went back on the road.

Esther eventually told Trevor that she could have coped but Lizzie couldn't. Lizzie would always mess up because she was so pathetic. From this time on, Lizzie had been in and out of the psychiatric system.

'I did ask Esther why, since she was a witch, she didn't just leave Lizzie and inhabit some other body,' Trevor told me. Esther never answered.

The medical records did show that Lizzie sometimes had delusional interludes in which she talked about an interest in the occult, and confessed to hearing the voices of witches. But these symptoms were put down as just the typical delusions you would expect of a schizophrenic. Lizzie embarked on her psychiatric career. Psychiatrists tried a variety of medications. Lizzie often absconded from hospitals and moved from one hospital to another. No one fought to get good care for her. She became a patient just as large numbers of patients were being sent out from hospital and into community care.

Lizzie never managed to establish a stable relationship with a man or with a psychiatrist. Trevor believed that he was the first professional to have extracted so much of her story. In her medical records, he found one note which queried whether she might not be suffering from bipolar disorder. Most of the time she was depressed and lethargic but, just occasionally, she would show great bursts of energy. Trevor thought it made sense to think that these were times when Esther took over.

He was both proud and frightened of what he was uncovering. It made him feel that he was a terrific therapist to have winkled out this history. He found it quite easy now to contact all three of the voices in Lizzie. There was no sign of any other voice and Trevor didn't do what American therapists might have done – say that he wanted to talk to anyone 'in there'.

Lizzie continued to be extremely depressed. He decided it was time to confront her with her own history. He prepared the ground as carefully as he could. Part of the preparation was to give her *The Three Faces of Eve* and *Sybil* to read. Trevor believes that it is important to make the patient as aware as possible of what is happening.

Lizzie remembered the books. 'I was a little disappointed,' she told me. 'I didn't understand why he was making me read them.'

After she had read the books, Trevor relaxed her deeply and told her as much as he had managed to piece together of her history. He was frightened she would run away again, and asked her not to.

Lizzie put her hands together and started praying. If she had done all those things, she felt it was terrible. She must be a real sinner. From this point on, she started going back to church.

Trevor tried to reassure her. She was ill, not wicked. He explained to her that all those three voices were parts of herself. Trevor also shared with the GP what he had discovered. The GP became extremely nervous. He first of all assumed that Trevor had suggested some of these bizarre events to Lizzie and he then asked if Trevor had behaved improperly. Had he slept with the Esther character? There were and are many concerns about therapists abusing their patients. Trevor was furious. The practice stopped sending him any new patients.

In a subsequent session, the third voice asked what could be done to rid her and Lizzie of Esther, who was still making their life miserable.

There is no happy ending to this case. Trevor has tried a number of tactics. Lizzie now knows in her head that there may be other entities in her and she finds the idea puzzling and distressing. Given her background, to be associated with a witch of any sort makes her feel as if she is being punished for something. And she's not sure what. She continues to go to church regularly.

According to Trevor, Lizzie has been put on a very heavy set of drugs by her GP in order, in effect, to keep Esther asleep. For the moment this is showing some signs of working, though Lizzie is not happy about the side-effects of the heavy doses of anti-depressants.

I asked Lizzie if she was now aware of other people inside her. 'In a sort of way, but they're not really me.' She is confused by what she has been told about herself.

The third voice is angry with Trevor. She has shared so much with him in the hope of getting Lizzie better and it seems to have got them nowhere.

It might possibly help Lizzie if she could get in touch with her parents again. But she would need to really search for them – and the last thing she remembers about them is their carting her off to the first psychiatric hospital. Like many ex-patients, Lizzie is living a half-life with only minimal contact with other people. Trevor is sure that when she has been picked up in strange situations by the local police, it's because Esther has somehow obtained control of the body again. But he doesn't see what he can do other than be there to talk to Lizzie and the other selves. How do you forge into one being a prim, religious woman in her early thirties who keeps her small flat empty and spotless, a witch, and a much younger angry 'voice'? He feels he hasn't even established which of these entities is responsible for the episodes of cutting and wrist-slashing that still happen to Lizzie.

As I left her, Lizzie was still toying obsessively with the scarf that covered her slashed wrists.

Lizzie is not 'cured' but, most of the time, in a slightly burnt-out way, she is – for now – less of a danger to herself.

CHAPTER 7

Silence and Suicide

The pioneers tend to complain of the way many patients have been misdiagnosed. In some cases, though, patients don't want to be seen as multiples. They present, Catherine Fine says, 'in a very constipated way'. In such cases, it takes a long time for any alters to come out. It's not surprising that some patients find the idea of suffering multiple personality disorder very frightening as Fine explained in Amsterdam (Fine 1995).

Naomi is still in treatment and Doctor Fine outlined many aspects of this case in discussions in Amsterdam. I refer to the two doctors involved as Doctor A and Doctor B.

Naomi is a petite woman in her early forties. She looks depressed and moves in a very lethargic way. She also has a rather vacant air most of the time, as if she is half in a trance. As we shall see, sometimes she puts herself in a trance without knowing it. Whether she does this to escape real life, no one is sure.

Naomi's parents moved to the States from Romania at the end of the 1939–1945 war. They were ambitious Jews. They had faith in the American dream. If they worked hard, they would succeed in the States. When they first arrived they had no money, so both parents had to work. To make that possible, they made rather elaborate child-care arrangements and Naomi was left at various apparently reliable kindergartens and child-minders.

When Naomi was a small child in the 1950s, parents didn't worry about whether child-minders might be abusers.

As Naomi grew up, her parents noticed that she was very quiet. But that didn't seem to upset them. Naomi was doing the one thing they cared passionately about – working hard in school and succeeding. They weren't bothered about her not having many friends. The Holocaust had left its mark on them. They knew that the outside world could be frightening. A Jew was never safe. Try too hard to make the outside world like you and you would encounter prejudice, abuse, even violence.

Naomi might have been quiet but she also seemed a devoted daughter. Nevertheless, photos of her in her teens show her as being very depressed. Her mouth is set down. The eyes look a little blank. What her parents didn't know was that as a teenager Naomi seems to have become involved in a rather strange sexual relationship.

When she was about sixteen, her parents decided that it might be a good idea to send her to Israel. She went to live, study and work on a kibbutz for a while. Again, she had some intense sexual relationships out there.

Then Naomi came back to America and finished college. Her life appeared to have sorted itself out. She graduated and she got married. But her wedding pictures don't seem to show a happy bride. The woman in them seems depressed. 'You'd think she was going to a funeral,' Doctor B joked. Despite all the problems, the marriage lasted. She became pregnant. Her first three pregnancies were unremarkable, though in her twenties Naomi seems to have sought some help for her recurring depressions.

Then, Naomi became pregnant a fourth time. This fourth pregnancy was extremely difficult. After giving birth to a second daughter Naomi became depressed again but she and her family seemed just able to manage.

On her daughter's fourth birthday, however, Naomi made a serious suicide attempt. It turned out that she had made some previous attempts. Her husband sought help and Naomi was admitted to hospital.

Initially, Naomi seemed to be suffering either from major depression or a borderline condition. Her doctors thought that her inert passivity, her being 'out of it' for long periods of time, was a form of aggression. The technical term was that she was passive aggressive. But what struck them more than this was how out of touch she seemed – as though she was 'not there'. Yet she had brought up a family, a family that had not reported any major problems. It seemed very strange.

The doctor in charge of her case initially suspected there might have been some child abuse. He decided to hypnotize her. He was fairly pleased with what emerged. When she was hypnotized, Naomi had some memories of being abused though the memories were not entirely clear.

Most multiple personality therapists now clarify that the first step in any treatment is to make the patient feel safe. Richard Kluft has developed a series of stages of therapy. He argues doctors must be very careful the patient feels secure and committed to therapy before taking a full psychiatric history. Otherwise, memories of abuse can come out too quickly. The patient panics. Naomi's first therapist was pushing the pace before Naomi felt safe about revealing her truth.

This phase is an interesting one. One complaint of the pioneers about the sceptics is that they always want *the truth* about abuse. There is literal truth, the kind that holds up in court, but there is also the truth you feel. If I feel I have been abused that feeling is true for me about me.

Once Doctor A had obtained Naomi's memories of abuse, he decided to confront her conscious self with them. He started to ask her questions based on the assumption that her parents had abused her.

The results were dramatic. Naomi denied that she had ever been abused. In effect the doctor had asked her to accuse her beloved parents. Naomi just wasn't going to do that at this point in therapy even if she had been abused. Doctor B is highly critical of the way the therapy had been done. She told me that using hypnosis in this controlling and intrusive way mirrors the initial abuse. 'It's the your-life-is-in-my-hands approach and I think that may recall what abusers do to children,' Doctor B said. It wasn't surprising that patients often rebelled.

Naomi's response to her therapist was simple. He had planted these wicked allegations of abuse in her mind while she was hypnotized. They were untrue. Her parents were good and loving. But Naomi also made a new – and serious – suicide attempt.

The hospital decided it was time to bring in another doctor. But the arrangements were slightly bizarre. Naomi would have three sessions a week with Doctor B but she would continue to have one session a week with Doctor A. The doctors became rivals. Doctor B complained that Doctor A was pushing the idea that Naomi was suffering from multiple personality disorder. When Doctor B tried to discuss that with him Doctor A became hostile. Then he refused to take her calls.

At this stage, Naomi hadn't mentioned any alters or any splitting. Yet at least one doctor assumed she was concealing these and resisting the diagnosis. Both doctors complained the patient's style was forcing them to work through the conscious host personality (which was the only personality they had seen) rather than through alters they assumed were there but hiding.

What both doctors really wanted to do was to find all the alters in her system, tease them out, learn what had traumatized them, work through each trauma and put each healed alter back in its niche in her personality. Then the self could be made whole in a classic way. But Naomi, being a difficult patient, was denying she had any alters and refusing to let either of her warring doctors get on with such basics as 'mapping' the personalities in her system; Chapter 11 will explore these 'maps'.

There is a different way of seeing this, though. Naomi wanted therapy to proceed according to her agenda. Therapists keep on repeating the mantra that there is so much to learn from the patient and yet all too often they seem irritated with the patient who doesn't fit their preconceptions. Naomi refused to fit the preconceptions. Passive but angry, she kept on flirting with thoughts of suicide. She would go on about these thoughts during many sessions so that Doctor B eventually issued a bit of an ultimatum. She was fed up hearing about death. Far too much therapy time was being spent on fantasies of dying.

Doctor B clearly continued to have problems with Naomi's attitude. Naomi would come into sessions and say almost nothing at the start. Often she would be distracted instead of focusing on the therapy. She would complain about irrelevancies. For instance, she moaned that her daughter was being dramatic and annoying her a lot.

One day Naomi complained about having burned herself at the stove. Doctor B was irritated because it seemed yet another detail which took them away from the main point of therapy. Naomi was always looking for a way out, Doctor B said. The doctor didn't pursue the subject of burning.

One day, finally, there was a spark of progress. Naomi started to talk about how conflict led to 'a dying place'. As her doctor was trying to make sense of this phrase, Naomi said she felt 'contrived'.

'What's contrived?'

'Focusing on death is contrived, I do that a lot.' Naomi went on to say that she noticed that Doctor B was refusing to play the game.

'She was right,' Doctor B said, 'I didn't want to get into the game she had been playing with Doctor A where she threatened suicide and he would have some sort of contract where she promised not to kill herself.' But Doctor B was interested in the fact that Naomi had talked about things being contrived, about games and about pretending.

'Oh, so you don't want to play the game,' Naomi said.

Doctor B repeated that she didn't. She also noticed that Naomi was in a strange state – half in a trance.

In a session soon after this, Naomi started to regress, to behave more and more like a child. Naomi felt threatened, she looked as if she was frightened and getting depressed. She looked very young and wide-eyed. Suddenly she started shaking and showing signs of intense fear, and Doctor B believed that she was regressing in age. She was going back into a child state. The one thing that was missing was any sense of anger. The feeling of fear was overwhelming.

Naomi had finally 'popped' one of her alters.

I didn't see Naomi in that state so I'm relying on what Doctor B said. Through the child state, she began to make some sense of the personality system that Naomi had so long blocked any access to. Eventually Doctor B discovered that this shaking child was one of a number of very scared child personalities. Through these child alters, she made contact with three other alters. Of these the most important was a man called Sam.

Eventually – and, again, I have to emphasize how in writing down these narratives they inevitably become more structured and logical than they are – the following story emerged or was remembered.

When Naomi was a little girl and her parents were relying on various child-care arrangements, she was often taken to kindergarten by Uncle Sam. He was a friend of her parents. Naomi suspected that Sam was very close to her mother, and thought that they may even have had an affair. He would often pick Naomi up from the child-minder. But he didn't always take her back to her parents' house. Sometimes, she remembered, he would take her to his own house. Sometimes she would stay the night there. Sam would say they were going to have fun, they were going to play games.

Sam was a thoroughly unpleasant alter. Doctor B thought him obnoxious and also belittling to women. He didn't persecute Naomi but he seemed to be doing his best to prevent her treatment progressing. Doctor B wondered if he was scaring Naomi's child alters because he didn't want anyone to find out what had really happened when they had 'fun'.

Having made these revelations, Naomi returned into a depression and wouldn't give any more information. She started to talk again about killing herself.

Then Naomi started to hear voices. She wasn't sure if she was hearing male or female voices. 'I felt confused with voices,' she said.

Doctor B couldn't decide if she was diverting attention away from her trauma by producing bizarre trance states. She felt her patient was bullshitting.

Then Naomi added, 'I don't want to lie.' Again, remember that this narrative is more structured than the memories. Essentially, Naomi revealed that when she was four – the same age as her second daughter – Uncle Sam would take her back to the local

Masonic Lodge. There Naomi would encounter what she called 'a lot of weird guys'. They would show pornographic movies. And the little girl would become a central figure in their games. The men would use her in a number of sexual ways. Some of them were, if not Satanic, at least sadistic. She was strapped down on some kind of surface. She was physically hurt. But she kept on being told it was part of a game. It was all contrived. A game she had to play.

It was contrived: Naomi spoke the word, the word that had started this little spurt of progress.

But while Naomi was speaking as if she hated it, in her memory the little girl was being told that she liked it. And if she didn't like it or if she didn't pretend to like it, they would hurt her. These memories, as Doctor B points out, are gruesome. Grown men were torturing a little girl, abusing her sexually and even on one occasion placing her in a coffin.

Naomi repeated that she didn't want to lie, she didn't want to edit. She closed her eyes. Doctor B tried to soothe her. 'If it's in your head, we need to pay attention to it,' she said.

Having recalled this, Naomi struggled to open her eyes again. She said that she felt she was in a trance. And then there was a new voice. It was very different. It was chanting, almost. As she described this voice, Naomi seemed to be going into a trance.

Then she said it was 'like that burn'.

Burn? Burn? Doctor B suddenly remembered that months ago there had been a mention of a burn in the kitchen, but she hadn't paid any attention to it because it seemed just another of Naomi's distractions. Naomi had burned herself badly in the kitchen because she felt no pain. Doctor B was now sure that Naomi was alerting her to the existence of an anaesthetic personality (like Usoffa). It was this personality who had split off when she had been abused as a child.

But no well-rounded alter of that sort came out to talk.

Naomi now kept on having dreams in which she saw images of abuse, and in one of these dreams she heard fragments of Romanian. Doctor B started to wonder whether these snatches were going to lead down a familiar path. The far-fetched stories of Uncle Sam would turn out to be a cover for a much more domestic story. The perpetrator of the abuse would be her father or perhaps her grandfather. As she told these dreams, Naomi still often shook with fear.

Then Naomi went on holiday with her family. One day while her husband and children were off doing something together Naomi was sitting outside in a café and reading. She loved reading, Doctor B added, as this too allowed her to escape reality. While Naomi was reading, a man walked by her. His presence made her uncomfortable. About ten minutes later, he reappeared, bent down and poked his head between her book and her face. (If true, it was remarkably intrusive, hardly the kind of thing you do to a stranger.)

Naomi was frightened. The incident triggered new thoughts of suicide. Naomi's husband rang Doctor B and asked whether they should return early from the holiday because Naomi was in such a state. Doctor B talked to Naomi and calmed her down. There was no panic return. But in the first session after the holiday, Naomi said that she kept on seeing this man's face. He flashed into her thoughts and dreams.

And Naomi mentioned masks.

'What masks?' said Doctor B.

Naomi then drew a number of masks and started crying.

Doctor B obviously hoped that Naomi would now reveal the root of her trauma, but instead Naomi again started talking about wanting to die.

The doctor said she would be happy to hear about dying but not today. This ultimatum had a strange effect. In front of her, Naomi changed.

Naomi then sent out a teenage personality who said that adults are all motherfuckers. 'You're supposed to be listening. I'm saying I'm going to die. But you're being mean. You want us to kill ourselves.'

'I want to understand,' Doctor B said.

'I think we're going to do it. And you can't do a damn thing to stop it.' She meant commit suicide.

Naomi had waited till the very end of the session – Doctor B looked at her watch and saw they were on the forty-fourth minute of a forty-five minute session – to bring out the teenage alter. She obviously hoped that this would confirm the fact that the wicked therapist didn't really care.

But Doctor B said she cared so much, it was so important, she would ask her next patient to wait ten or fifteen minutes while they talked some of it through. Doctor B reinforced this by saying that if she didn't talk about it, Naomi was in such a bad state she would need to be hospitalized. The mix of care and threat worked to some extent. Naomi revealed that she felt she had had enough and that the time had come to speak. But it was hard.

What really appalled Naomi was that if the men at the Masonic Lodge had really done some of the things to her that she imagined or dreamed they had done, she could not live with herself. She would be so dirty. Naomi hedged her bets slightly. She wasn't sure if these memories were real or were metaphors, but she had had images of abuse since she had been an adolescent. She was blindfolded. She was a small blindfolded girl whom these men were abusing. Some were wearing masks. She had been spread-eagled. She had been on some sort of medical trolley. The men had used instruments on her. Were they surgeons who were wearing masks?

Vivid and terrible as these memories were, it still wasn't clear exactly what happened or who perpetrated the abuse. Was it the Lodge or the doctors?

It's not hard to see why a story like this should provoke some scepticism. It's clear that both doctors were looking for alters from the start. But also both insist that they didn't plant any theories of abuse. After Doctor A's first session it was Naomi who raised the subject of abuse – something that Naomi confirms.

Her therapy is unfinished. Whether what she has remembered is true remains unconfirmed. But that is true of very many cases. One of the puzzles in the field is just when therapy is completed. It's a point I'll come to in Chapter 13.

CHAPTER 8

The Thin Thief

In many ways Alison's story is much less fantastic than Lizzie's. There are no occult entities here. It also seems much more likely that the final revelations here are close to the truth.

In the restaurant, Alison looked painfully thin. She had high cheek-bones and big staring eyes. She seemed to be one of those infuriating people who could eat as much as she wanted without putting on weight.

First, she wanted to know about me, about my project. She had no intention of being talked into something she didn't want to do.

She finished her hors-d'œuvres and said, 'Excuse me.'

Her boyfriend, Mark, shook his head.

'I don't have to explain to you,' she snapped, and walked off to the Ladies.

'She always does this,' Mark said.

The waiter asked if we wanted to wait for her to come back before he served the main course. It was quite a wait. Alison smiled as she came back. She had been so long in the toilet because she had been thinking about what she called 'my project', she said pleasantly.

She wanted to be sure no one would know her identity. She had insisted on that to her therapist. She hoped to inherit a large amount of money and she didn't want to do anything which might prejudice that.

'Inherit from whom?' Mark asked.

'One of my aunts.'

He shook his head again. They appeared to have a rather negative relationship.

Alison ate the main course as heartily as she had done the hors-d'œuvres but didn't touch the potatoes. Potatoes were totally fattening. Then she got up again.

'Don't,' Mark said.

'Fuck you,' she said.

'You know what the doctor said,' Mark reminded her.

'I don't find it particularly easy to talk with you around. It cramps my style.'

And, with that, Alison made for the Ladies again.

Mark said that I had no idea what it was like trying to sustain a relationship with someone like her.

When Alison returned, she smartly drank two large glasses of white wine one after another. 'I didn't ask you to come along,' she told Mark tensely. Then she turned to me. 'I wouldn't believe anything he says about me.'

This interview seemed headed for total failure. But then Mark suddenly got up and said if she didn't want to talk with him present, fine. He'd bugger off. He wouldn't ring her. She could ring him.

'You will,' she said.

Alison gave him a sarky wave. But she mellowed enormously once he had gone.

'He pisses me off. He likes the fact that I flake. It turns him on.'

Flaking was her word for dissociating.

As with the other narratives in this book, this one runs the risk of seeming more structured than the reality. Over a number of weeks, I talked to Alison, Mark and briefly to one doctor who had treated her.

Alison was quite forthcoming about her background. Her father had been a wing commander in the air force. He had retired in his late forties. Her mother had never worked. Alison had one brother. It wasn't a happy family. Her parents quarrelled a great deal. Her father was very demanding and seemed to think he could treat his family as if they were lower ranks. Alison remembered that she had erratic periods when she was a teenager. She associated these with the trouble she had with eating.

Then she leaned closer to me.

'I went to the loo to throw up. Binge, throw up, binge, throw up. I hate it. Sometimes I starve, but I like my food.'

As I was to find out, in some of her personality states, Alison had a sharp sense of irony about herself. She laughed. 'I'd like to have pudding but then I'm going to have to vomit. Would you like to be me?' But still she ordered a syllabub.

I told her that Richard Kluft said that one of his worst experiences had been with a woman he called Jennifer. The first time he saw her he had been appalled: she was filthy, flies buzzed around sores on her arms and legs and she stank. Kluft said that his first therapeutic reaction to this client was, I mustn't vomit.

Alison said she wasn't surprised, many therapists liked to avoid 'multiples'.

When Alison was about ten she developed a passion for acting. Her parents lived in East Anglia because her father had been stationed at one of the air bases there. Alison went to a private school, and when she was fifteen, she landed the plum part of Lady Macbeth in the school play.

'I was good.' She was young to get such a leading role. She laughed. 'And I did the sleepwalk beautifully.'

Alison had been obsessed with acting. She wanted to talk about the parts she had played. I listened for about fifteen minutes, reminded of Colin Ross' experiences with alters who love to discuss the occult. Nearing thirty, Alison was still stage-struck. It took persistence to nudge her back to her own history.

Alison wanted to leave East Anglia and go to London. Her father said she was day-dreaming. But Alison refused to go to university. She got two A levels, and then came the first of many awful family rows. She applied to two drama schools in London without telling her parents. She was sure she would get in.

'I fucked up the auditions,' she said. She was turned down by both RADA and another drama school. She couldn't face going back to see her parents. Her father would laugh and say he had told her she wouldn't get in. Her mother would be sympathetic but secretly glad. She didn't want to lose Alison. Alison could remember these feelings but she didn't remember what she did next.

Her next memory was totally disconnected. 'I was in Leicester. At the railway station.'

She knew the story now but she thinks she didn't really remember it. Her mother had told her it. What had happened was that she found herself in Leicester with no money and no ticket. She was upset. The only thing she could think of doing was to ring her parents. Her father answered and yelled at her. Didn't she care about worrying them? He supposed she'd been off with some man.

Her mother was calmer. She got British Rail to put her on the train for Diss.

Her father's first words to her were, 'You couldn't cope, could you?' He mocked her and kept on saying she should get a normal job. Alison started to drink heavily. She also started having an affair with the owner of a local restaurant, a much older married man. His wife was a friend of her mother's.

'I'm sure I did it to get back at them. We used to get plastered together. Joe had a little room above the restaurant where we made love. At first it was fun but then there were rows.'

Alison paused. She wanted to explain to me that she was an honest person. But since the age of about eighteen, she had been plagued with accusations of stealing. Even Mark accused her.

A few months after they had started their relationship, Joe rang her in a temper. Some of his wife's jewellery was missing.

Joe accused Alison twice of stealing small items of his wife's jewellery. His wife sometimes worked in the restaurant and usually took off her rings and bracelets while she worked and put them in a little cubby-hole. The jewellery wasn't that valuable.

'I hadn't stolen them. Whatever crap I'd gotten up to sometimes, I hadn't stolen them,' Alison told me.

The next day, however, when they had met, Joe found one of the rings in her handbag. She had no idea how it had got there. Alison defended herself saying that maybe his wife, who knew they were having an affair, had planted the jewellery on her.

These memories made her very upset. She suddenly got up and

went back to the loo. When she came back, she was ice-cool and rather brittle.

'I still don't know if I'll do it.' She wanted to know if she was worse than other cases I had talked to. I said I needed to know more.

Alison's psychiatrist was reluctant to tell me very much about her. She hadn't given him permission to talk to me. All she had said was that she would meet me and see.

Later that day Mark rang. He was sorry lunch had been so bitchy. Things were bad between them. They were always bad. He wanted to trust her but she always did something unexpected which hurt or betrayed him. He tried to understand. He knew it wasn't 'her' who did it. He knew that she didn't mean all the things that the bits, the different sides of herself – Mark certainly wasn't into using the American alter jargon – did.

'I know that with my head,' Mark said, 'but it's fucking hard to believe.' He felt she exploited it. Maybe she had always exploited it. He didn't know what to do about her. She had seen a number of doctors and none of them were succeeding in doing any good. In some sneaky way she enjoyed her condition. She wanted to be an actress, after all.

Mark's bitter outburst only emphasized how frustrated families and partners can get with people who dissociate. It reminded me of a case discussed in Amsterdam by E. Van Hoof in which a seventeen-year-old boy had to cope with his mother and her many alters. She was terrified of her husband, a reclusive carpenter, finding out anything about her multiple life, but he became jealous of her confiding in their son. Mark was expressing similar frustrations. He didn't know how to trust Alison because he had no idea what she might do from one moment to the next.

I asked him if there were times when she didn't acknowledge that she knew him.

'It's happened,' he said drily. He added that it was only when she wanted to get away from him. Rather than confront those feelings, she would just 'disappear'.

MORE STEALING

The next time I saw Alison she insisted that we meet at her small mews cottage. She and Mark weren't really living together, he had his own flat, but there were many of his things around. She made sure, she told me, that he would not interrupt. There were many things about her life that puzzled her but she couldn't bear him butting in and being Mr Know-All because he had talked to her mother and her therapist.

I took my notes out and tried to go back to the point we had reached in the restaurant. But Alison was distracted. She wanted to talk about the TV programmes I'd made. She didn't want to get back to her history so quickly. I didn't know what to do except wait.

Then, after a few minutes, she suddenly became very brisk and said that she knew what I had come for. She was going to help partly because she wanted to get her own history straight in her mind. She couldn't remember what part of her history she had reached so I reminded her. She had returned to East Anglia and had been accused of stealing.

'Joe suddenly got all huffy. His wife wouldn't do that kind of thing. She was the lady. I was the bitch.' It must have been ten years after the event but Alison was still blazingly angry about it. I wondered if that was because this had been the first sign that there was something wrong with her. She might argue that Joe's wife would try to frame her but she didn't really believe it.

'Do you now think you might have done it?'

'Not me.'

'Not any one of you?'

'Shit, do you want to play the "is-there-anyone-at-home game"? Maybe one of the spooks did it.'

'Who are the spooks?'

We had hit on a central issue. Just who are 'spooks'. Alison only knows from the outside – because she has been told – that they exist. She has no direct experience.

'I've been introduced to them, or to some of them, by a Gestalt therapist. He made me act some of them out. I've listened to tapes but you know they could be someone else. The voices don't sound like me to me.' For all she knew, they could have been the voices of other people.

'Tell me what you've heard.'

'A pathetic kid, someone who sounds like Miss Marple and . . .' she tailed off. She really didn't want to go into it, largely because she was still angry after all these years about the accusations.

Being accused of stealing depressed her. It seemed another unjust blow of fate. She knew she was innocent but Joe didn't believe her. After another huge row, she walked out on him. He took his revenge. He went and told Alison's father that she had stolen. Alison said that she suspected he had been such a creep because it gave him a way of making up with his wife.

'I was the witch, you see. I've always been the witch. Lady Macbeth,' she smiled.

Alison felt she had to get out of the village in East Anglia. She had no money so she asked her parents to lend her five hundred pounds. Her plan was to go to London, get a room in a flat and look for a job.

'My father refused. I couldn't believe it.' He had the money. She saw it as pure spite. She suspected he wanted to bargain over something. She yelled at him and ran into her room. She fell down on the bed and started crying. She was shaking with rage.

'One of the troubles with this is that you don't know what's real and what isn't. I think now that I saw myself in that room as a little girl. Five or six. Crying. But maybe someone who hypnotized me suggested that's what happened. I don't know.'

She had the feeling of being a little girl again. Two days later, her father flew into a rage. He wanted to know where his four hundred pounds was.

He accused Alison of stealing it.

'I hadn't taken it.' But her father didn't believe her. He said she had always been dishonest, she had always made him ashamed. He yelled he was going to search her room. She screamed it was private. He yelled he paid all the bills, and forced his way in. He threw her clothes all over the bed and, in the pocket of her leather jacket, he found three hundred pounds.

'I didn't steal it. I had no idea how it got there.'

He told her she was a liar. By now, he was beside himself and started to slap her hard.

'Mother stopped him. She said he was hurting me.'

Alison's mother made Alison give the money back and lent her three hundred pounds herself out of her own savings.

The next day Alison left for London. At the time, she did not believe she had stolen from either Joe or her parents.

She had only very fragmented memories of the next two years. She was lonely and depressed. She drank a lot. She was scared of getting fat. She drifted into a drug scene around Earls Court which also involved some masochism. She was literate and could be presentable so she had no problem getting jobs as a temp, but things would always go wrong. She would get bored. She would be lazy. She'd be accused of stealing from petty cash. She never held a job for long.

Broke, she saw an ad for an escort agency.

'I was really pretty, then. Thin and pretty.'

She found that she didn't have to try hard at the job. She found it easy to flatter men. And when she needed it there was extra money for sex. Again, it was the feelings she remembered as much as the incidents. And the feelings were strange.

Alison said that despite being attracted to the scene in Earls Court, she didn't feel very sexual. But she found that it wasn't that hard to have sex with the men she escorted. 'I could switch off. I just lay there, or stood there and tossed them.'

Again she had a feeling of being able to observe the scene. She was hovering in the room looking down on a thin pretty girl who was having sex for money.

'I'd see myself as doing something else. It wasn't me that was doing it.'

All kinds of images flashed through her mind. Some struck me as very odd. She was mending fuses. She was ironing.

Alison was convinced she was coping but she was relying more and more on cocaine. There were also niggles with the escort agency. Three or four times, there were complaints. Men had returned to their hotels in the morning to find that there was some money missing, or a ring or even a credit card. The women who ran the agency asked Alison to come to see them. They questioned her. Was she having problems? Did she have to spend a fortune on highs?

Alison was confused. 'But I kept saying I didn't have any reason to steal. I was making good money. I was having a good time.' They didn't seem to believe her.

The next time a client complained about having unaccountably lost some money, the agency gave her an ultimatum. If she wanted to carry on working for them, she had to see a doctor. There was obviously something wrong. None of the other girls got complaints like this.

'I told them to get stuffed. But they were nice, and they seemed to think I was sick.'

Bizarre as it sounds, the escort agency arranged for her to see a psychiatrist privately. Alison remembered a tall blond man who asked her whether she had been accused of stealing before. She told him no. The men who hired her were all deceiving their wives. Maybe they needed to accuse her to explain why they had spent so much money.

She remembered going to see this psychiatrist because he was so hateful. He thought he was so clever. He told her that she had to face the fact that she stole from the men she screwed. Maybe she hated them. She had to face it. It was, as she remembered it, surprisingly brutal.

'I wanted to leave but I listened to him. He said the escort agency wanted me to get well. Clients liked me. I was pretty. I was fun. But I had to deal with this.'

He asked her to think if she had any memory of the thefts. She hadn't. He asked her about her family. She told him about the tensions. He said then he could do one of two things. He could prescribe some pills – tranquillizers. Or he could send Alison to see a hypnotherapist. Most kleptomaniacs were middle-aged women desperately seeking attention. Alison was different. He suggested hypnosis might help – in particular it might help unearth memories. The first step to dealing with her thefts was for her to admit she was doing them.

Alison chose the tranquillizers. That weekend, she went away with a boyfriend.

The next thing Alison remembers was being interviewed by the local police. She was in a bleak interview room. A tape was going. There had been a fire at the cottage. Her friend had been badly burned. Where had she been when the fire started? She couldn't answer. Had they had a row? She couldn't answer.

The police knew he was a drug dealer and told her cocaine worth several thousand pounds had been fried in the fire. Someone had done them a favour.

Alison was sure she didn't start the fire. There had never been accusations of that sort before. But she was scared and shaking. She asked them about the fire. All they said was that they had picked her up about half a mile from the cottage. Someone had rung 999. Was it her?

They played her the tape of the call.

It sounded, she told me, like the voice she now recognized as that of the pathetic child.

'That's the worst thing about this. You end up not knowing what you're going to do next.'

She fled back to East Anglia. Her mother was pleased to hear from her but warned her she would have to be very tactful with her father.

'She came to meet me at the station. Alone.'

Later, Mark told me that her mother had told him she was terrified by the way Alison looked when she came back. She wouldn't eat. She often shook. She seemed unable to remember all kinds of things. She was often dizzy. Her coordination was poor. Her mother knew very little about drugs, thought she might be suffering from epilepsy, and took her to the local doctor.

'She wanted to sit in while I talked to him,' Alison said. 'I was twenty-four, twenty-five. Not a baby. But I just didn't want to talk with her there so I said I was fed up and depressed. I knew he'd give me tranx.'

At home, the atmosphere was sour. Her father kept on criticizing her. He kept on bringing up the past – the money stolen from him, Joe's wife's jewellery. She had done nothing with her life. She was a slut. But then she had always been a bad girl. Her father's face would get red and he would get het up as he yelled at her.

Then one day, after one of these rows, Alison said she had had enough.

Her father asked where she thought she was going.

Alison went back into her room and slammed the door. 'I felt scared. Tired and scared.' She lay down on the bed and started to shake. She must have started to scream. Alison's mother, according to Mark, heard her scream. Then it got worse. Alison started to bang her head against the wall. She hadn't done that since she was a child. Alison wouldn't let her mother in the room. Her mother did the only thing she could do. She called her GP.

Alison refused to let him into the room. She had locked the door. From outside they could hear her banging her head.

Her father finally announced that he had had enough and kicked the door down. They found Alison had slashed her wrists. She was taken to a hospital and admitted as an emergency patient.

Alison couldn't recall anything about what had happened in the room.

'Later, I was told that probably what had happened in my bedroom was that my child alter came out.' To anyone used to working with trauma, it wasn't surprising that this should happen. It was clear that Alison had a terrible relationship with her father which peaked in her provoking him and his rejecting her.

In the hospital, Alison became very withdrawn but slowly she felt restored. They got her to eat well, which she said was unusual. She decided she must try to get help. She returned to London and went back to see the psychiatrist the escort agency had sent her to. She was now ready to go for hypnosis.

'I was desperate,' she said.

Alison now seriously committed herself to trying to sort out her problems. Over a number of talks, she explained to me that she had slowly learned that inside her thin body there were a number of competing selves.

'I don't know if it's true. Sometimes it feels true. Sometimes it feels fantastic. I'm not a wanker.'

Alison had started to suspect that there was in her a frightened child. She had no idea, because she didn't really believe that she stole, that there was also a character she eventually called Fanny Fagin. She was told that when she was hypnotized, her therapist asked to speak to the sneaky thief in the system.

'Sneaky, some bit of me said,' Alison laughed. There was in her some kind of imp who had learned very young to steal all kinds of things. She started apparently innocently enough by gathering the coins that her mother often left on the kitchen table. But the thieving imp liked making trouble.

'He told me that children often do that when their parents aren't happy, which was good. I'd rather blame them,' Alison smiled. Fanny Fagin became an expert shoplifter. When she was young, she often nicked things from stores but did it so deftly she was never caught.

Alison admitted that made sense to her. It explained some of the clothes she had. Her mother had once found some blouses she hadn't bought for her and demanded an explanation. Alison couldn't explain. Her father suspected that she had stolen them, and beat her. She must have been eleven or twelve at the time. The next day, to spite him, she went out and stole more things. But she got better at hiding them.

'He told me that he had asked me when I was under if I knew why I was doing it. I didn't, apparently.' This alter had become extremely well established in the system. It made her feel she was getting her own back on an unjust world when she stole.

Under hypnosis, Alison revealed a number of other thieves besides Fanny Fagin. She seemed to have evolved a group of alters who enjoyed the tricks and power of stealing. To give her pleasure, though, the thefts usually had to be from someone she was involved with, someone who loved her.

'I knew there were bits of me that weren't very nice.'

In theory, this was the easiest part of the personality system to work on. If Alison didn't feel afraid of confronting people, especially men, then she would be able to hold her own in less underhand ways.

Alison was more surprised when in a subsequent session she appeared to reveal what she called a Sexpot. In many multiple personality cases there is a tart personality who often makes all kinds of sexual assignations and then disappears, leaving a confused host personality on the verge of sleeping with a total stranger. Alison's personality system was different. She had again had some sense of being an observer when she had worked as a prostitute.

'This was a bit I found fantastic, so he did record a voice, my voice, I suppose,' she said.

One of her voices claimed that she loved sex. She had been brought up to be respectable. Her parents never touched each other in public. But beneath the tart who wasn't really having any fun, there was another alter controlling the tart. This alter adored sex and got tremendous pleasure out of the whoring. The date was curious.

'He asked me if I thought I might steal things from men after I had a really good time. Just to show who was boss.'

There also seemed to be some link between this 'sexy' personality and Alison's fear of fatness. It was as if she feared she would lose some sexual edge if she put on weight.

Later, I told Mark what she had said. It made sense to him. She was, for all her spikiness, a wild lover when she was in the mood. But it pained him that it was never what he did that put her in the mood. Sometimes it happened; sometimes it didn't. It wasn't his skill or his seductiveness that provoked her lust.

Identifying this alter was double-edged. It had the possibility of making Alison happy and fulfilled, of freeing her about sex.

But the therapist said that wouldn't happen unless they could get to the root of the frightened child. These other alters weren't getting anywhere near the trauma. They were too easy to reach.

Like most patients, Alison had by now become persuaded of the model her therapist was using. It assumed there had been sexual abuse. But Alison found it impossible to think that her father would have abused her. But then she had a very vivid dream. She was a baby lying in her crib. She couldn't have been more than two. Her father came in in his uniform. He stroked her and petted her. Then her mother came in in a pink nightie. The nightie was transparent. She could see her mother's pubic hair. Her father kissed her.

Her therapist encouraged her to dream in this vein. But she found she couldn't for some weeks. Then she had another dream. She was a little bit older. Both her parents were sitting on her bed. Again, her father was stroking her. Again, her mother was watching.

Alison had always talked of remembering feelings rather than incidents. Her feelings around this dream were very strange.

'What I'm going to say now doesn't seem like it could be true but I felt that they came and petted me first and then they went off and did it.'

Her therapist began to put together a narrative, as he called it, of what might have happened. Until she was six or seven, when her father was at home, both parents put her to bed sometimes. Her father didn't abuse her in the normal sense of the word. But the act of stroking and petting her was for her parents a crucial element in arousing them. What had started out as a tender ritual, putting their baby to bed, had become an essential part of their sex lives.

Alison found the idea flabbergasting. Her parents were such respectable people. She desperately wanted to talk to them about it but she didn't know how to.

'My father had had a heart attack and I just couldn't see doing it.'

Her therapist said that she ought to talk to her mother, at least. She tried to rehearse her in ways of asking about it. Alison went along with it and twice went to see her parents.

'I bottled out.'

She felt completely stuck and started stealing again – from Mark this time. On a few occasions, she arranged to meet him and didn't show up. Or that was his story.

'I felt a lot was going on. I just couldn't handle it. I started going for long walks, I told myself I was going to sort it all out in my mind and I'd end up miles from where I thought I was.'

Her eating got worse. She starved herself for days and then would binge. 'I'd tried to deal with my problems and it had got me nowhere.'

Alison now had a piece of luck. One of her aunts died and left her the mews cottage where we were meeting. She didn't need to work for the escort agency any more. She felt a tremendous sense of relief and it gave her the strength to confront her mother.

She went back home for a weekend and finally after she had drunk half a bottle of brandy, she told her mother they needed to talk. 'I tried to be sensitive about it. I wasn't sure. I hedged round it.'

Alison wasn't prepared for her mother's reaction. 'She flew into a temper and said that she had no idea what could have given me such crazy ideas. It was years of whoring and taking drugs. It was lies, wicked lies that some trendy therapist had fed me. Nothing like that had ever happened.' Her mother's fury was so unusual that Alison felt sure she had touched some nerve.

'I told her I loved her. I said it was all a long time ago. I just needed to know. I was trying to get well.'

But her mother just snapped that her father was right. 'You are a slut. A bloody slut.'

Her mother wouldn't say any more. She just made Alison promise not to talk to her father about it. He was a sick man. Being accused might kill him.

Alison was sure now that something had happened.

'I started to dream about my mother saying it was true. I couldn't stop thinking about what might have happened.'

Then, her father died. Her mother decided to go on a cruise. She said she deserved it, and now that she had a bit of money she was going to spend it. She sent Alison endless postcards from the cruise, something she had never done before.

'She was also stirred up,' Alison said.

When she came back to England, she asked Alison to come up for a few days to see her.

'It was so sad I couldn't even be angry.'

Her mother told her that her father had beaten both of them. He had lost interest in sex after the children had been born. It made him furious. He beat his wife because he was impotent. He blamed everyone but himself. Alison often head-banged when she was a little girl and it woke her parents and her brother. Her father would fly into a rage and hit her. Her mother tried to calm him down. Sometimes, after hitting Alison, he would suddenly be potent. He would insist on taking his wife to bed. Alison had been left crying and bleeding a few times while her parents went to make love next door. Her mother felt so guilty because she did nothing to protect her.

It seems likely that it was in such a situation that Alison first split as a child. It was too much to be hit by her father and abandoned by her mother. Sometimes, when she was hit, Alison would run away. When her father found her, he would beat her again.

'Your father wasn't a bad man. I loved him,' Alison's mother said. But she was too ashamed to turn for help to their GP. So the violence went on. Alison is not sure her mother has told her all the truth even now. And even if this is the whole truth, it has not brought peace. Ever since her mother 'confessed', their relationship has been very difficult. Alison is angry and does not see how it will be resolved. She feels she is being realistic.

In one of the most pessimistic contributions in Amsterdam, Suzette Boon and Onno van der Hart asked why discovering the truth does not necessarily bring about healing.

But if one thinks of how people react to other traumas, perhaps that should be less surprising. When people suffer from post-traumatic stress after being hijacked or being in an accident, they know what happened. There is no mystery about the event. But that doesn't prevent them suffering.

I'm still in touch with Alison. She still isn't sure she's found the truth but she has stopped stealing – and forgetting that she steals. Fanny Fagin and her friends, at least, are at rest.

CHAPTER 9

Polyfragmented Pam

How many selves can you cram into one body, one person? Psychiatrists have coined a nice piece of jargon, 'polyfragmented MPD', to describe patients with fifty or more alters. Critics, again, sneer at the idea. You need to be utterly gullible or intellectually corrupt to believe that such fantastical notions could have any reality. The pioneers counter that polyfragmentation only shows how complex reactions to trauma can be.

The story of Pam, one of Colin Ross' patients, illustrates some of the problems. Ross (1994) has described many aspects of the case. It is worth examining in detail because it is remarkable and Ross has acknowledged – and did so again in Amsterdam – the need to learn from it. When you are confronted with a patient who seems to have hundreds of splits, alters, fragments, is there any meaningful way to speak of these as entities which are in one self? Are these alters not rather fleeting moods that somehow cascade through consciousness like a shower of meteors? I've suggested that multiple personalities often have a certain cartoon quality. They seem much like one-dimensional entities – the arty self, the angry self, the romantic self. These may be stereotypes but they have a certain stability. Hundreds of fragments don't have that at all. The right image to describe them may not be that of characters in a play but the showers of sparks from a firework. One fragment rockets into life, pours out its fairy lights and then vanishes. It's an image that comes out of the sheer energy of Pam's personality system.

Pam was twenty-six years old when she was admitted to the Winnipeg Hospital. She looked thin and distraught. She knew her way around psychiatric wards. In the previous six years, she had been treated thirteen times as an in-patient. Pam had usually been diagnosed as a borderline personality but her symptoms were complicated by the fact that she had a serious cocaine problem. No psychiatrist had ever suggested that she might suffer from multiple personality disorder.

When Colin Ross first saw her, Pam was sitting in a corner of the ward of the General Unit of Winnipeg Hospital. She was screaming, 'No, no, don't hit me.' To Ross, her voice sounded like that of a desperate child. He went over to sit by her and suddenly he found that she was talking to him as if he was her father. She seemed to have switched almost instantly. She had no memory and no awareness that a few seconds before she had been behaving like a frightened child.

Ross said that given his own beliefs, he was inclined to think that she suffered from multiple personality disorder. He had Pam admitted to the Dissociative Disorders Unit in the hospital and started to investigate her background.

There was nothing startling about her psychiatric history. Ross found out that before each of her previous admissions as a borderline personality, Pam had become very manic. She wouldn't sleep; she found herself much more interested in sex than she usually was. She would buzz with energy and self-confidence. Her sense of judgement would get a little divorced from reality, a common feature of mania.

After each of these manic bouts, Pam would collapse into a deep depression. Only as she was never depressed for as long as two weeks, the depression was never diagnosed. DSM III argues that episodes of depression need to last at least two weeks to qualify.

Ross discovered that Pam had about four such swings between depression and mania a year. But *who* exactly was having these swings? Ross became convinced the host personality was suffering from both borderline personality and manic-depressive psychosis. But her case was even more complicated.

As he had also seen Pam behave as a child, Ross told the nurses to look for changes in her behaviour that resembled the switch from child to adult that he had witnessed.

Ross explained to me that he soon discovered it wasn't Pam 'as a whole' who had these manic-depressive swings but only her host personality. Her behaviour on his unit was disturbing, but it fell into a clear pattern. There was a host personality and *three* alters.

Pam, the host personality, was a psychiatric patient, reserved, a bit confused.

The first alter was the frightened child Ross had first seen. The child alter mainly cried and screamed. Sometimes, it seemed scared of being abused.

The second alter was less personal. He was a Friend, a helper personality, but a rather ineffectual one. The Friend had good intentions but doesn't seem to have been strong enough to win control of the body for long periods. Ross recruited the Friend as a therapeutic ally but, as the Friend couldn't get control of the body very often, his good intentions achieved very little.

What made Pam special at first was the intensity of her third alter. Ross said that this angry alter was one of the most unpleasant entities he had ever encountered. This was a growling, spitting alter who insulted and sometimes physically attacked nurses and other staff on the unit. This self was also self-destructive. The alter often started violent bouts of head-banging.

The switches between the different alters were dramatic. Pam would change from the child into the self-abusive angry alter with almost no warning. It was very vivid. At the moment the abusive self took over, Pam would clutch her head, bend over and fall to the floor.

Sometimes Pam had some warning of what was going to happen. She would get a terrible headache, giving her enough time to stagger to the quiet room in the ward. As soon as she got there, she would fall over and start head-banging. This was so violent Ross had to send her to have X-rays. Sometimes, she had to wear a neck-brace.

The sheer intensity of the anger amazed Ross. The alter would yell, 'Die' over and over again. It would bite staff. This alter could never be engaged in conversation. The only good thing was that the fury did not usually last long. Often after less than two minutes of head-banging the alter would disappear inside.

After the angry alter had gone back inside, Pam would often swoon. As she recovered, a slightly dazed host personality would return to consciousness. But the host didn't know what was going on.

Ross offers an interesting anatomy of alters. He believes they are organized in systems. Angry alters are themselves often controlled by stronger alters that lie deeper in the system. Faced by an alter like Pam's, the psychiatrist needs to ask where real power in the system lies. Ross has sometimes found alters claim that the whole personality is controlled by Satan. Ross told me, 'You'll be told that Satan is very powerful, very important, he's not going to talk to you.' After all, Ross is a mere shrink, hardly on equal terms with an infernal power. He added, 'So I've had cases where I then ask where Satan is. And the alter will say that Satan is in a three-foot-thick steel safe protected by a river of molten lava. And I will say if Satan were so powerful, would he need to protect himself with all that? Real devils are strong in themselves. They don't need to hide.' But Ross added that he had one advantage. 'I know, after all, that Satan is just a child.'

So Ross was looking for ways to handle Pam's angry alter. The speed and violence of the changes as the angry alter appeared and disappeared were exhausting the staff on the unit.

Ross told me his aim was to have as quiet a unit as possible. He saw no reason why nurses should be assaulted by alters.

Coming into the unit may have accelerated the changes, for Pam would get the headaches and the abusive alter would appear two to four times a day. Ross did not manage to find out what triggered these appearances. With his staff increasingly under stress, Ross felt it was vital to get the angry alter under some form of control so that they could try to treat Pam. Ross tried to hypnotize the angry alter but without much success.

Their first breakthrough came when they realized that on those occasions when the angry alter came out twice in quick succession, it ran out of energy fast. These double performances were followed by wonderful periods of quiet which could last up to twenty-four hours.

Ross and his colleagues wondered if they could trick the angry alter to exhaust it, deliberately provoking the angry alter into appearing just after it had gone back inside. He decided to be honest with Pam's host personality and Pam agreed.

To force the angry alter out, the team had to be slightly abusive. The host personality, Pam, would allow herself to be physically restrained by staff. As she was held down the angry alter would often appear. So after one appearance of the angry alter, the staff got into the habit of holding down and restraining Pam. The trick worked. Usually, the restraint would provoke a new appearance.

Pam had been restrained a number of times during her psychiatric career. Whatever one may think of the tactic, Ross did get the host personality to agree to the restraint and he freely admits he could think of no better way of getting a quiet period.

The trick worked but it didn't lead quickly to what Ross had hoped would happen – some clue as to the origins of the trauma.

On the face of it this seemed to be a three-alter personality system. Ross had no idea though what the original cause of the trauma might be. He gave Pam a variety of EEG and other tests, including a neurological consultation which suggested that she did disassociate.

Ross and his team then decided to use sodium amytal to see if they could force out some of the other alters they were convinced were in there. Ross attacks the media version of sodium amytal as a truth drug. Rather, he claims, it helps liberate all kinds of memories. With Pam, who was blocked, using sodium amytal didn't produce new memories but contact with another alter. After she came round from the injection, there was a pause and then someone said, 'Hi.'

It was Midge. Midge was the first of Pam's alters who didn't emerge spontaneously. She was a talkative, excited young teenager. She knew all about the other four personalities. She had no idea, however, about how to cope with the angry alter.

Once Midge emerged she became very powerful. She established herself as a partner in Pam's life in the hospital, frequently taking control of the body. Midge was interested in events on the ward. She decided to redecorate Pam's room to make it livelier, so she hung it with drawings and posters. There was a slight priggish streak to Midge. She objected to Pam's smoking, for instance.

Contacting Midge under the influence of sodium amytal opened a real Pandora's box. Ross told me he was astonished when with every single session more and more alters started to appear. He had a feeling he hadn't had for a long while. When would it all end?

This incredible profusion of alters or fragments made Ross fear there just couldn't be any progress. His notes told him that Pam was exhibiting hundreds of alters or personality states.

In what was clearly an attempt to get back some sort of control, Ross asked Pam to produce a chart of all of these personality states. If she was to have any therapy, her personality system had to be mapped. And she was the only person who could do it.

Ross then asked Pam to group the different personalities into teams. I put it to him that this sounded quite fantastic. But Ross told me it was the only way of beginning to see how one might cope with the trauma. The members of each team shared a common theme or personality characteristic. There were two predictable teams or themes – one made up of frightened children who were terrified of being abused, and a second one of rebellious teenagers.

But Pam had more esoteric secrets to offer. One group consisted of personalities that were paranormal or mythological in nature. Another group consisted of intrusions from her past life or lives. These included entities who could fly above the hospital by astral projection. These paranormal alters were very keen to discuss large issues of the meaning of life, death, the universe. Ross says he was unfortunately seduced into spending hours talking metaphysics. He knew he shouldn't, but the paranormal selves wouldn't take no for an answer.

In this seeming chaos, there were two central figures called Sarah and Rebecca. Pam did not accept these as alters but claimed they were spirit-helpers and had a transcendental nature. They lived inside Pam, talked to her, guided her silently and partially controlled her personality system.

Pam also had a team of transsexual personalities.

Sarah and Rebecca were, Ross found, very helpful. They agreed that each team should have an internally appointed team-leader who would be the spokesperson for that team or theme. Only the team-leader would take executive control and all the work by the team would be funnelled into therapy through the leader. The system, Ross said, was necessary in order to cope with what was a chaotic situation.

This form of therapy seemed to be making some progress when there was a crisis. Pam said that her mother had been reported missing. She then added she was scared her mother had committed suicide. The police were called but they discovered nothing definite. Then Pam told the therapists that her mother had been found hanging in a barn belonging to some friends. She had been deeply depressed and had committed suicide.

Ross and his team prepared themselves for a slog of grief work, expecting Pam to fall apart. Rather to their surprise, she did not. Within a month Pam was able to talk about her mother's death. She was showing grief and anger.

There was soon another difficulty, however. Within this month the therapists heard from Pam that her father was living with another woman. This woman seemed to be grossly insensitive. On Pam's birthday, her father's fiancée, as apparently she now claimed to be, sent her a card which she signed 'Mom'. Pam told them she didn't know how her father had allowed her to do that. The treatment team were sympathetic. It did seem gross.

Focusing on her mother's death meant, of course, that no progress was being made in searching out the original trauma. Then during one session a new male alter appeared – Bob. Bob had only rather vague ideas about how to help, but he had one shattering revelation to make – shattering to the psychiatrists. Pam's mother was not dead.

Bob explained that Pam was having a great deal of difficulty dealing with the endless rows between her parents. If Pam believed her mother was dead, Pam wouldn't suffer from these conflicts. That was why Bob had planted the belief her mother was dead. He agreed that the strategy didn't seem to be working.

It was only at this point, it seems, that Ross and his team made any effort to corroborate what Pam had told them. Until then they had just been listening to the patient. There had been no checks with the police or any outside agencies partly because they felt that would undermine trust between Pam and the team. All the professionals involved were amazed to learn they had been duped. Pam had been so convincing. Her descriptions of going to visit her father and his fiancée had been so consistent. She couldn't have made it all up.

But it had all been lies. The team expected some major reaction when they confronted Pam with what Bob was saying, with what was clearly the truth.

When Pam was told what Bob said, she didn't treat it as a major revelation. She just shrugged her shoulders and acted as if it was all some kind of inner prank.

By now Ross and his team were a little confused. They were no closer to the heart of the trauma, when there was yet another drama. Pam appeared for therapy with shaven eyebrows and bad news. She had been diagnosed as having cancer. This time, Ross carried out a series of external checks. The local oncology clinic had never heard of Pam.

Frustrated by the patient's refusal to let them get anywhere near her reality, Ross began to wonder if the manic-depressive illness that Pam had presented might also be a myth. He concluded that it was. In other words, here was a patient who was making up memories, incidents and symptoms in a magnificently chaotic way. But why?

Ross sadly admits that he never managed to get an answer. The atmosphere clearly deteriorated. After the cancer scare, an angry alter started to make death-threats against Ross. He really didn't feel he wanted to put up with that. After not much soul-searching, he abandoned therapy.

Ross tells me that despite all these traumas and apparent failures, the latest information he has is that Pam is surviving. She has not returned to psychiatric treatment but it is obviously the case that she was not ready to be treated. The trauma was not ready to be faced.

Ross says that he learned much from the case and it helped him see that one could not trust as literal truth the very consistent and believable 'facts' and memories that patients brought into therapy. In *The Osiris Complex* (1994), Ross claims that working with patients like Pam also made it clear that one has to look at allegations of Satanic abuse with a sceptical frame of mind.

To those critical of the multiple personality diagnosis that looks very much like a fast move to avoid embarrassment. As the evidence for Satanic abuse has come under more and more question, no one sensible wants to be too closely associated with claims it exists.

I'm not sure the critics are being fair, and one of the things that must be said in favour of Ross and a number of other pioneers is that they seem very willing to discuss cases which they must know will look like failures to the outside world.

Pam wasn't, after all, cured in Winnipeg. She was too much for them. It takes some courage to report that.

It is not easy, of course, for psychiatrists to admit that they have been fooled. The sceptics point to cases like Pam as an instance of less than thorough work. Why didn't they check her claims about her mother's death when she first made them? Therapists reply that constant checking requires more time than they have and that it would undermine the therapeutic relationship if they were forever doing detective work on what their patients told them. In many of the well documented cases like Jonah, Naomi and, of course, Eve and Sybil, there was a great deal of checking.

CHAPTER 10

Changing Room

Most multiples are not conscious of having alters so you can't ask them the key question. What does it feel like to change from being one personality to another? Those of us who don't disassociate have to rely on comparisons. What does it feel like to have new clothes, a new hairdo, the world's most total makeover?

The language in which the pioneers today express the idea of changing from one alter to the next suggests it's very sudden. Where Thigpen and Cleckley talked of Eve's slow transformation, with ripples, almost as if they were describing an extremely slow mix in the cinema, alters now 'switch' from one to another. They take 'executive control'. They 'come into the body'. Some psychiatrists now say that they don't need to rely on hypnosis to get alters to emerge. Often, all they have to do is to address the patient and say something like, 'I want to talk to Frank, or Jude,' or whatever.

Then, on cue, that alter will be there 'in the body', ready to talk.

For most people, the only chance to see any changes like those I have described in the various case histories is when you see a hypnotist in action.

SVENGALI IN CAMDEN

The Prince Albert, the rough end of Camden Town. Saturday night. The coming of a hypnotist hasn't set the place alight. After eight, some sixty people drift in, pay their four pounds admission, drink as normal.

The audience is ambivalent. The men scoff. The girls – most of them in miniskirts – are more curious. They might just be persuaded it's going to be interesting but they're not going to show it. No one wants to let on they're so naive as to believe in the Svengali spiel.

Martin, the hypnotist, is thin, blond, a little nervous. He's wearing a suit which makes him the most formally dressed person in the pub. The Disco Man doesn't want to leave the stage. He thinks Svengali is uncool dressed in a suit and tie.

'I'm just going to wander round to get them on my side,' Svengali says, and starts to walk around the tables to do a bit of close-up magic. But even the girls aren't that interested. They start to giggle.

'I don't want someone looking into my mind.'

'They might ask me to take my knickers off.'

'I've seen it all on the telly.'

'I'm not going to look daft.'

'Go on. Give it a go.'

He's asking for volunteers now. Five people up on the stage so he can get going. Foolishly, he introduces his act by saying he isn't about to put them in a trance or to sleep. No occult magic. No secret words. They'll do what he asks them to do because of 'social pressures'. 'Social pressures' makes them laugh.

'It doesn't hurt,' Svengali says.

Two bullet-heads come in, promising to behave. They don't, and start making fun of him at once. But the landlord's too lazy to do anything about it.

The show starts badly. The pub crowd don't want to know Martin's theory of hypnotism. They want maximum weirdness, to be amazed by the strangeness of what he can make people do.

First trick. Svengali's finally coaxed three girls and two lads to sit in chairs facing the audience.

'Clasp your hands.' They go along with it but laugh.

'After I've said "Xanadu", you're going to find that you can't

CHANGING ROOM

unclasp them. Try as hard as you can, you can't. They're locked together. Xanadu. You can't unclasp your hands.'

For a moment, he's got the audience's attention.

The trick's crap. Total disaster. Four of the five unclasp their hands at once. The pub laughs. Are we about to witness an ultimate prat? One girl has a struggle but you can see she's putting it on because she feels sorry for Svengali. Then, slowly, she pulls each hand free of the other.

The next trick doesn't work either. The bullet-heads guffaw he can't do it. They want their four quid back. The crowd laugh. Svengali rounds on them to be quiet if they want to learn something. It's a mistake. This is not a lecture in a college. He has trouble getting new volunteers on stage.

Finally, he gets five to agree, but three are taking the piss. They make silly faces. He gets rid of them, coaxes three others up on the stage. He's working the girls because he thinks they're more likely to be suggestible.

'Look, folks, if you don't keep quiet, you don't give it a chance.'

It's Saturday night, not keep-quiet-to-be-impressed night.

I'm beginning to panic a little for him. What if no one is hypnotized, no one ever does a weird and silly thing and we're here sixty minutes later still waiting for the black-magic arts.

I give him credit for trying. Another go at the clasp your hands and you'll never unclasp them. Finally, he gets his first ray of light.

One lad does seem to have his hands stuck, fixed rigid. Is he larking about? Mark is squat and he's got a squashed face. Mark doesn't look too bright, which may be why he isn't taking the piss up there. It's a new experience for him to be the centre of attention. He seems to be enjoying himself.

Svengali makes sure Mark gets a big round of applause for having his hands stuck together.

In the next thirty minutes, Mark becomes a star – or some part of him does. For example, Mark finds that he can't remember his name even when he's told his name as part of a sentence.

'Mark, tell us what your name is?'

Mark can't. He stammers, looks blank. The pub falls apart. They're beginning to be intrigued.

165

The basic trick is always the same. The hypnotist tells Mark that when he hears a particular word – 'Xanadu', 'Arsenal', 'Ping' – he will break off whatever he is doing and respond automatically like a robot. So in the next half hour, Mark stops whatever he is doing and goes automatic. On automatic, Mark puts on one tie after another so that he's got five ties knotted round his neck. On automatic, Mark dances sequences out of 'Singing in the Rain'. He plays an imaginary violin. He says 'Ping' every time he hears someone else say 'Pong'. He's robotic.

Mark even starts to strip. He's been told only to take off his shirt but he has to be stopped from taking his pants off too.

This is the only time I wonder whether Mark's pretending. Is he having too much fun? Later on, Mark swears he wasn't pretending. He had no idea why he was doing the things he was doing. He had never met the hypnotist before. I believe him.

When Mark stops to a word of command, his reactions are interesting. These are moments of change. Mark is in the middle of dancing the sequence out of 'Singing in the Rain'. Swinging an umbrella in the middle of a Camden Town pub. Playing at being Gene Kelly. Then, the word of command. Mark snaps out of it. Snap is too quick. Mark slowly stops his performance. He looks around. He's still shaking a bit to the music. Then, he looks at his hand. Why is he waving an umbrella?

For a comic, it would be a perfect double take. What am I doing here? How did I get in this mess? But Mark isn't a comic. He doesn't look puzzled at the umbrella. Yet he's enjoying this. He enjoys it even though each time he wakes up, he has no idea why he's doing what he's doing. And that's when you get these light, rather charming, moments of transformation.

It's the moment of change that arrests the audience. He turns into something different. He's an idiot becoming a person again, becoming himself again.

The bullet-heads jeer he should strip again. Mark's in the spirit now and willing, but the hypnotist stops him.

I wanted to describe this scene at length because of the many links between hypnosis and multiple personality. Moments of transformation aren't always like this in hypnosis. People can be very emotional when they wake. But I think it's important to retain that image of lightness, of playfulness, to balance what we think happens when patients 'switch'. The image of Jekyll and Hyde remains. In Stevenson's book Jekyll had to swallow chemicals and foul-smelling potions for the change to occur. He went into grotesque seizures that mimicked the reactions of the grand hysterics Charcot and Janet studied.

But why has it become easier for patients to switch? It may be that multiple personality syndrome and the way it is acted out is being influenced by some contemporary models in psychology – especially by the notion that different networks in the brain operate independently of each other. A leading advocate of that view is Robert Ornstein.

MEGASTAR OF THE MULTIMINDS

In 1976, Robert Ornstein published *The Psychology of Consciousness*. He has not stopped being interested in consciousness since. Since then he has argued that the brain is not a unity but a number of competing entities or competences. He calls these multiminds and finds they battle constantly for what he calls 'executive control' – the ability to take decisions and initiate actions. Can such different entities or competences be compared to alters? Some multiple personality researchers think so and have started to talk of switches of executive control as patients switch from one alter to another.

Going to meet Ornstein, I was aware of my selves. When I was twenty, before we were married, Aileen called me MogulBelly, as I had a belly and often fantasised about fabulous deals I would make. It was definitely MogulBelly who on discovering that there was no public transport from San Francisco Airport to Palo Alto bought a solo ride in a white Lincoln convertible, having agreed to pay the extortionate price of \$110 for a thirty-minute journey behind black-tinted windows. And it was my HaggleSelf who complained that, at $110, there were no drinks in the gold drinks cabinet and that the TV wasn't working.

MogulBelly arrived and had to give way to Serious Journalist as I went into Ornstein's office.

Ornstein is large, friendly and very sure of his opinions. He has worked his theory out from the inside. Experimental data on how people do things and some sophisticated experiments on which areas of the brain control what activities led him to see the brain as a multimind. It wasn't patients, trauma, inner selves, sinner selves or alters but the daily grind of the cortex.

'People don't seem to get just a personality,' Ornstein told me, 'they seem to get lots of different components of everything, so the best way to put it together is to think about it as multiminds. Or later in the evolution of consciousness to talk about simpletons and various special purpose proto-humanoids or humanettes that just go out and do things you need done – get you through traffic, for instance.'

The key word is 'components'. I suggested to Ornstein that all such theories leave us bewildered as to where the true self is. Most of us, even many people with multiple personality disorder, have a sense of having a core identity.

This true self, for Ornstein, is 'a useful placebo for people. I think it's one of the things that all of us including myself want to live by'. But Ornstein thinks we should grow up and dump our illusions. He added, 'I think it's a great idea. I just don't think it makes any sense in truth.'

Ornstein may be radical about the self and core identity but his model doesn't require anything radical when executive control switches from sub-brain A, controller of decisions about shopping, to sub-brain B, verbal wizard and quick solver of crosswords. Nothing melodramatic takes place at the instant of switching. The eyes don't roll; there are no seizure-like contortions, no touch of the Jekyll and Hydes. The process is ordinary because, of course, such 'switching' in Ornstein's theory takes place all the time. One multimind blends into another. The process Ornstein describes is very different from the one that the pioneers like Frank Putnam saw.

In the early 1980s when Putnam first tried to categorize what happened when there was a switch, Eve was very much a role model. He saw that often the eyes first rolled upwards. There were then a series of grimaces which looked like polyfragmented Pam's seizures. Clever patients would sometimes turn away or hide their face in a newspaper to mask the change. (Putnam 1989)

When child personalities appeared, there were often visible changes of posture. Children might come on with heads bowed and their toes pointed inwards. Angry alters were usually contorted in fury with violent grimaces. Putnam says that the impact of these changes is dramatic. The voice is different; the way of standing or sitting is different. And sometimes there's a curious kind of commonsense in the midst of this seeming madness. If a woman has a male alter, for instance, that alter often will not appear unless she is dressed in trousers. Clearly patients don't want to seem too silly. They need the observer to believe. Many women also sport severe haircuts which allow them to be male and also make it easy for them to put on a wig in case one of their alters is a flamboyant floozy.

These kinds of change are really dramatic, suggesting that it is traumatic to make the switch from one personality to the next. In some cases, like Pam's, it's still true, but listening to many of the presentations in Amsterdam I sensed two things. First, often people zap from one alter to the next without too much difficulty. Second, many papers by Colin Ross, Onno van der Hart and others, seemed to be finessing the subject of hypnosis.

Ross told me, for example, that he thought it was possible to talk to alters without all the hypnotic drama. 'I often just say to someone, "I'd now like to talk to this alter, to this personality." ' And, without any fuss, they are in contact as if the alters are there, just below the surface, so easy to touch and reach.

Van der Hart also warned about not relying too much on transformations that happened while patients were hypnotised. Putnam told me there had been a radical shift. Hypnosis was often contraindicated.

Sceptics say that this move to achieve a certain distance from hypnosis is a ploy to win scientific respectability. Others, like Carol North (1993) suggest that everyone who is interested in the field in the States is concerned by the fact that new multiples often seem to model their performances on what they have seen on television. Trudi Chase, a woman who claims to have ninety-two personalities, started to reveal them after seeing the real Eve on a television show. Alters are making their act slicker because they're basing it on other acts.

The way people express psychiatric symptoms is always influenced by the culture around them and the expectations of psychiatrists. In one way it stands to reason that patients need to switch faster and more glibly. You can hardly zap – and 'zap' as in zapping the TV remote is the word – through three hundred selves if it takes hours of agony as you dissolve from one self to the next. There is much less of a long struggle to excavate the alters out of deep trauma.

For the pioneers, this shows that they have become more expert at dealing with the condition. For the sceptics, this shows that patients have learned to produce quickly and efficiently the symptoms their shrinks want to see.

The battle rolls on.

CHAPTER 11

Maps of the Personality

Imagine *The Book of Imaginary Selves*.

It lists human beings who exist fleetingly, occasionally taking control of the body – the high point of their existence.

Some of these Imaginary Selves have names and are individual. But few are that whole. Some flicker and cascade for only a few minutes. Do they then die or go back into soul hibernation? What words can we use, given how we normally use the word 'self', to make sense of that idea?

Other Imaginary Selves are types, like stock characters in melodrama – the young lover, the old nurse, the frightened child.

The Book of Imaginary Selves is not truthful, however. It is just a list of those selves that have agreed to be named. The more powerful ones, who control the whole system, never allow themselves to be seen. They are concealed controllers.

It's not enough to have one map of the personality system, a map which describes all the different selves. You need a second map which pinpoints where the real power is. It's only when you heal the trauma of the most dogged, most hurt, most powerful alters that you will heal the patient.

The pioneers have tried to make their subject more scientific by categorizing common types of alters. These alters express typical feelings and reactions that occur in childhood trauma, so one would expect to find them in a number of different patients.

Critics have a very different view. They say it's not surprising that the alters should be so similar. If therapists believe that their patients have been abused and are traumatized then obliging patients will present on parade alters who fit the shrinks' theories. (Tom Fahy suggests doctors 'mould' the diagnosis.)

They can hardly let their poor doctors down.

Top of the list is the:

HOST PERSONALITY

The most multiple multiple has to present a routine face to the world. That is the host personality. The host tends to be rigid, repressed, conscience-stricken. Usually, host personalities are innocent and don't know a battle of identities is being waged within them. When therapists tell a host personality the truth, the host is almost always surprised as well as upset.

CHILD PERSONALITIES

A typical alter is the frightened child. You can feel that fear. The child personality is often the victim of abuse. He or she is withdrawn and sometimes displays extreme withdrawal. Child personalities curl up in foetal positions, suck their thumbs. Many are completely silent. Often, they start to hurt themselves. They head-bang. They hurl themselves against walls. They act out typical reactions to abuse.

There are a few reports of sweet, untroubled child personalities but there are virtually no reports of playful child personalities.

PERSECUTOR PERSONALITIES

Psychoanalytic theory suggests that victims often take on some of the characteristics of those who persecute them. Anna Freud called this 'identification with the aggressor'. If a child is the victim of abuse, then alters often appear who are what analysts would call introjects of the abuser. These alters are the image of the abuser as the child sees it. The child then injects this image into itself, i.e. it introjects. Inside the child's mind, this split-off self can be even more vicious than the 'real' abuser. Some abusers do offer children a strange tenderness. They charm them, wheedle them, even love them in order to be able to abuse them. But any love or tenderness the abuser may offer is usually split off into another alter. The persecutor, as multiple personality practitioners see it, is only evil, angry, aggressive, completely black.

Persecutors can cause hallucinations. They may bully, and even chase patients across internal landscapes. One patient had a persecutor who was her father. As a child she often saved herself by climbing up a tree in their garden. He couldn't follow her. In her adult dreams, she was still fleeing from him.

Often the persecutor tries to hinder any treatment out of fear that the true story of their abuse will come out.

Some therapists think persecutor personalities can be persuaded to help in therapy. If they understand that they are really frightened children who have been abused they will want to get well. But many therapists are not that optimistic.

DEMON PERSONALITIES

Thomas Szasz, the famous critic of psychiatry, has argued that many witches who were said to be possessed were probably suffering from what would now be labelled mental illness. Szasz claims that we label deviants as mentally ill. In the nineteenth century, some patients who suffered from multiple personality symptoms claimed to have been possessed by demons. Ross argues that this is not fanciful. He says he has had a few encounters with such demon personalities but, sadly, the quality of demons has declined. Ross did not find he was talking to grotesque gargoyles of great power but to alters that were children who were furious and talking very tough.

SUICIDAL PERSONALITIES

Therapists constantly worry that patients with multiple personality will try to kill themselves. Putnam found that 71 per cent of his sample had made suicide attempts; Ross found that 72 per cent had made such attempts. Ross claims that the more severe the abuse as a child – especially if there was rape – the more likely it is that there will be a suicidal alter.

PROTECTOR AND HELPER PERSONALITIES

Few patients are totally self-destructive. There is some part of them that wants to live, and wants to live healthy lives. Many therapists claim that this tendency, the health instinct, comes through protector and helper personalities. The label speaks for itself. Female patients often turn out to have male helpers. These splits usually sound clear and balanced but they often turn out to be less helpful than one might expect. Often, with the best of intentions, they don't actually manage to get control of the body very often.

Sometimes a protector plays one very limited role, like a child personality who essentially runs away and hides from an abusive father.

In a way, it's not surprising that helper personalities are quite ineffective. If that part of the personality were strong, would someone be fragmenting in order to deal with their pain?

CROSS DRESSING PERSONALITIES

Sex and multiple personality is a fascinating topic. Some alters seem to exist to let fairly uptight patients act out sexual fantasies. Male multiples (who are much rarer than females) sometimes develop, as James Carlson did, a lesbian alter. Female multiples have rather duller male alters who often have a clodhopping quality. They tend to be handymen, carpenters, mechanics.

One interesting pattern that some therapists see in male multiple personalities is the appearance of female or older or good mother figures. Some would see these as clear examples of Jung's mother archetypes. Others see them as expressing a need for a safe kind of love that was never received.

PROMISCUOUS PERSONALITIES

Eve Black was a party girl but she never went too far. The only time she ever slept with someone was with her 'husband' Ralph when they went to Florida. With the explosion of multiple personality cases many women multiples have developed a promiscuous alter. I mentioned in Chapter 8 the simple pattern that emerges here. The 'tart' personality cruises in a bar, picks up a strange man and sets up a date. Often the date has clear masochistic overtones. It's a date for bondage, say. Then, just as the action is about to begin, the alters switch. A rather confused host personality finds herself in a compromising situation. The 'tart' has vanished.

The man wants sex: the woman wants to escape. The result is chaos, misery, and a host personality who often thinks of herself as frigid. Some feminist therapists object to descriptions on these lines but they don't usually dispute the basic behaviour. It is telling, though, that often promiscuous personalities pull back just before there is any sex.

OBSESSIVE COMPULSIVE PERSONALITIES

These tend to have a variety of fetish-like behaviours. There is a disorder known as obsessive compulsive neurosis which Freud described in detail.

SUBSTANCE ABUSERS

Many therapists report alters who have drug or drink problems that the host personality claims to know nothing about.

AUTISTIC PERSONALITIES

These are mute child-like personalities who usually say very little but cry and withdraw. Occasionally they head-bang.

PERSONALITIES WITH SPECIAL TALENTS AND SKILLS

Sybil is the classic case as many of her alters showed great artistic talent.

ANAESTHETIC PERSONALITIES

These are personalities that don't feel pain. They are the splits who often suffered the initial abuse and who went into denial. Usoffa, who couldn't feel any pain, and Naomi when she was burned, are good examples of this sort.

INTERNAL SELF-HELPERS

These are alters who want to be healthy and try to make sure the patient gets the best available help. Some believe this is the 'true' voice of the patient.

The list doesn't exhaust the types of alters but they are the most common ones. Describing the system in this way is only a small advance as these descriptions tell psychiatrists very little about who actually controls the system. Ross argues that fights between different alters often occur. If, for example, you persuade an angry alter that it makes no sense for it to beat up a helper personality by exposing it to danger, you may find that the angry alter is itself attacked by a more powerful controlling entity deeper in the system. These are issues I will return to in dealing with treatment.

Throughout the book I've tried to suggest that those who have dissociative disorders or multiple personality aren't freaks. I have also tried to show how ordinary people often play different roles which can make you feel you're hosting a number of selves. That means you sometimes blink and wonder why you're doing or saying what you're saying. Is that really you?

You're not nuts, but who was that speaking?

Welcome to the sublime, subconscious, subterranean world of your subpersonalities.

CHAPTER 12

Subpersonalities

'In every fat man, there is a thin man struggling to be let out.'

I was always rather ambivalent about being called MogulBelly by Aileen when we were in our early twenties. She always said it was affectionate. I couldn't deny that I really was a bit podgy – at school one unkind master had called me Heffalump, but as I was an immigrant who'd never read *Winnie the Pooh* I had no idea who or what a Heffalump was except that it obviously wasn't sleek. So much for the Belly. The Mogul, as I have said, was because I was really in love with wheeling and dealing as I tried to carve out a career in film and television. Neither of us realized it at the time, but MogulBelly was just the kind of name that some therapists would encourage their clients to give to one of their subpersonalities.

Note that we're talking here about clients – not patients. The whole field of subpersonality has nothing to do with psychiatry. It's a product of alternative and humanistic therapies, though one reason why there are few multiple personality cases in the United Kingdom compared to the United States is that British psychiatrists working in the Health Service can't possibly afford to have such demanding patients. There are no reliable studies of how long National Health psychiatrists see their patients on average but very few get the hours of therapy that some American patients get courtesy of their medical insurance.

A chapter on subpersonalities finally allows us to focus on the reader who wants his or her self explored in the hope of finding more depth and more complexity.

If you wonder whether there's more to you than meets the eye or the usual personality tests, this really is the chapter for you.

It is not only psychiatric patients, however, who have different sides to them.

In his *The Ego and the Id* (1923), Freud outlined the first of many theories to posit dramatically different aspects of personality in normal people. Freud's ego, id and super-ego have a certain cartoon stereotype to them. The late Don Bannister, a well known psychologist, personalized them nicely. The ego was, he said, a referee trying to keep the peace between the impulses of a sex-crazed monkey (the id) and a prim but tigerish Victorian granny (the super-ego).

It's not hard to make sense of cartoons like Popeye with that frame of reference. Popeye is sane and knows he needs spinach to turn himself into a superhero. He, the ego, is always battling with the Fat Sailor, a nice representation of the id, for the unlikely favours of the prim Olive Oil who has many of the attributes of the super-ego.

Jung had different divisions of the mind. He argued we all had an animus, which he defined as the masculine principle, and an anima, which he defined as the feminine principle. Jung also believed we could all contact archetypes. He argued (1954) these were pre-existing forms of experience and were made up out of the basic human experiences common experiences through the ages which somehow – he never explained how really – took on the shape of a personality, rather like Aladdin's genie. Some were protective, like the Father; some expressed creativity, like the Magician; others were evil. The Shadow, for example, was the individual's potential for evil, which could become actual. After it became necessary to distance himself from Nazism, Jung argued that it grew out of the rise of the Shadow.

Many of Jung's archetypes have found an odd life in American cartoon comics. The Shadow, for instance, became an American cartoon figure in the 1930s in which a Batman-like hero was at the mercy of his own shadow, who would sometimes take him over and perform acts of incredible evil. In the comic, the Shadow often breaks through in exactly the circumstances of high stress which can act as triggers of switching between personalities.

Jung was probably never aware of his influence on American popular culture, but it's evident enough.

Take a third theory – Transactional Analysis. Eric Berne argued that in each of us there warred a Parent, an Adult and a Child. These characters were a little like Freud's super-ego, ego and id turned into something homely that suburban America could identify with.

These theories all offered splits among normal minds and personalities. All implied that for someone to be whole and healthy, to be able to work and to love, tensions between these elements had to be kept in balance – and that might be achieved by adjusting one's inner controls.

If you, Mr Artist, could get freer access to your anima, maybe you'd paint a masterpiece. If you, Mr Uptight Manager, could strengthen your ego, maybe you would panic less and so make those you manage a little less anxious.

A forgotten paper from 1924 by Morton Prince offers an excellent anatomy of a normal person's different personalities. In 'The Four Sides of Jack', Prince described a twenty-two-year-old student who was clever, conventional and not suffering from any psychiatric disorder. Prince recruited him as a subject for some experiments in hypnosis. Jack was not that suggestible. He refused to do anything bizarre under hypnosis.

But when he hypnotized his subject, Prince discovered there were unsuspected sides to the young man. There was a 'gay' (in the 1920s sense) fellow who cracked jokes and saw himself as a jester with an eye for the girls. Prince described that side of Jack as a Lothario. This personality would toss his clothes around the room and make indecent suggestions. Such behaviour was not at all like Jack.

Jack had a third, unpleasantly violent side. Prince named this Jack the Ripper. This side of Jack wanted to inflict pain. Ripper-Jack often asked Prince if he could stab him. He wanted to see what it was like to draw blood from another human being. Once Prince caught Jack taking a penknife out of his pocket and was sure his subject was about to commit the ultimate crime of attacking the experimenter. There was a fourth character in Jack – a depressed, lethargic personality.

Jack described the experience of being these characters as very odd. He felt he was looking at them through a magic lantern. He seems to have had a sense of alienation, and yet all these personalities were within him. Prince was not treating him so there was little risk of suggestion. If Jack was tired, drunk or stressed, Prince found, these sides were more likely to appear.

Prince did not elevate these four personalities into four separate selves. He did not dismiss them as different moods Jack might be in. He concluded that though Jack was normal and did not suffer from amnesia, they were different sides of his personality, so different from each other as to have some similarity to the alters of true multiple personality cases.

After its publication in 1924, little notice was taken of this paper. But Prince seems to have stumbled upon something that is now becoming very chic – unearthing your subpersonalities. In this context I want to look at the work of one British therapist, John Rowan. His work illustrates an important point. Rowan builds on both Freud's and Jung's notions of different tendencies in the mind.

SUBPERSONALITIES

Rowan does not quote 'The Four Sides of Jack', but many of his ideas develop Prince's notions although Rowan doesn't speak of 'sides' of the personality. Rather, Rowan speaks of *subpersonalities* and he celebrates these even quirkier entities, these different aspects of the personality. I think it's easy to forget what a remarkable shift this is.

Most therapy till the 1980s hoped to get people to conform so that they could manage to lead 'normal' lives, hold down a job and a marriage. That was why you could get it on the National Health. Even radical psychiatrists like R. D. Laing were not that different. In *The Divided Self* (1961) Laing offered a startling view of schizophrenia but he still saw the therapist's job as healing this divided self by making it whole.

Today, a growing number of therapists celebrate the divided self. Creating a whole seems to matter less than helping the various voices in the personality to express themselves.

Before examining Rowan's work, I should add in fairness that Rowan and I have not always seen eye to eye. When I edited *Psychology News*, he sent us an extremely rude letter saying that the magazine wasn't worth reading apart from one contributor, Aileen La Tourette, and so, he explained, he wouldn't renew his subscription. I published the letter. But there is undoubtedly somewhere in me a get-own-back-on-Rowan side to my personality which I shall do my best to keep in check.

Rowan was one of the founders of the Association of Humanistic Psychology. He has been considerably influenced by Jung. In 1974, after a number of Gestalt therapy meetings, Rowan began to be interested in his own subpersonalities. He came to realize that he was talking essentially about aspects – often contradictory aspects – of his own personality. He then took an LSD trip, saying, 'I regarded myself as something of an astronaut of inner space,' with the explicit intention of getting into each of these subpersonalities. He had – and I like the precise touch – eleven questions to ask each of them. Rowan came to believe he had touched on something important in terms of self-understanding. His subpersonalities mattered to him.

Next, Rowan gathered a group of fourteen different people who wanted to explore the topic with him. All had some experience of group work and self-examination; all acknowledged the unconscious aspects of themselves. The group held six meetings. They found the range of subpersonalities per person was 0 to 18. The mean was 6.5. Rowan concludes that anywhere between 4 and 8 subpersonalities is perfectly normal for any one of us to have. In *Human Inquiry* (Reason and Rowan, 1981) Rowan reported new research, and then he wrote up these ideas in *Subpersonalities* (1985) and *Discover Your Subpersonalities* (1990).

Rowan approaches the whole subject differently from the

enthusiastic American psychiatrists. He does not deal with sick or dysfunctional individuals who have a long history of psychiatric care. The people he discussed and explored ideas with were equal members of a group who wanted to seek out their subpersonalities and dialogue with them. They weren't being crippled by alters. Rowan's partners had control and choice over what they were doing.

It's not hard to see why one might want to meet some of one's subpersonalities. Many of us like to think we're deliciously complex. Some subpersonalities could be useful. If I get anxious when I go for an interview, I'd love to turn on that confident self who could sell snow to the Eskimos. Equally, I'd love to handle my mother's anxieties by meeting her with a Mature Self.

In *Subpersonalities*, Rowan playfully introduces ten of his own subpersonalities. His descriptions make it clear each tends to fulfil a particular role in his psychological make-up – a role he understands better as he's worked on the topic. Here is his list:

Big Eggo – a dominant male figure who was the main executive personality. He appeared as Old Reliable. Being influenced by Jung, Rowan saw this subpersonality had some characteristics of two important Jungian archetypes – the Magician and the Clown. Rowan has now trimmed the macho elements so that Big Eggo is more PC and less dominant than it was before.

Jean Starry – a mixture of two earlier characters, Brown Cow, a natural, sensual woman who could let things happen, and Mr Commitment, who used to be Rowan's only lovable 'self'.

Black Dwarf – a nasty put-downing creature. Rowan believes this destructive character became less powerful as Rowan stopped trying to destroy his mother. It was a subpersonality very much like Jung's Shadow. Rowan sees this subpersonality as intensely destructive.

Behemoth – Rowan's creative self. It was very changeable, unreliable and brilliant. Rowan discovered that Behemoth could also appreciate creativity.

Father – a patriarch figure who was just like Jung's Father complex. He sometimes appeared as Archbishop Makarios, by whom I presume Rowan means the Greek Cypriot leader of the 1960s. Rowan did not deal with him till he had finished the research but found him important when he did.

Lilith – a slim dark woman in a shiny dress who reminds Rowan of his mother when she was young.

Just Me – a subpersonality Rowan described as having links with his Real Self, Loving Me and Centred Me, but one that he still had to finally sort out his relationship with.

Babette – a magical girl-child who also appeared as a Fairy and a Magical Child. Rowan needs her less now. Once upon a time she was the only subpersonality who was lovable. As Rowan's self-work progressed, that changed.

The Dome – Rowan's transpersonal self. After the first time he made contact with it, it became more accessible and that had a big impact on his life.

Little Lady – a grandmother figure who appeared once as a pair of elderly sisters. She was precise, knowledgeable and very good with her fingers.

Rowan argues discovering one's various subpersonalities, the people inside us, may provide important tools for both therapy and personal growth. He snipes at Melanie Klein and the object school, saying that 'it does not do justice to the complexity of these internal objects which are more in reality than internalized mothers or good or bad breasts' (p. 57).

Rowan emphasizes that many other therapists use giving subpersonalities a voice as a technique, among them the American therapist Richard Schwartz, who works with what he calls inner voices. Gestalt therapists routinely get clients to act out situations from different perspectives. So do psychodrama therapists.

It can hardly be an accident that just as psychiatrists are discovering more multiple personality cases than ever before, there is growing interest in subpersonalities. There was plenty of evidence before for the existence of both phenomena but cases were seen as great oddities. So why should this be happening?

HOW MANY SIDES ARE THERE TO YOU?
DIARY OF MANY SELVES 2

Let's return to the diary of the thirty-seven-year-old mother-persecuted lecturer I can easily identify with.

In my first extract from his diary, I just scratched the surface of his different personas. A number of them brought his hostility out into the open There is much social and emotional pressure on all of us to suppress hostility. 'Don't be rude' is one of the first rules we're all taught. I've internalized this well. I dislike being rude. Yet there have been plenty of times when I have been rude. Sometimes, my rudeness has caught me by surprise. Some years ago I contributed to a series in a Sunday paper. One of the people I was working with had a story on the front page one week.

When I came into the office on the Tuesday after, I said, 'I saw your byline on the front page and so I didn't read the story.'

I had no idea I was going to say that, to be so rude. There was no way back, no unsaying what I'd said. I didn't know I felt so hostile to this woman or that I was so jealous of her front-page story. We had been drinking together, flirted a little and a friend was trying to set us up. As soon as I said the offending words I knew two contradictory things:

It wasn't me speaking.

I felt every word I'd said.

I would never say this was an instance of multiple personality but it was clearly a different bit of me speaking.

It's this kind of experience I want to look at, and so in the spirit of exploring our tendency to hop through many different selves during the day, I now come to the questionnaire. I hadn't originally planned to put one in this book, but as I've been writing and talking to friends about what I've been writing, I've had a reaction I've only had once before – when I was writing a book on the experience of being a man. Say to people that you're writing about multiple personalities and it often provokes slightly nervous laughter.

People hesitantly say, 'I've got a few personalities in me,' or, 'My friend's going out with a bloke who's a real split personality.' This nervous laughter suggests two opposing twitches. If I admit that there are different bits to me, am I admitting I'm weird, or, worse than weird, actually disturbed? The idea that split personalities are a form of schizophrenia remains deeply embedded in our popular culture. If this is negative, however, all our fascination with therapy, changing ourselves and shopping around in the Self Bazaar – why not try out this new self, madam, you look so good in it? – may make many of us feel boring and uncool if we don't have seriously conflicting elements in our personality.

Be truthful in answering the questions. This is not a test. It is not better to have more or fewer sides to your personality. You can be an interesting human being even if you always feel you are yourself. The test that follows has not been validated by any research. I make no scientific claims for it. Rather, the questions should act as triggers. They should trigger your imagination, self-analysis and self-exploration.

THE DIFFERENT SIDES QUESTIONNAIRE

1. Are you surprised by the way you behave:
   a. *often*
   b. *occasionally*

    c. once or twice

    d. never

2. If you have answered a, b or c, does such surprising behaviour occur when you are under stress?

    a. no

    b. yes

3. Do the following descriptions seem very strange to you:

Janet is worried because she has caught herself at work behaving in a way that seems odd to her, not like herself. She is in charge of a department and thinks of herself as a competent manager. Inevitably, at times, she has to reprimand members of her staff. Sometimes, when she does so, she is concerned because it doesn't really sound like her doing it. It's almost as if there's another voice doing it.

John has gone out to have dinner with Sally. John is married but not very happy with his marriage. He hasn't told his wife, of course, that he's having dinner with another woman. The dinner is going very well. Plenty of eye contact. He thinks he's in with a definite chance. Just before they have dessert John goes off to have a pee. As he stands at the urinal looking at the blank tiled wall, he wonders just what he is doing here with this strange woman?

You are not likely to have had exactly similar experiences but the descriptions outline a particular feeling of dislocation from the normal self.

Have you had a similar experience of being distant or dis-associated from your surroundings:

    a. never

    b. just once or twice

    c. often enough to recognize a pattern

    d. very often

4. If you have answered b, c or d, write down the particular circumstances in which you have had these experiences because they may well reveal something about what triggers them in you.

5. For the next question to make sense we need to define a daydream. A daydream is a sequence of thoughts and feelings

that occur while you are awake. A daydream is connected. It isn't just a flashing thought. It will last at least two to three minutes during which you remain aware of normal stimuli but your focus is miles away. The notion that a daydream is some form of connected story is important. Daydreams can be about anything but often they are about ambitions. If, for example, you think it would be lovely to win the lottery, that's just a moment of fantasy. But if you see yourself getting the big cheque and working out how you will spend your money so that you decide, for example, what you'll buy your wife, what you'll treat yourself to and whether or not you'll give up your job, that's a 'proper' daydream. Do you daydream:

a. *often*
b. *at least once a week*
c. *hardly ever*
d. *never*

6. In your daydreams, do you ever imagine that you are a completely different person:

a. *often*
b. *hardly ever*
c. *enough for me to know my unconscious is trying to tell me something*
d. *never*

7. Is the person you fantasize about being:

a. *always much the same – i.e. you worry that you're a wimp and dream of being a hero*
b. *one who changes a great deal*
c. *there is no such fantasy being*

8. Does this fantasy self or fantasy selves:

a. *solve problems that you recognize in your life*
b. *seem not to be connected to your usual problems. He or she is a playful projection*
c. *there is no such fantasy being*

9. Do you sometimes fantasize that:

a. *you are of the opposite sex*
b. *you are a child*
c. *you come from a different culture*

      d. you come from a different planet, star system or galaxy
      *e. you come from a different time period – e.g. you are
      living in the sixteenth or twenty-fifth century*

10. Do you get so caught up in these fantasies sometimes that you feel:
      a. it affects your normal everyday life
      b. you are never caught up

11. Are there aspects of your personality you really dislike? It's important to be honest. An example may help. George, a friend of mine, once confessed to me that he was disturbed by a pattern in his behaviour. As a teenager, George enjoyed stealing. In his twenties, he worked as a civil servant but he missed the thrill of breaking the law. He became a fare dodger. He didn't need to fiddle his fares but he enjoyed it. In his thirties, he got a divorce and he started to steal from women he was dating. It was never very much. Two or three pounds, a tenner. He despised this part of his personality but he also liked the feeling that he was getting away with it. He sometimes fantasized about being destitute and wondered what life on the streets would be like. He couldn't understand why he should have such fantasies but he thought they had something to do with his thieving. A few nights before talking to me, George had stolen ten pounds from a woman he was dating. He liked her and he was worried she would guess it was him and end the relationship. Stealing was no longer a lark. It was grubby. Yet he did it and enjoyed it. But George did not like the part of himself that did and liked it.

    Do you feel there are aspects of your personality you don't like?
      a. there are no such aspects
      b. you don't see any such aspects as part of the 'real' you
      c. there are one or two such aspects
      d. there are so many of them you'd rather not think about it.

12. Do you forget things that you have done:
    a. *never*
    b. *sometimes*
    c. *very often*
13. If friends draw your attention to things or events you have forgotten, do you:
    a. *always remember what you did when they mention it*
    b. *usually remember*
    c. *feel confused*
    d. *often feel concerned because you don't remember*
14. Do you have feelings and thoughts which frighten you and don't seem to really belong to you:
    a. *never*
    b. *quite often*
    c. *very often*
15. A couple who are friends of yours reveal that sometimes, to spice up their sex lives, they pretend that one of them is somebody different. Catherine calls herself Lindy. Do you think:
    a. *this is very weird*
    b. *rather envy their freedom to be so imaginative*
    c. *laugh that this is plain silly*
16. You have to go to a function which your parents, your boss and your partner will attend. Do you feel:
    a. *perfectly comfortable*
    b. *a little worried because you know that each of these important people sees you in very different ways*
17. Would you describe your behaviour as:
    a. *predictable*
    b. *changeable*
    c. *you often only know what you are going to do after you have done it*
18. Do your friends tell you that they didn't think you had it in you to do something:
    a. *often*
    b. *sometimes*

     c. hardly ever

     d. never

19. Have you ever looked in the mirror and not recognized your-self:

     a. yes

     b. no

20. Do you sometimes wake up in a state of confusion because:

     a. you're not sure where you are

     b. you're not sure what you were doing last night

     c. you're not sure what you have to do today

     d. these situations very rarely happen

21. Are you aware of behaving differently when:

     a. you are with your partner

     b. you are at work

     c. you are with a parent

22. Do you think that that is:

     a. perfectly normal, reflecting the fact that these are differ-ent situations

     b. a little surprising

     c. it worries you because you are so different with each of these people

23. Do you have a sense that there is a core personality to you:

     a. yes

     b. no

24. Are there people close to you that you find it frightening to reveal that core to:

     a. yes

     b. no

25. You will have read in this chapter of Rowan's description of his own subpersonalities. Have you had experiences like that:

     a. when you feel there are subpersonalities in you that you know quite well

     b. when you feel there are different fragments of your self but you don't know who or what they are

     c. this isn't a feeling you have

26 Do you sometimes find yourself remembering snatches of
events that you can't place:
  a. never
  b. sometimes
  c. quite often

27. Which of the following adjectives best describes the feelings
that go with these memories:
  a. curiosity
  b. fear
  c. surprise

28. Do you talk to yourself:
  a. never
  b. sometimes
  c. quite often

29. Do the case-histories you've read so far in this book make
you feel:
  a. these are totally bizarre people who must be mad
  b. interested
  c. uncomfortable
  d. you can't personally connect with them at all

30. Do your hostile feelings towards some people sometimes
take you by surprise:
  a. never. You know who you hate.
  b. sometimes
  c. quite often

31. Do you sometimes find you have lost things without having
any idea of how that might have happened:
  a. often
  b. sometimes
  c. once or twice
  d. never

The answers to these questions aren't right or wrong. They do
indicate something about the extent to which you feel there are
different sides to you, your fantasies about that and your ability
to tolerate conflicts consciously.

SCORING

1. *a.* 4, *b.* 3, *c.* 2, *d.* 0
2. *a.* 0, *b.* 2
3. *a.* 0, *b.* 1, *c.* 2, *d.* 4
4. open-ended
5. *a.* 4, *b.* 3, *c.* 1, *d.* 0
6. *a.* 4, *b.* 1, *c.* 2, *d.* 0
7. *a.* 4, *b.* 4, *c.* 0
8. *a.* 4, *b.* 4, *c.* 0
9. Score 3 points for each answer you said YES to
   TOTAL POSSIBLE FOR THIS QUESTION: 15
10. *a.* 4, *b.* 0
11. *a.* 0, *b.* 4, *c.* 2, *d.* 3
12. *a.* 0, *b.* 2, *c.* 4
13. *a.* 1, *b.* 2, *c.* 3, *d.* 4
14. *a.* 0, *b.* 2, *c.* 4
15. *a.* 1, *b.* 4, *c.* 1
16. *a.* 0, *b.* 2
17. *a.* 0, *b.* 2, *c.* 4
18. *a.* 4, *b.* 2, *c.* 1, *d.* 0
19. *a.* 5, *b.* 0
20. Score 3 points each for saying YES to either *a*, *b* or *c*. Score 0 for *d*.
    TOTAL POSSIBLE FOR THIS QUESTION: 9
21. Score 3 points for each answer you said YES to.
    TOTAL POSSIBLE FOR THIS QUESTION: 9
22. *a.* 1, *b.* 2, *c.* 4
23. *a.* 1, *b.* 4
24. *a.* 4, *b.* 1
25. *a.* 4, *b.* 4, *c.* 0
26. *a.* 0, *b.* 2, *c.* 4
27. *a.* 1, *b.* 4, *c.* 2
28. *a.* 1, *b.* 2, *c.* 4
29. *a.* 1, *b.* 2, *c.* 4, *d.* 0
30. *a.* 0, *b.* 2, *c.* 4
31. *a.* 4, *b.* 3, *c.* 2, *d.* 1

Pay particular attention to the open-ended questions because they tell you a good deal about both the kinds of fantasies you have and the triggers that will provoke them.

Clearly anyone who scores above 90 out of a total possible of 144 feels their personality can change and is rather unpredictable. There is nothing pathological in such feelings. Nor do they necessarily indicate that you have subpersonalities that you should discover. But what that kind of score does indicate is that you are more likely to play with your sense of identity than many other people. This should at least make you sympathetic to what I'll call the weak case for multiple personality – that in the complex modern world we're bombarded by different pressures, conflicting role models and a lack of structure. These things make it easy to imagine how one would develop an awareness either of 'subpersonalities' or, to avoid the jargon, of different, radically different, aspects of oneself. It also means you can consider the bizarre notion of multiple personality with an imaginative eye.

A score between 90 and 60 indicates a certain tendency towards a sense that one's personality can change and fluctuate.

A score under 60 means that you are pretty fixed and stable in your sense of your own identity.

Ian Hacking quite rightly points out that most tests of dissociative tendencies are not scientific. I've offered the above test just as a way of getting you to think about your own personality.

Where I disagree with Hacking is in his faith in other personality tests. In devising 'instruments' (that nice scientific-sounding word) to measure multiple personality, the pioneers are just playing the scientific psychology game. You can't blame them for that. If they want to stay in mainstream American psychology, they have no option. But even IQ tests (which Hacking thinks are serious) have many flaws and are only useful at predicting a fairly narrow set of skills. Hans Eysenck, who is a fan of them, observed to me once that it takes much more than a high IQ score to do well in life. Otherwise, MENSA (the club for high IQs) would not be full of so many losers. In 1995, MENSA sacked some of its staff for running some sort of private business from their offices. The staff, all high-IQ-niks, hadn't taken the most elementary precautions to cover their tracks.

Questionnaires are not chemical equations. At best, they illustrate a few points about intelligence and personality. A complete moron is unlikely to get an IQ score of 140.

It's now time to return to the serious psychiatric research and the controversies which surround tests of dissociation and multiple personality. Again, one sees more of a battle than a cool scientific inquiry.

Ross' test puts eleven specific questions in the midst of a standard psychiatric questionnaire. The eleven questions are sensible. They deal with whether individuals have ever lost or found objects in an inexplicable manner, whether they feel 'unreal', whether they suffer severe memory loss, whether they hear voices. Ross reminds subjects to exclude experiences they have had when drunk or on drugs. Ross stresses that he is not talking about ordinary forgetfulness. I may not remember if we had dinner last Tuesday or Wednesday without that being a 'symptom' but if I have totally forgotten seeing you last week that is more than mere forgetfulness.

Ross also seems scrupulous in the way the questions are set. Many of the eleven questions like 'Do you feel that there are people inside you?' require subjects to give a rating from 1 to 5. For this question in Ross' test, 1 stands for 'never' and 5 for 'very often'. Psychometric research shows subjects are more likely to tick 1 because that is the first box in a row. Well-designed tests make sure that box 1 is not always a positive response as that would distort the results. Ross has produced a respectably designed test, not one which uses psychometric tricks to boost the numbers of dissociative patients or symptoms.

Hacking also ignores more recent tests like the American National Institute of Mental Health's SCIDD. None of this will convince sceptics, but to claim there are no useful tests of dissociation is unfair. The condition is complex; the tests are fallible; there is nothing unusual about that.

PSYCHOLOGY FOR CHANGE

As therapy has become part of more people's lives, it has affected attitudes to change. We no longer think we have to be desperately disturbed to want to alter – the use of the word is deliberate – aspects of our life or personality.

Some years ago, I worked on a film on mid-life crises. We found that many people in their forties did try to change their lives radically. One man who had been a carpet salesman was increasingly fed up with his narrow life. He sold up his share in the family business, moved to the north of England and decided to see whether he could make a living as a singer. He was trying to live a new life, trying to forge a new identity.

In another case a woman decided to adopt a baby even though she didn't have a partner and it meant giving up her career. She claimed that she was much happier in her new life than she had ever been in the old one.

John had worked in the Royal Air Force as an air traffic controller. One of his jobs was to guide planes in on targets. He told us that as he knew he was going to lose his job he became deeply depressed. He toyed with killing himself. Then he decided that perhaps he shouldn't see the change as a calamity but as an opportunity. He realized that he was quite interested in caring for people. In the air force he hadn't expressed that side of himself very much. He decided in his mid-thirties to take up nursing. It was hard on his family but he was eventually very glad to have done it.*

Looking back, many of those interviewed felt their lives had changed dramatically because of what they decided to do. Most saw the changes as positive and something that they had chosen to do. After people go through a mid-life crisis, they often don't understand why they didn't take steps to change their life much earlier. Our sense of personality is much more flexible. You can re-invent yourself. You can, as Rowan recommends, use your

* Fortysomething was directed by Lindsay Knight; I was its executive producer.

subpersonalities to help achieve that goal. Rowan's work has developed in a climate in which it is much easier than ever before for people to try out new personalities, new selves, new roles. It is hard to believe that this cultural climate has not influenced the whole multiple personality debate.

CHAPTER 13

Testing the Treatment

Many of the psychiatrists I have talked to suggest that they know how to treat multiple personality sufferers. In this chapter, I want to look at the kind of treatment being offered, at some factors that seem to complicate the treatment of multiple personality disorder, and to ask a basic question. Has all the work done since 1980 led to better treatment? I have been sceptical about the sceptics, but I think it is fair to ask why fifteen years after large numbers of cases started to be reported there are still no really good studies of how well various forms of treatment work.

Experts like Ross emphasize that multiple personality is a reaction to trauma. But the treatment of trauma is not a newfangled psychiatric speciality. Before the boom in multiple personality, there were studies of techniques designed to cure some sorts of trauma. In 1922, for example, the British Army commissioned a report into shell-shock or battle-shock. Over five hundred British soldiers were executed for cowardice in the 1914–1918 war. Some military doctors feared a great injustice had been done. Many of the 'cowards' were ill; some were mad. The gruesome conditions at the front had traumatized them. Millais (1924) reported on what happened when he talked to survivors. Many could remember nothing; many felt ashamed. Millais eventually gave soldiers sodium amytal to dis-inhibit their memories. He found that after talking out their terrifying experiences, many started to recover.

Talking is not a panacea. In 1972 at Buffalo Creek in West Virginia, a dam burst flooding the valley below. The flood left 125 dead and 654 injured. An American court commissioned a study from the University of Cincinnati. It found 90 per cent of survivors suffered from post-traumatic stress. They had flashbacks, nightmares, memory loss – some of the symptoms that also are typical of multiple personality syndrome. Survivors were angry. They asked, 'Why me?' Many became depressed and lonely. The psychological damage they suffered was estimated at nine million dollars. Kai Erikson of Yale University (1976) followed up the victims and reported on how effective the treatment they received was.

Controversy about the results of treatment is not new. It is being fuelled in multiple personality disorder now by the lack of treatment studies that everyone accepts. I believe the reasons for this lack of outcome studies are complex and some involve the perils and ironies of being a psychiatrist.

SAD SHRINKS

The humorist James Thurber in his satire on psychoanalysis, *Let Your Mind Alone*, betrayed a soft spot for the figure of the sad shrink who is defeated time after time by the misery of the human condition and the absolute determination of his patients not to get better.

Multiple personality experts often seem to be sad shrinks. Many seem to need a multidisciplinary squad to protect them from the awful, sometimes awesome, behaviour and demands of these patients. These are not good patients. They lie, cheat and connive. Consciously, unconsciously, subconsciously.

It is hard to believe that this doesn't affect the psychiatrists.

One illustration of the less than lovely attitude of these patients.

The emergency room of a New York hospital. An ambulance brings in a thirty-year-old woman who has taken a serious overdose. Two women accompany her. One is forty; the other is twenty-five and dressed far more smartly. She has short-cropped hair and wears a trim jacket. She looks out of place in the emergency room. The two women don't speak. In the next thirty minutes, the nurse gets a bizarre history. Each woman claims to be in a stable monogamous relationship – a gay marriage – with the woman who has taken the overdose. Each woman seems sincere. It becomes clear that the woman who took the overdose is an ace manipulator and dissembler. She turns out to be a multiple personality.

Such patients have no qualms about manipulating their therapists, testing them and crossing all kinds of therapeutic boundaries. After all, multiples also have the perfect punch line to any criticism:

'I didn't do it, it was one of the others.'

So it's your fault, shrink, for not controlling my alters properly. Don't blame me.

As one patient put it, 'Let's stop all this crap about therapy. I'm not in therapy. I only bring her here.'

It's not surprising, then, that many psychiatrists are ambivalent about such patients and a little ashamed of that. After all, doctors are healers. This adds to the pressure, for many already feel defensive as colleagues attack them for being either gullible or greedy. As I have said, Ian Hacking and others believe many therapists are doing well out of multiple personality, an allegation doctors like Kluft and Fine deny with an 'I wish . . .'

The media also are a menace. On the one hand, they always lust for The Big Story: THE SERIAL KILLER WITH FIFTEEN IDENTITIES. On the other hand, they are always liable to become pious: SHOCK! HORROR! PARENTS FALSELY ACCUSED OF CHILD ABUSE BECAUSE OF MAD OR STUPID SHRINK.

Spare a thought for the psychiatrist, then.

STAGES OF TREATMENT

In most disorders, the first step is to take a detailed medical and psychiatric history. In dealing with dissociation, however, the first imperative is to calm the patient so that they can accept the very idea of therapy. If that isn't done, therapy itself can appear as a new form of abuse. Most psychiatrists think it essential to make a contract which will include getting permission to use hypnosis.

Hypnosis or some form of deep relaxation is essential because in 80 per cent of cases the psychiatrist sees no switching between alters. The symptoms aren't that obvious and could be symptoms of other psychiatric conditions. If you suspect a case of dissociation, you need to probe for alters. Over the last ten years, psychiatrists have learned to be patient and not to rush into probing.

Different therapists use different models of treatment but there are some important similarities. Kluft outlines the stages most seen as:

Establishing contact
Reducing immediate symptoms
Making the patient feel safe
Taking a psychiatric history
Mapping the personality system
Metabolizing the trauma
Preparing for integration
After integration

Establishing contact is often hard because many patients show up angry or withdrawn. They are in a world of their own, re-living traumatic memories. Richard Kluft said one patient was writhing on the floor when he first saw her. He felt he couldn't touch her. He just sat by her and asked at intervals of fifteen minutes, 'What are you going through?' He added, 'I'm very persistent.' Eventually she said, 'Rape.' He was glad he had stayed two hours.

In other cases, he was appalled, as in the example of Jennifer, mentioned in Chapter 8, who was so filthy he had to be careful not to vomit!

One 'technique' for reaching the withdrawn, Kluft told me, is to sit by the 'not there' patient and whistle. It's a form of teasing. Once, facing a woman in distress, Kluft eventually heard a different voice say, 'Don't you see the anguish she's going through, and you whistle.'

'I didn't know you were listening,' Kluft replied, establishing more contact than he had hoped for.

PSYCHIATRIC HISTORY

Kluft advises against taking a psychiatric history at once. Many patients have had disastrous experiences in the 'system'. Taking a history before they are ready to confide in the doctor can make them panic. The doctor has to start by providing reassurance, medication if necessary, and a sincere promise to listen. Much of what has to be heard will be confused and far-fetched.

There are surprisingly few psychiatric studies of the voices that patients hear. This is very curious. History, ancient and modern, is packed with famous and infamous characters who have heard voices. Voices inspired Joan of Arc. Many murderers like Ricki – a man I interviewed in Creedmoor Hospital, New York – who pushed an innocent stranger in front of a train have claimed that voices told them to do it. Hearing voices is a first-rank symptom of schizophrenia but multiple personality patients also hear them. As I have said earlier, Colin Ross argues there are important differences between voices. Multiple personality patients experience their voices as if they are coming from inside their heads. They are, Ross suggests, the voices of alters trying to break through. Hearing voices from outside the head, however, is a classic symptom of schizophrenia.

Schizophrenics feel creatures from outer space, devils and other frightening entities are speaking through them, giving them orders. I put it to Ross that the best accounts of the experience of schizophrenia, like R. D. Laing's histories in *The Divided Self* (1961), suggest something different. Laing saw the voices of his patients not as meaningless but as expressions of current conflicts. Laing trawled the literature and found that one famous example of 'mad' jumbled speech reported by the German psychiatrist Emil Kraeplin (1856–1926) was, in fact, a protest about being demonstrated in front of a class of medical students. Many of the voices Laing's patients heard were attempts to make sense of family conflicts. Ross was not convinced, and insisted on the difference between voices inside, and outside, the head.

Despite Ross' strong views, the origin of the voices is not seen by all multiple personality workers as a key issue. If a patient presents with the usual symptoms of headaches, memory loss, blank spells and voices, psychiatrists today will ask three central questions before making a diagnosis. These are:

1. Is the patient a woman aged between twenty and forty?
2. Has she been unsuccessfully treated for years?
3. Have other psychiatrists claimed she's suffering from border-line personality?

If the answer to all these questions is yes, psychiatrists who believe in multiple personality disorder are likely to diagnose the condition.

Recent research complicates the picture. Some patients seem to suffer from both dissociative disorders and other psychiatric illnesses. Ross (1995) claims that 41% per cent of dissociative patients also had symptoms of schizophrenia. In a separate study Beth Brodsky and colleague claimed 47% of dissociative patients had major symptoms of depression. Ross argues over 50% also had symptoms of borderline personality. For Ross, these combinations reveal the major role of childhood trauma. The age at the start of the trauma and the precise nature of the trauma will determine the precise mix of symptoms.

Sceptics, however, do not accept that patients with other illnesses are also suffering from multiple personality syndrome. They tend to ridicule the idea of distinguishing voices from inside the head and voices from outside the head.

Yet the nature of these voices highlights an important issue. If the voices are part of the patient trying to communicate, if they are signals, rather than symptoms, it is not very sensible to suppress them with drugs of the kind given to schizophrenics. The voices need to be heard. They will have information about the original trauma. To censor them is the last way to achieve a cure. The alters need to be found, reassured and coaxed to speak.

Taking what 'mad' voices say seriously goes against the medical model that so many psychiatrists practise. The phrase 'the medical model' came to be used in the 1970s for an approach to psychiatry that relies heavily on drugs. Since victims are 'mad', their particular symptoms do not have any meaning. Many caring psychiatrists believe in the medical model; they don't believe patients have any insight into their condition. What their voices say is psychic garbage, not revealing.

Multiple personality patients, however, are not as out of touch with reality as schizophrenics. Might not this mean their voices have something important to say? That essentially is Ross' position. They offer a way of starting to map out their personality system, which is a first step to effective treatment.

MAP OF THE SELF

Among the case-histories I've given is that of polyfragmented Pam. Ross told her to produce charts of her 335 personalities and the main themes among them. Critical psychiatrists can hardly stop themselves giggling. Dr Tom Fahy of the Institute of Psychiatry in London told me it just showed how silly the diagnosis was. He added that Pam had now been trumped by someone in the States who claimed to have four thousand alters – and was probably selling their story to Hollywood. But mapping the personality system isn't a foolish procedure. Maps are useful. Therapists have to know who is in the system, the part each alter plays and what each alter 'holds' of the trauma. As these inner relationships become clear, it may be possible to make alliances and get some alters to work together for the good of the whole personality. Drawing a map of alters is like drawing a map of a country in the dark. You don't know your way around. And the easiest technique for revealing alters is highly controversial.

Ever since Puysegur discovered waking sleep two hundred years ago, scientists have quarrelled about the status of hypnosis. Alan Gauld (1992) has charted these arguments in detail. From the 1850s hypnosis was used on stage by magicians in music hall and variety shows. So hypnosis has long had a touch of the freak show. This makes it simple for critics to dismiss. Among the many excellent barbs, snipes, swipes and other academic moves I've come across in writing this book, my favourite is by Ray Allridge Morris, super sceptic. Allridge Morris (1989) has it in for an Italian psychiatrist, Morselli, who used hypnosis to study one multiple personality case. The reason? Morselli took mescalin. Mescalin, Morselli wrote, once made him change into a werewolf. For Allridge Morris, that sums up the risks of using hypnosis in science. Soon many members of the Royal Society will start baying at the moon. In fact, Isaac Newton believed in ghosts and tried to communicate with angels. Yet he also described laws of the universe in a way that was not improved upon for three hundred years.

The fact that bizarre individuals use hypnosis does not make the technique useless. Sensible hypnotists pay attention to the very real risks of suggestion and compliance. Gisli Gudjuddson (1993), for example, has devised personality tests which identify individuals who are especially compliant and suggestible. Such individuals are more likely to make false confessions under pressure in police stations, as in the case of Judith Ward in Chapter 1. They are also likely to comply under hypnosis and produce whatever they think the therapist wants. Hypnosis creates its own social pressures. Psychiatrists need to be aware of research like Gudjuddson's and to stress over and over again that there is no need to produce a troop of alters. You won't be a better patient if you do that.

Speakers in Amsterdam accepted hypnosis has to be handled with more care than it had been in the past. Frank Putnam warns that any alter needs to appear at least twice under hypnosis before a therapist should accept him or her as a genuine part of the personality system. Onno van der Hart said that therapists should not give patients the impression that any memories evoked under hypnosis are true. The fact that they were repressed doesn't make them true.

These reservations about hypnosis seem to many sceptics to be another sign of appeasement. The pioneers are so desperate for scientific respectability, they will ditch hypnosis. But these anxieties coincide with a peculiar development. As I have emphasized it is no longer so hard to contact alters. Many seem to bubble just under consciousness. Colin Ross claims that often all a psychiatrist need do is relax the patient and invite alters to come out. Most alters will oblige and pop out. No need to bother with hypnosis. It's only if the personality system is very complex or well defended, if the therapist suspects he is far from finishing the map because some alters just will not co-operate, that hypnosis is necessary these days.

Sceptics take a very different view of these newly accessible alters. Patients know they are supposed to produce alters and so they comply. I can understand the scepticism, but some patients do see it very differently. One told me she had learned to relax better in therapy. She found she could picture in her mind the part of her that wanted to speak. When she was normally conscious she couldn't do that, but it now didn't take anything as baroque as hypnosis to free her up to do it.

None of this is likely to convince sceptics, who remain certain that hypnosis is a dubious procedure and allows manipulative patients the joys of malingering. In a letter to *The Bulletin of the British Psychological Society*, Tony Armond announced his magic cure. If he ever met a patient who claimed to have a multiple personality, he told them all their personalities would be held responsible for everything any of them did. All alters, selves, personalities were equally guilty.

With more alters per patient and anxieties about hypnosis, mapping the personality system isn't simple. And these aren't the only obstacles.

VIOLENT ALTERS

The history of medicine is full of heroes who were ridiculed only to be proved right in the end. Multiple personality pioneers identify with this scenario. But perhaps they need all the comfort they can get, because they have to deal with the continuing problem of the violence of some of the alters. Many psychiatrists admit to being scared of some alters. As we have seen, Ross stopped therapy with Pam after receiving death threats from one of her 335 alters. Ross is not unique. The American Psychiatric Association recommends making a contract with multiple personality patients. An essential clause, according to the APA, is for the patient to promise, 'I will not kill myself.'

Dramatic as this clause is, Frank Putnam does not believe it goes far enough. He points out the need to make a contract with every one of the alters. Otherwise, one or more of them will cheat. This contract has to specify that none of the alters can behave violently or run away. This is something they tend to do when treatment gets close to the heart of the trauma. Child personalities may well not understand the contract, Putnam adds, so it has to be explained very carefully to them. They must not be left any excuse for destructive behaviour. After he has made a contract, Putnam will make a formal announcement. He says, 'I want everyone in there to give me their full attention.' Now is the time for those who object to the contract to speak.

Managing the violent tendencies of alters is a real problem. Ross told me his staff at the Dissociative Disorders Unit in Dallas, Texas, were getting too stressed out because they had so many assaults to deal with. The basic rules Ross enforces are simple. Patients cannot attack staff physically or verbally. Patients cannot attack each other. Ross uses many groups in treatment. He has also tried to re-name some groups because he thinks the right name encourages the right attitude. So the group for angry and destructive child alters and persecutor personalities is now known as the Resocialization Group. The emphasis of the group has shifted from getting alters to express all their anger to teaching them to behave in acceptable ways. Ross is more willing now to threaten patients with disciplinary sanctions. If they are violent, they will be moved out of the Dissociative Disorders Unit and on to the hospital's general wards. He told me he is also more willing to use physical restraint if he has to.

Ross claims these techniques have cut violent incidents on his unit by 50 per cent. They have done so, he maintains, without making patients so resentful that they clam up. The less violence, the more chance to get on with treatment.

BOUNDARIES

Patients in many conditions don't respect boundaries. Psychiatrists argue that this problem is especially acute with multiple personality cases. But here there is more ambivalence about what to do. Patients are sometimes in severe crisis. Crises can be used to make breakthroughs. Putnam argues the psychiatrist must not be too rigid about boundaries in such a situation. It is no good sticking to the conventions where the patient comes to the therapist's office for fifty-five minutes. Putnam reports visiting patients' houses, going out with them and cancelling the appointments of other patients. Psychiatrists become very ambivalent about such patients. Many therapists in Amsterdam complained of the demands the patients made. They turned up without appointments; they left interminable messages on the therapists' answering machines; they wanted their therapists to go shopping with them; they were outrageous in their demands. Surprisingly often, they got their way.

For sceptics like Tom Fahy, the readiness of therapists to go along with all this shows many of them have become so fascinated with these flashy patients they are 'over involved'. Fahy told me he didn't know whether to laugh or cry when one therapist who rang him to ask for advice said he couldn't talk for long because he had to pick up his patient's children from their playgroup. Fahy warns of the dangers of collusion between patients who want endless attention and therapists who are too much in love with the disease. The doctor stops being objective.

Such demanding patients can also be very seductive. Many anecdotes suggest therapists have slept with multiple personality patients, but none of the doctors I talked to had, or were willing to reveal specific instances. Putnam may be willing to put himself out for patients but he is very firm on this issue.

He writes (1989): 'I have been sexually harassed by some

alters. I regard this exactly the same way as I regard outbursts of violence. It's a form of aggression towards the therapist. I deal with this exactly the same as I deal with violence.' Putnam summons other members of staff so that he has witnesses and the therapy ceases to be private. Putnam argues it is crucial for therapists to deal with this issue. It is often a replay of the initial abuse. Sometimes, the only way an abused child can exert any control is to appear to be the seducer. That way she keeps some initiative, some feeling of not being a victim.

Multiples are manipulative, scared, confused, sometimes violent and make endless demands on their therapists which makes mapping the personality system, therefore, not a simple business.

Before looking at Kluft's next stage, metabolizing the trauma, I want to ask a simple question. Given the demands these patients make, why do shrinks persist? Is it just professional devotion? I want to argue there is another motive – and an unusual one.

There is no glamour in most psychiatric disorders. Psychiatrists do not fantasize about being depressed or schizophrenic. Only R. D. Laing at his most radical in *The Bird of Experience* suggested there was anything to learn from the 'journey' of the schizophrenic and he at times denied he had such a romantic attitude. (Laing, 1994). Multiple personality disorder does have a certain glamour however. I don't mean to suggest that it is fun to suffer but some of the symptoms are similar to a pleasant fantasy many people have, the fantasy of having a second life or a secret life. In '*The Lavender Hill Mob*', for example, Alec Guinness played a meek bank clerk at the Bank of England who masterminded a daring bullion robbery. Then he can lead, and leads with great style, the playboy life he always had in him. In *The Captain's Table* Guinness played a captain who lived a staid Brit-life in Gibralter with one wife and an exotic, erotic life in Tangier with a second wife. The fantasy of trading places is the plot of many movies. These fictions are popular because we dream of a different, a better life.

Psychiatrists are only human – or, at least, some are – and, therefore, curious. That may explain some of their willingness to accept so much from their patients. By contrast take the Capgras syndrome. In Capgras, people think objects and significant others have been replaced by replicas. It's supremely weird but no one gets that involved with it.

The phrase used for the next stage of treatment reveals a pathetic desire to please 'Science'.

METABOLIZING THE TRAUMA

The next stage has nothing to do with chemistry, however. Metabolizing the trauma is really an old therapeutic practice. By forcing the alters out into the open therapists hope to get the repressed material on to the surface and into consciousness where they can deal with it, alter by alter.

When alters appear, therapists usually ask their name. If they don't have a name, they usually give them one to make it easier to get their history even though this risks boosting the alter into imagining him or herself as a distinct personality rather than one part of the whole personality system.

'I always try to get an alter to tell me when they were born, what the circumstances were and, crucially, I try to find out how much they know of the whole personality system,' Frank Putnam says.

No one can predict how long it will take to contact all the alters either through hypnosis or other techniques. Some alters may be frightened to appear. Others may enjoy hiding from the therapist and love playing hide-and-seek. Often the hide-and-seek is a power game. Some alters are more equal than others. Some are more powerful. Many think that the earliest, most damaged alters are the strongest because they have so much fear and rage. They will send out 'lesser' alters to make contact with this strange shrink in this strange situation.

One patient told me that she was scared before a session. Scared because often she felt extremely 'turbulent'. Such fears aren't exaggerated. Ross has found that if an alter is sent out and does something an alter higher up in the system doesn't like, there can be consequences. He said, 'Those alters can get beaten up.' The idea that Alter John A who won't appear will attack Alter John B 'invisibly' inside the body sounds strange, but alters do often complain that other alters want to kill them.

Kluft said that if he hears of such threats, he asks how the murderous alter would feel if someone planned to kill them. He finds that this sometimes calms things down.

As more patients turn out to have more alters, psychiatrists find it harder to make sense of the 'map' of personalities. Having managed to contact and 'out' all the alters, therapists need to identify what each of them represents. In theory this should be simple.

There's a nice image that suggests this process better, I feel, than the chemical one of 'metabolizing the trauma'. Imagine each alter as a tortured soul in its own little space, a confined space. The soul is in an aquarium. The alter is brought out of the water. We find out what hurts it. We talk it through. We talk out the pain. We then put it back in a larger aquarium. There it will be joined by the other alters as they, too, are healed. And once they are all healed, they will dissolve and re-form into a mighty fish.

Even maybe a dolphin.

Unfortunately for my nice poetic image, there is always resistance in dealing with abuse – resistance because there was so much betrayal, resistance because some have actually come to live with themselves as victims.

Jane told me she found it impossible to think of her uncle, who she remembered as a sweet grey-haired man who liked to play the piano, as also the man who exploited her, fondled her, caressed her. She was furious with her parents – especially her mother – who she thinks suspected what was going on but did nothing about it because she didn't want to create family tensions. The woman was more furious with her mother than she was with her uncle. They should have protected her. Once she dealt with the reasons for her trauma, she still had her anger with her parents to deal with.

Victims of abuse often feel that they sometimes brought it upon themselves. That only makes them more angry and defensive, feelings that persecutor personalities express. Some therapists believe these alters are angry children terrified at what happened to them. It feels as if it is still happening to them. They become violent to protect themselves, and self-destructive because they hate themselves. Harnessing that energy can be therapeutically useful but these alters do not trust. They have to be convinced that therapy is not a new form of abuse before they can become allies.

Turning pain into positive, usable anger requires enormous skill. There is no formula for how to achieve it. Patients often find what they are remembering incredible. As sessions continue, a hierarchy of alters is found. Deeper, more hidden in the system, there are the true controllers – the splits to which it really happened.

As I said in Chapter 9, Ross finds that these deeply hidden alters often think of themselves as devils or Satan figures. He often tries a very matter-of-fact approach, given that while they may think of themselves as Satans, they are also children. He tells them he knows that they are in there and says that everyone – Satan, the shrink, the host – could 'all be saved a lot of trouble if you come out and I can speak to you directly'. It's important to offer hope, to appeal to that part of the personality that wants to get well.

Richard Kluft also believes it's important to remember that in some sense alters are children. 'You do sound rather authoritarian sometimes.' He sees some alters almost like Talmudic imps. The truth is it is hard to make contact with all the alters, and harder still to unwrap each of their traumas. Treating multiple personality cases is a slow process. All kinds of defences protect the memories of the abuse and the pain. Patients often get confused, backtrack or even leave therapy. One woman told me she hated it when the therapist told her conscious self what she had said under hypnosis. She could not live with herself if it was true.

All these complications go to show what a misleading pseudo-scientific phrase 'metabolizing the trauma' is. Liquids and gases metabolize in seconds, minutes, perhaps hours – not over days, weeks and months.

As therapy continues, there is another potential trauma.

PLEASE DON'T FORCE ME TO GET WELL

Patients can always sabotage progress, consciously and unconsciously. Freud saw patients had 'secondary gains' from being ill. It's an idea which has spread widely. Research into heart attacks, for example, often asks what a victim would have been doing if he or she had not had a heart attack.

The ordinary tricks of patients are simple compared to those a multiple can play. Patients may forget appointments, turn up at the wrong time, leave town to avoid a heavy session as well as pester therapists in the ways I have described before. Some alters go in for nasty childish pranks. Patients may find that their wardrobes are full of new clothes, or else that some of their favourite dresses have been cut up.

The sabotage can be much more serious. Many psychiatrists have treated patients who have a promiscuous alter as described earlier in the book. The promiscuous alter hits town, makes a hot date, often promising some sado-masochistic activity. The date starts steamy. A fumble in the bar and then back to his place where the poor man is not prepared for the transformation. The come-on alter switches into Madame Mega Prude. After a moment's confusion or a trip to the bathroom, the date finds he's trying to bundle a cold and unwilling host personality into bed. For the host it's a nightmare. She doesn't know who she is with or how she got there. Sometimes, she is attacked. This process isn't always unconscious. One therapist speaks of an alter who when confronted with that scenario thought it was perfectly just. The alter said, 'I had to take it for her when she was little. I now want her to feel what it's like.'

Alters can also try to kill through suicide. Every therapist I talked to had had cases where one alter was suicidal and made a number of serious attempts.

Suicide attempts often interrupt treatment. Whatever the attempts to deflect therapy, the therapist has to press on with the main task – talking through the original trauma. Every doctor I talked to stressed the need to be gentle and supportive. Every doctor stressed the need to encourage empathy and co-operation between the alters to prevent the kind of sabotage I've been describing. Ross has been trying to use techniques based on cognitive therapy to persuade alters not to be destructive and to trust the process of therapy.

Ideally each alter should come to understand why he or she had to be created. Ideally, each part of the system should love and pity the others. In reality what happens is that the unconscious battles to control the body now become more conscious. Every member of the cast demands his, or her, time in the spotlight when they are in control of the body.

Often, the therapist has to act as a go-between. Frank Putnam has compared what he does to being an arbitrator. Often, alters complain of the fact that it isn't fair some of the others have so much time in the body. Many therapists say that this is a perfect time to intervene and negotiate.

In some ways this looks like taking a step back from integration, but it seems to be necessary to any further healing. Therapists stress the need to give all the alters time to settle down and get used to the situation when they know of each others' existence.

INTEGRATION

Ideally, talking through the trauma will pave the way for the creation of a new personality. When you put it like that, when you remember what Eve eventually went through, it becomes clear that this is the best, a magical outcome. It was not until the 1980s, when she was quite old and had been in and out of treatment for about thirty years, that she really fused. Sybil turned out to be more of a success. She didn't write books that demolished her therapist's account of treatment. There may not have been the spontaneous appearance of a new figure like Jane in *The Three Faces of Eve* but Sybil's sixteen personalities were integrated into one person. It is increasingly clear, however, that relatively few cases have such happy endings.

In analysing the success of treatment, it is also necessary

to look at the political context of the multiple personality debate.

THE POLITICS OF RECOVERED MEMORIES

The question of whether memories recovered under hypnosis are true or produced to comply with the therapist's theories has become a political issue as well as a scientific one. Those who argue against hypnosis sometimes raise the research on the 'experimenter effect'. This shows that subjects often produce the results they believe the experimenter wants. My shrink needs me to have had a traumatic childhood. I can't let him down.

Critics claim that such problems are fatal flaws. Memories of abuse recovered in hypnosis are all too likely to be false memories. As I have said, in America in 1992 and the UK in 1994, Foundations for False Memory were started by parents who felt they had been wrongly accused of abuse by their children. Many thirty- and forty-year-olds in therapy had suddenly remembered appalling incidents from their past. The parents quickly gathered a number of psychiatrists and psychologists as allies in the United States and in Britain. After a number of harrowing cases, it is clear that multiple personality pioneers are very nervous, and also clear, as I have said before, that accusations of Satanic abuse are not to be relied on.

One paper in Amsterdam gave fifteen therapeutic precautions to help prevent false memory allegations. The list is clearly designed to help therapists stay out of legal trouble. It's worth summarizing it.

Don't be quick to accuse an individual of sexual abuse
Don't over estimate the accuracy of repressed memories
Don't tell your clients that you know their memories are true
Don't tell your clients to cut off their families
Don't lead your client in the recovery of his or her memories
Don't recommend books or support groups that you are not
    familiar with

Don't breath confidentiality

Don't encourage the premature confrontation

Don't encourage clients to take out legal action or to take retribution on their abusers

Don't look on your clients as a subject for a possible good article or good book

Don't search for repressed memories if there is no good therapeutic reason for doing so

Your role is that of the therapist, not a police officer

Document the history of the recall of the repressed memories (Subtext: you may need that evidence in court!)

Be willing to educate your client in the processes of memory (Subtext: you must inform them of the fact that memory is not a clean and logical process. It's affected, and infected, by wishes, dreams, etc.)

Be willing to refer a client to someone else if that is in her or his best interest

Falsely accused parents are bound to be terribly upset and angry. But in our concern to find the truth, it's important not to lose sight of another truth. There is plenty of evidence of child sexual abuse. The police are constantly frustrated by the difficulties of bringing offenders to trial. (In 1995, the British government announced a review of how child abuse allegations should be investigated.) It has been estimated that less than 10 per cent of cases result in any kind of conviction. It will not help children or victims if the concern to be fair leads to a situation where people play down the likelihood of abuse. Sceptics who accuse those working with dissociation and multiple personality of inciting false memories of abuse themselves run the risk of being too complacent.

The division into those for and those against 'false memories' is, I think, a very dangerous development. It would be much better to emphasize the psychological evidence which shows memory is not perfect but a process of construction and reconstruction. Memories need to be sifted and examined critically.

What is certainly true is that for some years believers in multiple personality theory were naïve. They should have expected the problems, because the stakes were large. And many pioneers showed their naïveté by accepting too easily tales of Satanic abuse. Ian Hacking snipes that some of the tales made Stephen King seem tame. There were too many masks and giant phalluses waving around by the light of flaming crosses in the moonlit woods. Too many people dressed as goats dancing diabolically to the beat of tom-toms. The stories were getting too incredible. Hacking claims that in a nice political move the multiple 'movement', as he calls it, stopped talking of Satanic abuse and started talking of sadistic abuse.

There were plenty of signs of that kind of retreat in Amsterdam, plenty of anxiety about cases where parents are now countersuing the therapists for 'inserting' false memories.

Hacking believes that as the moral panic about abuse fades, the multiple movement will get weaker. As I hope I've shown, that would be a pity. People have a right to know what their families did to them – if there really was abuse. There is no sign as yet of the debate becoming more reasoned, only of fear.

It also seems important, however, to address the question of what therapists are doing if they heal 'false' traumas. If someone who produces memories of abuse hasn't been abused, what does that mean? As both sides stake out their positions, the critics accusing therapists of encouraging patients to dream up lies, no one is paying attention to this point.

OUTCOMES

In the light of the saga of Eve and concerns about false memories, one has to be wary about claims of successful treatment. Colin Ross says it takes an average of twenty-one months of intensive therapy to achieve integration. Others are warier of putting a time on it. One problem is that there are few good statistics on the outcome of treatment. Ian Hacking has argued this is a serious problem – and perhaps a curious one, given that it has been such a lively field for over ten years. I would like to be able to disagree with Hacking but what remains striking about the situation in the States is how few good outcome studies there have been. The Netherlands has produced the most comprehensive study but it is far from optimistic about the results of treatment.

First the optimists. Ross reported one follow-up in which they found 53 out of 103 patients. This is not that brilliant a follow-up rate. But of those who were found, Ross claimed that 32 had achieved integration and, six months later, seemed to have maintained the improvement. Their scores on various tests of depression like Beck and Hamilton's were much like those of a normal population. The patients who hadn't integrated, however, were still showing a plethora of symptoms. Ross challenged critics to come up with as good cure rates for their conventional treatments of conventional disorders.

But there is also a pessimistic view. For some patients, dealing with the trauma fully is never going to be possible. The best option is a holding-job. The late David Caul, a leading figure in the field, suggested it was utopian to think you can always – or even often – achieve integration. It was better to think of trying to get the alters to understand the situation and make compromises so that they could live with each other. A United Nations of the Self. A co-operative of selves where different entities need time, space and freedom to be themselves. It's not a perfect solution but it's better than a saga of never-ending splits.

At the international conference in Amsterdam in 1995 papers by Onno van der Hart and Suzette Boon suggested early claims of success were maybe exaggerated. The first studies in the 1980s seemed to show over 50 per cent could integrate. But Boon told the conference some patients were so damaged and so lacking in ego strength that the best outcome one could hope for was to achieve some stability. Then, patients could live with the pain and with their dissociative symptoms. Those who were least likely to get better were those who were still in abusive relationships. Research on victims of abuse shows many continue to choose partners who will abuse them. They are caught in a vice. Abuse is still abuse but it is also a way they are used to feeling loved.

Both Boon and van der Hart concluded that the evidence so far is that no more than a third of patients ever achieved true integration. This actually fits Ross' results reasonably well if one assumes that most of those who did get better responded to his survey. His 32 'cured' patients would then be 32 out of 103 – roughly a third.

Boon and others own up to this pessimism because it has become very clear that patients get some advantages out of their alters. It allows them to avoid certain situations and certain crises. They can juggle two lovers; they can express their anger without feeling shame. Once they have integrated they won't be able to play such games any longer. Teaching patients how to cope with life after they lose their multiple personality is something all sensible therapists stress.

But the critics have a point. With thousands of cases and many centres studying the phenomenon, there should be better information on what treatment has achieved and on what makes for good treatment.

Could it be that because many therapists feel doing therapy with multiples is such a struggle, they aren't pressing as hard as they should for large outcome studies? That maybe they find the work so hard that it somehow lets them off trying to find such proofs?

I said earlier that there was a lot of humour, perhaps too much, in Amsterdam. There was also a lot of suffering. Jean Olson presented a long paper on how therapists could cope with the difficulties and disappointments of treatment. In a remarkable exchange between Richard Kluft and Catherine Fine, who are friends and colleagues, Kluft challenged her about how much dealing with such patients took out of her. She said she did often feel depressed, almost dirty, after hearing endless stories of cruelty and abuse. She admitted she took too much of it home with her and found herself ringing Kluft after work. He countered that he didn't suffer the same way and suggested that the key difference was that she was easily hypnotized while he wasn't. She naturally absorbed more of the pain. It bounced off him more easily.

For many patients, too, the process of treatment feels very long and arduous. Many often try to give up, and one woman told me she felt she was never going to conquer her problems.

At present, one difficulty with the form of treatment that is being used is that it has modelled itself on treatment of other traumas. Most people who suffer other traumas, however, are in reasonable shape before the war or the disaster that changes their lives. I was surprised by the way so few of those interested in multiple personality had thought about that.

It's worth summing up what seems to me to be a complicated situation. There are signs of progress. Therapists now have a model of the stages of treatment and they know they must not rush patients. There is enthusiasm about some new techniques. The most promising of these is EMDR, Eye Movement Desensitization. Pierre Janet suggested long ago (1907) that recalling traumatic memories led to rushes of energy. One sign of this is very rapid eye movements which flounder all over the place. Using behaviour therapy techniques, some therapists teach their patients to relax and control their eye movements when they are recalling traumatic events. This makes it easier to evoke memories calmly. EMDR seems to help some patients.

Psychiatrists have also found better ways of managing patients' angry behaviour. They have become less naïve about using hypnosis and more careful to distinguish what is true for the patient from what is true objectively. But it is also important to remember the negatives. Studies which claim to show successful treatment are really not yet very substantial. And no attention is being paid by most of those who treat dissociative patients to the meaning of sincerely produced false memories.

Having said all that, I think it is important to make one other point. Doctors like Colin Ross are very honest in reporting failures. Ross has claimed that on average it takes twenty-one months to achieve integration but he has reported many cases where he has failed. In *The Osiris Complex* (1994), only eight of the fifteen cases seem to have really successful outcomes. Critics seize on this as an example of how dubious the whole field is. In most areas of medicine and science, understanding failures is an important step to devising better methods and theories. I would feel more confident in saying that, though, if it were not for the over-confident claims that have been made rather prematurely – for that just repeats what happened in the case of Eve.

CHAPTER 14

Carry on Nurse

DIARY OF MANY SELVES 3

I'm a good Jewish boy. I started the Diary of Many Selves with my mother and I'll end it there.

9.30 p.m. I rush over to my mother's flat. For the past twenty-four hours she hasn't answered the phone. She goes out often, but I'm worried. She's eighty and her eyesight is very poor. When I get to the block of flats, she doesn't answer the doorbell.

I let myself in through the front door of the block. But I can't open the door to her flat. Her key is in the lock and won't budge. I yell. I bang. I ring the bell again. No answer.

I ask the porter to call the police. I'm careful not to panic. Basically, I think my mother's indestructible. But I panic.

9.45 p.m. We're still waiting for the police to come. Inside the worried son, the journalist speaks. Is there a story in how slow the police are being? How many old people die unnecessarily because the cops are too busy with paperwork?

10.00 p.m. Two constables arrive. They're very reluctant to break in. I bottle the worried son and journo and become the concerned citizen urging them to do their duty. Finally, they agree to break in through the back door. This is the worst minute. She might be dead. I don't want to look. Is this panic, shame, fear? But in the midst of this, I realize that the pathetically young cops themselves are frightened of finding her dead.

She's alive, but unconscious. She's probably been lying on her bedroom floor for twenty-four hours after she fell.

10.30 p.m. We get to St Mary's casualty. The ambulance men think she's had a stroke. The doctors agree. But I want to make sure that I'm told everything so, pompously, I tell them I'm a psychologist with a doctorate. Don't pull the wool over my eyes. I become the self-important professional.

Over the next few hours, part of me is preparing for her death. She is eighty. She falls a lot. She's unconscious. I try to make peace with my feelings. I love her, I hate her, and I'm impossibly irritated by her. We very easily accept relationships have different sides.

As she gets better, I see a person recover herself. The process is far more understandable than in the case of the Reverend Hanna, but some of the stages aren't dissimilar. My mother starts to wake up. She can move. She first speaks German, then French, then English. She confuses me with my son. She confuses Julia, my partner, with Aileen, my ex-wife.

As she recovers physically and becomes herself again, she becomes impossible again. She complains about the nurses, who care more for the millionaires than for her. A Mrs Goldberg in the next bed is apparently fed intravenous strudel and also has bottles of brandy smuggled in.

People are dying on the ward: some groan constantly with pain. A man opposite has lost speech for over twenty days and can only sing. My mother's hands hurt badly, but her main problem is constipation. But she describes herself as '*la plus misérable des misérables*', the most wretched of the wretched. She's an eighty-year-old whiney baby.

In the scene I described at the beginning of the book, I felt frustrated that though I was an adult, she was making me feel like a five-year-old by complaining my hair was too long. And Oedipus didn't want to go to the barber's.

Now, in the hospital, the roles are more than reversed. She is a child. I have to be not just my age, but the mature sensible adult to her child. It's an easy role. I tell her not to be frightened. I negotiate with the nurses. I bring one of the treats she wants – feta cheese – but withhold another – castor oil. For her constipation. The only stuff that will shift it.

One evening as I leave, I catch the eye of the staff nurse. We've smiled a bit at each other. She tells me that my mother's been nagging her to have an enema. I tell her not to humour her Central European bowel kinks. Suddenly, the nurse smiles at me, touches my hair – 'You got wet in the rain, didn't you' – and gives me probably the least expected hug of my life.

Suddenly, with this hug, I'm reminded I have another self – a sexual one.

I return the hug and leave the ward, feeling pleased. And inside the man in his thirties, there's a sixteen-year-old smiling.

CHAPTER 15

Multiple Solutions

For a country with such a distinguished history of theatre, Britain has a curious fear of the theatrical. British psychiatrists seem to resent the histrionics of multiple personalities. In the late 1960s, before these issues were as defined as they are now, one of Britain's most senior neuropsychiatrists, Sir Charles Symonds, declared: 'Whenever I meet any hysteric, I treat them as a malingerer.' (Quoted by Bliss, 1986.)

In 1994 John Davis, a psychologist at the University of Warwick, told me that when he and his wife tried to set up a study of dissociation and multiple personality in Coventry, they met great resistance from the local psychiatrists. They were not allowed to interview any hospital in-patients.

And yet Britain is hardly lacking in histrionics.

DON JUAN OF THE LEDGERS

If Anthony Williams, who was found guilty in 1995 of having defrauded Scotland Yard of over five million pounds, had lived in America his lawyers might well have pleaded on the following lines.

For thirty-five years every morning Williams went to work in Scotland Yard. He was an accountant whose task it was to manage the secret police funds used to pay informers. Cashiers at the Midland Bank in Victoria were apparently given instructions to pay in cash and transfers whatever Williams instructed. He seemed to be a dull bureaucrat chained to routines, a pen-pusher who would be deskbound until he retired.

A competent American lawyer would argue, however, there was another self inside Williams. This second self was daring, histrionic, risk-taking. It does take imagination and balls, after all, to steal Scotland Yard's money. Sherlock Holmes' great foe, Moriarty, couldn't have pulled off a more stunning exploit.

For six years, using Scotland Yard's money, Williams cashed large cheques himself or wrote them in favour of companies he had set up. He used the cash to create a second life for himself in Scotland. He bought an estate and invested £100,000 in a small village, Tomintoul. The people there loved him because he created forty jobs and attracted investment. Williams was an important, dashing figure, nothing like his dull London civil-servant self. The second self also had social pretensions, for Williams bought himself a title. He became Baron Williams of the Chirnside.

Baron Williams was also an unlikely sex-pot. He kept a string of mistresses who purred to the press he was a stud – especially for his age. Three hours of passion were nothing for him even though he was fifty. He was the Cashbook Casanova, the Don Juan of the Ledgers.

No one tried a defence of multiple personality. In Britain, given the enormous scepticism, it almost certainly wouldn't have worked. In America it might have been successful. Williams' story is a reminder of how inside conventional men and women there are rogues, risk-takers and dreamers.

In five years or so, even British lawyers might toy with such a defence because there are signs of change even here. I believe it is possible to predict some future developments.

THE SEARCH FOR A JUVENILE SYBIL

Addressing the Amsterdam conference, Colin Ross painted an optimistic picture of an ever more scientific discipline. Only bigots had any doubts about the existence of the diagnosis. Ross offered new studies as proof. Schultz had just reported on a large group of 355 patients with multiple personality disorder.

Eight-five per cent had suffered sexual abuse, 82 per cent physical abuse. It fitted well with Frank Putnam's and Colin Ross' earlier studies. But the problem with all these studies is that they are retrospective, dealing with the distant past.

In the last ten years, there has been a vast expansion of child and adolescent psychiatry. Hundreds of hospitals in the States are full of teenagers. Children are regularly given medication. There are now reports from America of ECT being given to a child who was only eight years old. Even in Britain there is concern about the subject. A pressure group called Young Minds has been set up with a base in London to monitor, among other things, how children are dealt with by psychiatrists.

As part of this effort, it is clear that psychiatrists have been looking for a juvenile Eve or Sybil. When those cases were studied, both women claimed that they had split their alters very young. One would think that by identifying a vulnerable population early on, one could find children who were already showing signs of multiple personality.

The interest in child psychiatry has made it easier for some psychiatrists to do studies that would once have been seen as invasive – studies which look for early signs of dissociation and child abuse. A number of research projects are under way. Yet the results are a little disappointing.

As early as 1984, Fagan looked at four children who seemed to be showing such signs but the cases seemed rather thin. Dell and Eisenhower (1990) also reported some cases.

The most detailed study so far is that of Hornstein and Putnam (1992). They looked at sixty-four children in two different samples. They found many symptoms. These children showed high rates of amnesia, anxiety, problems in physical co-ordination, eating disorders, hallucinations, sexual problems, aggression, sleep disturbances. A number of them saw ghosts. What is missing, however, is any sign of alters appearing even under hypnosis. The psychiatrists could regress these children very quickly under hypnosis to an earlier age and ask them what problems they suffered. But multiples did not appear or, at least, are not mentioned.

The one case history presumably closest to a multiple is again rather thin.

One child reported having a 'guy inside me' who was called Bad Joey. Just as Fraiberg's patient, described in Chapter 4, had a wicked playmate, Bad Joey was blamed for anything wrong that Joey did, especially his acts of violence.

The child explained what was going on to the psychiatrists in these terms: '"Bad Joey" hears someone call me names then he would get me to do something. I'd be saying NO to my legs Stop but they'd keep going. Then my arms would go at the other kids. But I couldn't stop it.'

Joey was exhibiting automatic behaviour. As Usoffa had protected Jonah, Bad Joey was protecting him. But there are differences. Jonah the adult knew nothing of Usoffa exactly as Eve White knew nothing of Eve Black. Joey, however, seems to have been conscious of Bad Joey. He knew what he was doing. Bad Joey was more like an imaginary playmate than an alter.

Hornstein and Putnam (1992) found that 95 per cent of the children in their sample had well documented histories of physical and sexual abuse. The children sometimes referred to themselves in the third person; they had high dissociative scores. Given that they had all the right symptoms, why did none of these children actually manifest any alters? Was it because they were already in treatment? There are no answers so far to these questions. Putnam (1994) accepts that many child clinicians report 'grappling with more ambiguous dissociative presentations' which, he teases, end up with the label DDNOS – Dissociative Disorder Not Otherwise Specified. Psychiatrists will continue to look for children who have alters and may find them. If they don't, the critics will crow. There is another possibility we should consider. Initially trauma leads just to denial and repression. It is only later that the alters are created. Any such theory would need a lot of evidence to make sense but it is a way of interpreting the information we have so far.

ABUSE

Colin Ross also claimed in Amsterdam that professionals were slowly being converted. Two studies – one of 180 psychiatrists and one by Dunn of the US Veterans Administration of 1,120 psychiatrists – showed progress. In the smaller study, 56 per cent said they had seen a case of dissociation. In the larger study 85 per cent said they had seen a dissociative case and 80 per cent said they believed in the syndrome.

Therefore 5 per cent of psychiatrists had seen a case and didn't believe in the existence of the disorder. An interesting 5 per cent!

Ross pointed out that only 12 per cent in Dunn's sample were sceptical and dismissed the diagnosis. Seven per cent were still unsure. For Ross, this study was a sign of the victory to come. He joked that when that 12 per cent of ageing and obstinate shrinks retired, the battle would be won. He insisted multiple personality was not a wacky American syndrome. It was not the product of fevered Protestant imaginations. How many Protestants were there in Turkey where the diagnosis was becoming well accepted? How many in Japan?

It seems clear to me that the effort to design and research new tests of dissociation has been worthwhile. Psychological tests are judged partly on how reliable and partly on how valid they are. A test is reliable if a group of subjects will return more or less the same score each time they do the test. Inter-test reliability refers to the relationships between scores on different tests. You would expect individuals who scored high on one dissociation test also to score high on others if the tests were any good. The SCIDD (the Structural Clinical Interview for Dissociative Disorders) has high inter-test reliability – superior to that of many tests of depression, Ross added a little aggressively.

Ross and many others in Amsterdam were annoyed that those who believed in multiple personality were being asked to provide more proof than psychiatrists provide for other conditions. Pity the poor shrink caught between demanding colleagues and demanding patients. Ross argued that the latest follow-up – of 53 patients out of a group of 103 – was spectacular. Two years after leaving treatment, those who integrated were almost entirely free of psychiatric symptoms, according to tests and clinical assessment. Less than a third of the patients (32) were in that happy state. The others were still depressed and thought-disordered. 'The burden is on the sceptics to show that they can get superior results,' Ross challenged. The follow-up is, in fact, not that impressive. It tracked down just over half the sample. Usually, those who can't be contacted are assumed to have done worse than those who can. And curing a third is good but not that good.

More curious than Ross' claims is something he told me in discussion. He wanted to raise a million dollars to investigate his hunch that many patients with schizophrenia and depression have also suffered childhood trauma. But he was not pursuing the funds that vigorously. He told me he was not too optimistic because there was still so much hostility to the idea of dissociation. It seemed to be an example of that odd ambivalence and lack of confidence so many psychiatrists showed while trumpeting the importance of their findings.

DEFUSING DISSENT

Dissent in psychiatry is not new. Some of the acrimony reflects the fact that child abuse is a very emotive subject and multiple personality and child abuse are now linked. I suggested earlier the dissent reminds me of battles between psychiatry and anti-psychiatry like those fought by R. D. Laing, David Cooper and Thomas Szasz.

I have argued it is wrong to think of anti-psychiatry as a movement that failed. Laing and Cooper are now seen as failures. The biography written by Adrian Laing (1994) portrays his father as a desperately sad man. But did anti-psychiatry really fail? It highlighted many human rights abuses. It also changed the way ordinary psychiatrists deal with many patients. It's routine now to talk with families. Despite the discovery of the so-called schizophrenia gene, many doctors accept emotional stresses can trigger psychotic episodes. Medicine has recognized the importance of psychological factors. It would be very odd if psychiatry was the one branch of medicine not to.

It seems very possible something not dissimilar will happen with multiple personality and dissociation. The work reported in this book will start to influence ordinary psychiatry. I suspect the realists in the multiple movement were wise to drop the 'multiple' label. Psychiatrists are more comfortable talking about 'dissociation'. They find it even easier to talk about 'dissociative states'. No one denies patients do sometimes forget, fantasize and get into very peculiar frames of mind.

Language matters. Few people will quibble with statement 1:

1. Patients often get into temporary frames of mind which are completely out of keeping – and character – with their usual frames of mind.

But plenty will quarrel with statement 2:

2. Patients have different personalities, different selves, which manifest themselves at different times.

How you describe what you see matters critically in this controversy, and there are many signs now of linguistic compromises. As I showed in Chapter 1, the enthusiasts still clearly believe in multiple personalities. But they have also pulled back on what that means. It no longer seems to mean that I have in me a variety of different self-contained, solid, autonomous selves. Rather it seems to mean I have fragments of my whole personality. Fragments that don't know of each others' existence, fragments that are contradictory. (Tom Fahy has rubbished this move as being merely an attempt to diminish the 'absurdity of their model'.)

It may be useful to use once more the image of Dr Jekyll and Mr Hyde to clarify the change that is happening. Dr Jekyll used a noxious chemical formula to transform himself into Mr Hyde. He was one person or the other. Jekyll knew about Hyde and Hyde knew about Jekyll but each character existed in full. Colin

Ross and others don't claim multiple personalities are like that. It is more as if, within the body of Jekyll & Hyde, there are times when Jekyll-ness is dominant and other times when Hyde-hood rules. Ross now insists all the fragments and alters express different aspects of one whole personality system. These are layers of the personality system. The alter ego isn't quite as robust as he or she was.

It may also be precisely because alters are only parts that many of them have a cartoon-like quality. If you want to make a mark quickly, you emphasize a few strong traits or images. Goofy is goofy; Popeye is absurdly strong. A few graphic characteristics is how you remember them.

Once the enthusiasts start speaking like this, it conjures up different images from those which have been traditionally associated with multiple personality. I'd like to take as an image that of the dancer. At the start of the show there is one dancer holding the stage. The dance is being filmed on video and we have a full battery of special effects available.

Out of the dancer, there MIXES a second dancer. This dancer looks identical to the first but the way he, or she, dances is different. Dancer 1 is doing modern ballet à la Martha Graham. Dancer 2 is classical, a study in pirouettes. Dancer 2 does its turn and then folds back into the body.

Dancer 1 continues with modern ballet but Dancer 3 now emerges. This time Dancer 3 emerges from the left foot. Using our special effects, we ZOOM in on Dancer 3. Dancer 3 is a strange self because it is essentially contained in one foot. As this is a cartoon, this foot develops a set of basic human characteristics. The sole of the foot becomes a face. This is the foot self. It feels it carries the weight of the whole body. It is also an angry self. Its dancing is nothing but furious stamping. It stamps and stomps. It reminds me of the song 'These boots were made for walking and . . . they're gonna walk all over you'. After a few minutes of enraged dancing, Dancer 3 also folds back into the body.

Dancer 1 now takes her bow. She deserves it. Dancer 3 was part of her repertoire.

I hope this image helps clarify some of the differences between seeing multiple personalities as really different people, as William James believed he had found in the Ansel Bourne case, and seeing them as fragments of a whole.

Despite the vehemence of critics like Tom Fahy, I think one can see the kind of compromise that may occur. There will be more talk of dissociative states. It will be accepted that high levels of stress often trigger such episodes. Psychiatrists who recognize a role for the unconscious will come to see this as another strange way in which the unconscious speaks. A cultural analysis might even suggest it's no accident multiple personality first made a splash in Paris when the can-can was popular and then reappeared in the States around the time of Elvis Presley.

The influence of dance on expressions of multiple personality – a promising Ph.D for someone.

British psychiatrists will continue to resist and get into battles with therapists. In 1996, the second meeting of the British Society for Dissociation takes place. There is one surprising speaker who has agreed to address them – John Morton, head of the Medical Research Council's Cognitive Development Unit in London. He is a very empirically minded psychologist. He told me he had been intrigued by the evidence and was convinced there was something to study. He had a feeling that multiples were people who found it hard to accept the contradictions in themselves. They took the radical step of turning themselves into separate beings. But sceptics remain sceptical.

Fahy told me he had been treating a woman who had spent five years in treatment as a multiple. He had started to see her when she came to the United Kingdom from California and had found the key to treatment was to get her to talk without anxiety about the problems she faced. These included being very histrionic – something that being diagnosed as a multiple in California had actively encouraged in her.

But if Fahy remains a fierce critic, there are others at the Institute of Psychiatry who are beginning to see that the issue is interesting and important.

James MacKeith and Gisli Gudjudson are in the process of

doing a study on parents who claim to have been falsely accused of child abuse. It is a reasonable bet the parents will report their children behaved in ways that suggest they were suffering from dissociative states.

For the sceptics that will explain why they made false accusations. But for others it will also be a small move to accept the reality of dissociation. MacKeith, who is a friend of mine, has been gently persuaded by what I have told him that the issue at least needs more study.

I suspect that as the American evidence sinks in, psychiatrists will have to face the issue of the long-term impact of childhood trauma. Feminist psychiatrists are asking why so many female patients report childhood histories of abuse.

THE QUESTION OF SATANIC ABUSE

One obstacle will disappear fairly quickly, I believe: fascination with Satanic abuse. One British psychiatrist told me that one reason why he didn't want to show any leaning towards dissociation was the company he would be keeping. He didn't want to be connected in any way with the Satanic abuse fanatics.

Even the pioneers are being much more careful about Satanic abuse now. Colin Ross claimed that through the case of Pam, he learned to be more sceptical about such claims. Catherine Fine agreed some of the stories did seem ridiculous. Ross added they never now encouraged patients to confront their parents. I don't think it's fair of experts like Ian Hacking to suggest they are backtracking just out of embarrassment or fear of being sued. It's possible to see their revisions as honest, the result of more clinical experience. The fifteen therapeutic precautions outlined in Chapter 13 seem to be the result of that.

But as people believe less in Satanic abuse, I suspect many experts will come back to a harsh reality. Child abuse exists: it is not always domestic. There is evidence of organized rings and gangs of paedophiles. As I write, a nine-year-old boy in Bristol has been found dead; he was abducted by a paedophile gang who abused and killed him. According to the local paper, *The Western Mail*, many local people deeply ashamed because the boy was seen in public, obviously struggling to get away from the men who were holding him, and no one lifted a finger to help. Attempts to find and prosecute paedophile rings have rarely met with success in Britain. There is a lucrative trade in child pornography. Children are filmed in strange costumes and locations. It is true that Jean La Fontaine (1994) found none of the eighty-eight cases of Satanic abuse in Britain had been proved to be 'real'. But to use such research to suggest there is no organized abuse is irresponsible and risks more children getting hurt.

The British government is concerned about the way child abuse has been investigated, according to a research report published in June 1995. Many researchers accept that one reason it is hard to get convictions for child abuse has little to do with the truth of the allegations. It is not easy for children to stand up in court and reveal what happened to them. Social workers are often very concerned that by getting a child to relive the trauma they cause more, not less, damage. Despite this, there has been a rise in the number of successful prosecutions brought for abuse over the last five years.

As we move to a more rational view about child abuse – and in the 1980s it had all the disturbing hallmarks of a moral and medical panic – and as the pioneers make less extravagant claims, some of the controversy will fade. Some will remain, but the extreme positions on either side will come to seem untenable and become less popular. I think that will be a sign of progress.

Pious Hopes

In which the author reveals a new subpersonality he wasn't too familiar with – Therapy Freak. Perhaps even Holy Therapy Freak.

Over the past hundred years, as Western societies have become more and more influenced by ideas of therapy, we have formed an image of what it is like to be a healthy person. We speak of people being 'well adjusted' and 'well integrated', of individuals 'working through their problems' to become whole.

We can pray to St Whole, patron saint of therapists. Let me one. Let me be healed. Let me whole.

A whole person is top notch, top hole.

This vision of wholeness often sounds pious so part of me can't help but mock a little while another subpersonality, Therapy Freak, the Susan Howatch fan who gets enthralled by her novels about the Church of England, thinks only those who are afraid to be themselves act so defensive. I want to suggest an alternative vision which also has its roots in a tradition of therapy and I'll put it as a prayer, but it is a prayer clearly addressed to oneself.

A PRAYER

Over the past hundred years, as the world has become therapeutic, we in the west have formed an image of what it is like to be a healthy person. We speak of people being well adjusted and well integrated.

It's easy to devise a simple prayer.

I pray I will be one, I will be healed, I will be whole.

A whole person is the best kind of person there is.

I want to suggest an alternative vision for which there is also plenty of tradition in therapy – a vision which can also have its prayer.

I pray that I will be everything I am, that I will be aware of the conflicts and of the differences in myself. I know there are times when I act differently, feel differently, respond differently to many things. I pray not to be afraid of that.

Long ago, Gurdieff, part charlatan, part guru, put it well: 'Man is a plural being. When we speak of ourselves ordinarily we speak of "I" – but this is a mistake. There is no such "I" or rather there are hundreds, thousands of little "I"s in every one of us.'

Ian Hacking in his book *Rewriting the Soul* (1995) ends his attack on the whole multiple movement on a moral note. The very idea encourages a false consciousness. If I can get away with pretending to be many selves other than myself, I stop being a decent person. I weazle my way out of my responsibility. I can get away with murder as, indeed, some people have tried to do by pleading multiple personality. As Sir Charles Symonds said, it is all malingering.

Hacking is right to suggest we have choices about this. But I think there is another equally legitimate view of being a person. In this view, being a person requires us to recognize the conflicts, the different dreams, possibilities and wishes that exist in us. Part of me, for instance, regrets not being an Orthodox Jew whose main aim in life would be to get his relationship with God right. Occasionally I go to synagogue and get a whiff, a nostalgic whiff certainly, of that self. But it's there. I'll be buried a Jew.

Being aware of such different potentials does not have to be an excuse for bad or corrupt behaviour. It doesn't have to be escapism. Hacking writes as if the real reason for the popularity of multiple personality is corruption of the soul. If we are lots of different beings, we can get away with all kinds of selfish and bad behaviour. But being aware of those different feelings and fragments also gives me a sense of the complexity of that true – my true – self.

I think part of what we have been struggling to learn since Freud is to accept such complexity, not to disown the Others or others in ourselves. We may not like these bits of us but they are part of us. It could be argued that those who have multiple personality syndrome do two things. They remind us of those different fragments in ourselves and they also highlight, in an extreme way, the dangers of being cut off from them.

A well-integrated person may not actually mould all these different fragments into one coherent self but rather may just know that they are all there. You know that the lawyer who gives a brilliant performance in court is also a man who is terribly frightened of confronting his son about his drug-taking.

We shouldn't be afraid of accepting our divided self or, in John Rowan's terminology, our subpersonalities. We have to learn to live with the conflicts within us. That is also part of becoming a person. For many people, it's frightening to look inside and see the fears, disappointments and betrayals, the parts we prefer to forget and keep under wraps.

As the world has become more complex, as we all have to play more social roles, it becomes even more important not to blind ourselves to those inner differences, to examine and accept ourselves for what we are.

One reason for the interest in multiple personalities has always been that those who suffered from it seemed freaks. But they are freaks who light up some uncomfortable truths about the rest of us.

I find myself surprised by my conclusion since I've tended to write sceptically about therapy for many years. Once I would have mocked subpersonalities as yet another example of New Age nonsense. Yet I seem now to feel there's something potentially valuable in it.

Did I write that?

Or was it some alter ego?

I do want to make one final point.

Any mistakes or errors in this book, of course, aren't my fault. I blame one of my alter egos.

Bibliography

Allridge Morris, R. B. (1989) *Multiple personality – an exercise in delusion*; Lawrence Erlbaum; London

Barglow, R. (1994) *The crisis of the self in the age of information*; Routledge; London

Berne, E. (1973) *Games people play*; Penguin; Harmondsworth

Bliss, E. (1986) *Multiple personality and allied disorders*; Oxford University Press; Oxford

Boden, M. (1995) in ed; J. Kahan *What is Intelligence*; Oxford University Press; Oxford

Brodsky, B., Cloitre, M. and Dalit, R. (1995) 'The Relationship of Dissociation to Self Mutilation' American Journal of Psychiatry, vol 152, 1788–92

Carlson, E. B. and Putnam, F. W. (1993) *An update on the dissociative experiences scale*, Dissociation, 6, 16–27

Cattell, R. B. (1965) *The scientific analysis of personality*; Penguin; Harmondsworth

Charcot, J-M (1887) *Leçons sur les maladies du système nerveux*; Progrès Medical; Paris

Clare, A. (1976) *Psychiatry in dissent*; Tavistock; London

Cohen, D. (1985) *The development of laughter*. Unpublished Ph.D thesis; University of London

Cohen, D. (1988) *Forgotten millions*; Paladin; London

Cohen, D. (1993) *The development of play*; Routledge; London

Cohen, D. and MacKeith, S. (1991) *The development of imagination*; Routledge; London

Crabtree, A. (1985) *Multiple man, explorations in possession and multiple personality*; Collins; Toronto

Dell, P. F., Eisenhower J. W. (1990), 'Adolescent multiple personality disorder'; Journal of American Academy of Child Adolescent Psychiatry, 29, 356–366

Dennett, D. (1994) *Consciousness explained*; Penguin; London

Deutsch, A. (1948) *The shame of the states*; Harcourt Brace Jovanovich; New York

Diagnostic and Statistical Manual of Mental Disorders (1980); American Psychiatric Association; Washington D.C; known as DSM III

Diagnostic and Statistical Manual of Mental Disorders (1987); American Psychiatric Association; Washington D.C; known as DSM IV

Draijer, N. and Boon, S. (1990) *Multiple personality disorder in the Netherlands*; Swetz and Zeitlinger; Leiden

Ellenberger, H. (1970) *The discovery of the unconscious*; Basic Books; New York

Erikson, K. (1976); *Everything fell in*; Yale University Press; New Haven

Eysenck, H. (1967) *The biological basis of personality*; University of Chicago Press; Chicago

Eysenck, H. (1986) *The decline and fall of the Freudian empire*; Penguin; London

Fagan, J. and McMahon, P. P. (1984) 'Incipient multiple personality in children, four cases'; Journal of Nervous and Mental Disease, 172, 26–36

Fahy, T. (1988) 'The diagnosis of multiple personality disorder, a critical review,' British Journal of Psychiatry, 153, 597–606

Fine, C. (1995) Presentation at Amsterdam Conference on Dissociation

Fraiberg, S. (1959) *The magic years*; Scribner; New York

Freud, S. (1923) *The ego and the id*; Hogarth Press, London

Freud, S. (1936) *A disturbance of memory on the Acropolis* in *Collected Works of Sigmund Freud*; vol XXII, p 236–251; Hogarth Press; London

Frith, U. (1993) *Autism*; Blackwell; Oxford

Gardner, H. (1994) *Multiple intelligences*; Basic Books; New York

Gauld, A. (1992) *A history of hypnosis*; Cambridge University Press; Cambridge

Gudjudson, G. (1993) *The psychology of interrogations, confessions and testimony*; John Wiley; Chichester and New York

Greaves, G. B. (1980) 'Multiple Personality 165 Years after Mary Reynolds,' Journal of Nervous and Mental Disease, 168, 577–96

Gurdieff, G. (1950) *Meetings with remarkable men*; Routledge; London; original publication Paris 1921

Hacking, I. (1995) *Rewriting the soul*; Princeton University Press; Princeton NJ

Henningsen, G. (1983) *Basque witchcraft and the Spanish Inquisition*; University of Nevada Press

Hornstein, N. L. and Putnam, F. W. (1992) 'Clinical Phenomenology of Child and Adolescent Dissociative Disorders,' American Journal of Child and Adolescent Psychiatry, 31, 1077–1085

Janet, P. (1887) 'L'anaesthésie systematique et la dissociation des phénomènes psychologiques,' Revue Philosophique, 23, 449–72

Janet, P. (1907) *The major symptoms of hysteria*; Macmillan; London

James, W. (1890) *Principles of psychology*; 2 vols Holt; New York

Jung, C. G. (1954) *Archetypes and the collective unconscious*; Routledge; London

Kampman, R. (1976) *Hypnotically induced multiple personality*, International Journal of Experimental and Clinical Hypnosis, vol XXIV, p 215–228

Kendler, H. H. (1981) *Psychology – a science in conflict*; Oxford University Press; Oxford

Kenny, M. (1986) *The passion of Ansel Bourne*; Smithsonian; Washington D.C

Klein, M. (1948) *Contributions to psychoanalysis (1921–45)*; Hogarth Press; London

Kline, P. (1990) *Psychology Exposed*; Routledge; London

Kluft, R. P. (1984) 'Treatment of multiple personality disorder,' Psychiatric Clinics of America, 7, 69–88

Kluft, R. P. (1993) 'The treatment of dissociative disorder patients, an overview,' Dissociation, 6, 87–101

Ladurie, E. Le Roy. (1978); *Montaillou*; Scolar Press; London

La Fontaine, J. (1994) Report of an investigation into 88 cases of child abuse; Dept of Health

Laing, A. (1994) *R. D. Laing*; Peter Owen; London

Laing, R. D. (1961) *The divided self*; Penguin, Harmondsworth

Laing, R. D. (1968) *The bird of experience*; Penguin; Harmondsworth

Latz, T., Kromer, S., Hughes, D. (1995), 'Multiple personality among female inmates of a state psychotic asylum', American Journal of Psychiatry, Vol 152, No 9, 1343–1348

Ludwig, A. M. (1972) *The objective study of a multiple personality*, Archives of General Psychiatry, 26, 298–310

Lynn, S. J. and Rhue, J. W. (1988), 'Fantasy Proneness, Hypnosis, Developmental Antecedents and Pathology'; American Psychologist, vol 113, p 35–44

Masson, J. (1980) *The assault on truth*; Collins; London

Merskey, H, (1995) Multiple personality editorial; British Journal of Psychiatry, March 1995, vol 160, p 281–284

Millais, J. (1924) 'Shell shock'; Journal of Nervous and Mental Disease, 54, 98–104

Modestin, J. (1992) 'Multiple Personality Disorder,' American Journal of Psychiatry, vol 149, p 89–93

North, C. Ryall, J. E. Ricci, D. R. Wetzel, R. D. (1993) *Multiple Personalities, Multiple personality, Psychiatric classification and media influence*; Oxford University Press; New York and Oxford

Ornstein, R. (1976) *The psychology of consciousness*; Penguin; London

Ornstein, R. (1985) *Multiminds*; Macmillan; London

Piaget, J. (1952) *Play, dreams and imitation in childhood*; Routledge; London

Pitcher, E. G. and Schultz, L. H. (1983) *Boys and girls at play*; Bergin and Garvey; Mass.

Prince, M. (1905) *The dissociation of a personality, a biographical study in abnormal psychology*; Longmans, Green; New York

Prince, M. (1924) 'The Problem of Personality', Powell Lecture at Clark University, reprinted in Prince, M. (1975) *Psychotherapy and Multiple Personality*, Harvard University Press, Harvard

Putnam, F. W. (1994) 'Dissociative Disorders in Children and Adolescents' in Lynn, S. J. (eds) *Dissociation*, Guildford Press, New York and London

Putnam, F. W. (1989) *Diagnosis and treatment of multiple personality disorder*; Guildford Press; New York

Putnam, F. W. et al (1986) 'The Clinical Phenomenology of Multiple Personality Disorder; a review of 100 recent cases'; Journal of Clinical Psychiatry, 47, 285–93

Rogers, C. (1939) *The clinical treatment of the problem child*; Houghton Mifflin; Boston

Rose, L. (1986) *The massacre of the innocents*; Routledge; London

Ross, C. A. (1989) *Multiple personality disorder*; Wiley; Chichester and New York

Ross, C. A. (1994) *The Osiris complex*; University of Toronto Press

Ross, C. A. (1995) Presentation to the Amsterdam conference

Ross, C. A. Heber, S. Anderson, G. (1990) 'The Dissociative Disorders Interview Schedule,' American Journal of Psychiatry 147, 1698–99

Rowan, J. (1985) *Subpersonalities*; Routledge; London

Rowan, J. (1990) *Discover your subpersonalities*; Routledge; London

Rowan, J. and Reason, J. (1981) *Human inquiry*; Routledge; London

Schreiber, F. (1973) *Sybil*; Regnery; Chicago

Sidis, B. and Goodhard, S. (1904) *Multiple personality*; Appleton, New York

Singer, J. L. and Streiner, B. F. (1966) 'Imaginative Content in the Dreams and Fantasy Play of Blind and Sighted Children,' Perceptual and Motor Skills, 2, 475–82

Shelley, D. and Cohen, D. (1986) *Testing psychological tests*; Croom Helm; Beckenham

Sizemore, C. C. and Pitillo, E. (1977) *I'm Eve*; Doubleday; New York

Sizemore, C. C. (1989) *A mind of my own*; Morrow; New York

Smith, O. (1995) 'Adults with a history of child sexual abuse', British Medical Journal, vol. 310 p. 1175–1178

Sperry, R. (1974) 'Lateral Specialisation in the surgically separated hemisphere' in Schmitt F. and Warden F. G. (eds) The Neurosciences; third study programme; Cambridge Mass

Stevenson, R. (1886) *Dr Jekyll and Mr Hyde*

Szasz, T. (1983) *The manufacture of madness*; Routledge; London

Szasz, T. (1987) *Insanity, the idea and its consequences*; John Wiley; Chichester and New York

Thigpen, C. H. and Cleckley, H. (1954) 'A case of multiple personality', Journal of Abnormal and Social Psychology, 49, 135–51

Thigpen, C. H. and Cleckley, H. (1957) *The three faces of Eve*; McGraw Hill; New York

Thurber, J. (1936); *Let your mind alone*; Hamish Hamilton; London

van der Hart, O. and Boon, S. (1990) 'Contemporary Interest in Multiple Personality in the Netherlands'; Dissociation 3, 34–37

Walrond-Skinner, S. (1986) *A dictionary of psychotherapy*; Routledge; London

Ward, J. (1992) *Ambushed*; Vermilion; London

Williams, S. (1988) *Psychology on the couch*; Harvester, Brighton

Index